MORRIS

MORRIS

CHRIS KUELL

atmosphere press

AUTHOR'S NOTE

Several years ago on a family vacation, we came upon one of those little free libraries where you are invited to take a book, leave a book. My wife selected a mystery and was taken aback when reading the author's note. It basically said that if you read this book without paying for it, you are essentially stealing and should burn in hell for eternity. I'm paraphrasing, but at the time I did think, "Dude, you are going about this all wrong."

So, if things go as planned, there is a good chance that somebody gave you this book. This book is a collection of short stories about people in their daily lives and work. Sometimes there's a guitar serving as a witness to their joys and struggles. I hope you read and enjoy it. If not, I apologize, and hopefully the next one will be more to your liking. If you do like it, I'd appreciate it if you would purchase a copy and pass it along. It's my little version of paying it forward, which I hope is more appealing than the fiery pits of eternal hell and damnation.

Happy reading. Feel free to visit and drop me a note at chriskuell.com.

TABLE OF CONTENTS

THE GIFT

"Yeah, some folks inherit star-spangled eyes
They send you down to war
And when you ask 'em, "How much should we give?"
They only answer, "More, more, more"

– "Fortunate Son" by Creedence Clearwater Revival

I spent hours hand-chiseling this piece of American mahogany. Whittling off smaller and smaller fingernail-sized slivers, followed by smoothing with various grits of sandpaper until it became the neck of a guitar. Sleek and strong and beautiful as a ballerina's calf. My back was sore from leaning over, my hands tired and cramped from the endless sanding, yet I kept going. Closing my eyes, running my dusty fingers down the length, I thought about the transformative nature of wood. Trees are the fundamental building block of human society. Early tools, canoes, shelters, weapons, wagons, furniture—you name it, and wood has been involved in one way or another. The Smithsonian has wood carvings estimated to be 10,000 years old. Totems to gods, gifts to leaders, meticulously crafted with nothing but sharp stones for tools. Fortunately, we've come a long way since then.

Despite sanding for half an hour, I felt something with the tip of my ring finger and stopped, moving back again until I located it. A bump, less than half the size of a grain of sand, but a flaw. Somehow, there are always flaws. If not in the wood, then in the lacquer or the clear coat or a nick resulting from rough handling or the first time somebody drops it.

Sometimes, your best is all you can do.

o o o

Beer-soaked carpet, cigarette smoke, a woman's drunken laughter, and a slight but noticeable whiff of weed greeted Rick and me as we walked into O'Brien's on a chilly December night. We welcomed the warmth and familiar buzz created by the locals inside. "The Ballad of the Green Berets" played on the jukebox, and a lonely string of Christmas lights were draped over the mirror behind the bar.

We edged into the crowd, and heads turned our way. Unlike the regulars, dressed in jeans and flannel shirts or peasant blouses, most of the men with long hair hanging beyond their shoulders, I wore my freshly laundered military blues. My hair was shorter than my father's, a fact that made him immensely proud. It certainly made me stand out at O'Brien's.

"Johnny Appleseed!" someone by the pool table shouted.

"That's Sergeant Appleseed to you," Rick shouted back, pulling out a stool and parking us at the bar.

Dana, who tried to look cool with his shaggy hair and round, blue-tinted glasses, greeted us from behind the bar. "You really did it," he said with a grin and a left-handed salute. He drew a couple of drafts, setting them in front of us. "On the house, fellas." He wiped a rag across the bar. "How long you home for?"

"I ship out on Monday."

Dana nodded, sipping the tumbler of Wild Turkey he kept for himself under the bar. I took a long draw off my beer and scanned the crowd. Most of the faces were familiar, either from school or just shooting pool most Friday nights. And, sure, the uniform, clean shave and haircut made me stand out. But there was something more than that. Like some organ in my body had shifted and could never go back to where it used to be. Sort of like taking a road trip. You stop somewhere—Gatlinburg or the Grand Canyon or Mount Rushmore—and then move onto somewhere else. Physically, I was still on the same barstool with its vinyl seat and faded green duct tape where I'd sat a hundred times before. But it felt like my ass didn't fit quite right anymore.

"She's not here yet." Rick put a fiver on the bar and ordered us a couple more Schaefers.

I almost said "who," but I was talking to Rick, my best friend ever since we'd got detention together in seventh grade. We'd played hockey together, hunted together, and talked endlessly about our two favorite subjects—girls and escaping this boring town. He understood me, and didn't give me grief about joining up.

The *she* in question was Allison King. I'd had a crush on her forever. We'd gone out a few times, and she still made my blood boil every time she walked by. She had dirty blonde hair, brandy-colored eyes, and a smile that could stop a train. Rumor was she liked to skinny-dip in Sherwood Pond on full-moon nights, and I was dying to find out if it was true.

As if I'd willed what happened next, the bar door swung open. A cold breeze blasted in, along with three fine females. In the lead was Robin Davis, who was short but had a great figure and an even better voice. She was the lead role as Eliza in last year's musical, *My Fair Lady*. Behind her was Veronica Johnson, dressed in a short skirt and too-tight sweater that was totally inappropriate for this weather. Not that anyone would complain about it, except the ogling guys' girlfriends. Last but not least was Allison, in a blue skirt and colorful blouse, making her eyes even brighter. Her hair was tied back with some sort of flowery bandana. As I stood, she gave me a wide smile.

"Hi Johnny," she said softly, as I pulled her close, my hands circling her narrow waist.

"Hey, Allison." The rest of the room faded when I fell into

those eyes of hers.

She reached out and touched my chest, playing with one of the flashy brass buttons. "Don't you look handsome in your new uniform."

"Thanks." I struggled to say more. It's not like I'd never kissed a girl, but Allison, well, Allison was special. "You're looking—"

A hand nudged my shoulder. I turned to see a guy probably in his late twenties, with stringy black hair and a long beard. He looked as if it had been a while since he showered.

"I know you," he said, the smell of cheap whiskey and unfiltered Camels strong on his breath. "You're the kid who works the stand by the orchard."

"Yup," I said, wanting this guy to disappear. "Andrew's Apples, that's my father's place."

"You get drafted, or join vol-un-tarily?" He drew out the last word like it pained him.

"USMC volunteer," I said. "Finished basic at Parris Island a week and a half ago. Ship out on Monday."

His eyes changed as though he was working a puzzle and couldn't put the pieces together. "Why the hell you want to go kill Vietnamese when you could stay here and pick apples."

The girls moved down the bar to order drinks. Rick was talking football with the guy on the barstool next to him. This hadn't been the first clown to ask me about joining up, and with tensions boiling over in this country these days, he certainly wouldn't be the last. But tonight was supposed to be a celebratory sendoff. I wasn't in the mood to debate.

"My grandfather was a Marine. My father was a Marine. My uncles were Marines. It's our duty to serve our country. You don't get it, and I don't care." I returned to my stool, drained my beer, and signaled Dana to bring another round.

o o o

I was busy admiring Allison's backside when Rick handed me another beer. "This one's on Joel," he said.

I accepted the frosty draft and nodded my thanks to Joel, who was busy cutting a rug with Ronnie. "Windy" played on the jukebox, and while it was new and not bad to dance to, I was in the mood for some serious rock-n-roll. My attention returned to Allison. I reached for her hip and gently guided her through a gaggle of people over to the jukebox. I dug a quarter from my pocket and put it in her hand.

"Play anything you want."

"Anything?" She was a little drunk and gave me a devilish look.

"Anything." We flipped through the jukebox selections. Beatles, The Rascals, Otis Redding, Buffalo Springfield.

"The Doors!" Allison clapped. "I love the Doors!"

She slid the quarter in and picked "Light My Fire" and the flipside, "The Crystal Ship." We watched the guts of the machine moving through the protective glass, then the speakers crackled with the drumming and keyboard, followed by Jim Morrison's dark, haunting voice. Allison yanked the beer out of my hands. She set it on a nearby table, put her arms around me, and started to dance.

I'm not a great dancer, but at that moment, I didn't care. I just followed her rhythm. That's one of the things I love about rock-n-roll, you can just groove any way you feel. As Morrison sang, "Try to set the night on fire," Allison put her arms around my neck and kissed me. Not a peck, but a real kiss, soft and velvety at first, then wild and unrestrained.

When the song finished, we downed our drinks and returned to our spot for the second song. "Crystal Ship" was a slower number. I put my hands on Allison's hips and brought her close. She put her head on my chest and I held her as we swayed to the same rhythm, like conjoined boats in the sea.

"Don't you just love the Doors?" Allison asked.

"I do now." I kept my eyes on hers.

"When I have kids," Allison said, "I'm naming the first one Morris, after Jim Morrison. Jim is too common, but Morris is far out."

"What if it's a girl?"

She laughed and snuggled in close. I smelled the apple scent in her shampoo. Even though I was pretty buzzed, I was sober enough to etch this moment in my head, my heart. This feeling, this beautiful girl, close and warm in my arms, would help me through the tough times ahead.

o o o

I ordered us another round of drinks. Somebody stumbled into me. I turned. It was whiskey breath, looking more than three sheets to the wind.

"'Scuse me, GI Joe," he said.

I didn't respond, just looked at Dana, who was busy filling pints.

"Ya know you're just a pawn in the fuckin' military machine."

It was getting harder and harder to ignore this asshole.

"Killing innocent women 'n kids. Fuckin' kids, man. Fuckin' napalming little babies, and for what? Tell me that. For what?"

I got in the guy's face, clenching my fists. He outweighed me by 50 pounds, but I was a Marine, and Marines don't take shit from nobody.

"I'm here having a few drinks with my friends, and I don't want any more of your bullshit. Got it? Now, take a fuckin' hike."

My buddy Rick appeared from nowhere and wedged himself between us. Then I felt Allison pulling me from the bar, through the crowd and out the door.

"Ignore that cretin," she said. "Jesus, it's freezing out here. You got a car?"

"Yeah," I said. "My dad's Chrysler's over here."

The chill of the night, the peace of the woods around us, stars bright in the sky, calmed me down. I started the engine to get the heat going, and Allison cuddled next to me. We kissed, then she asked, "You sure about this, Johnny?"

"Damn straight," I said.

"Not this, silly. I mean Vietnam. The war. I don't want you getting killed over there."

"Me neither." I smiled, then kissed her nose. I knew there were guys going to college just to defer their draft, or to Canada to avoid the war altogether, but that wasn't me. I was raised to be proud of our country. To defend our freedom. I knew the danger, and I accepted it fully. "I'm not sure of much these days, but inside I know this is what I need to do."

She kissed me again, her tongue electric on mine. Elvis crooned on the car radio. I kissed Allison's lips, her neck, her jawline, her breasts. Thoughts of Vietnam and napalmed babies and the shitty swamps that were waiting for me vanished as my hands searched her warm, soft flesh. *Love me tender, love me true...*

o o o

Anybody who ever read a newspaper knows that Vietnam's mostly a shithole. But if you haven't been there, you can't know how goddamned hot it is. Beyond hot. And the humidity. It's like living in a steam room. A steam room that smells like an open latrine with occasional whiffs of smoke and cordite and rot and the acrid, unforgettable stench of blood. Way too much blood.

Yes, welcome to Nam, where you get to live in filthy dirt holes with big rats the size of house cats. You can go without food or water, wear the same clothes for weeks and fire your weapons at complete strangers, and hopefully, God willing, kill them.

My platoon just returned from doing a sweep when a recon team called the CP for help. Word was they got ambushed and four of our guys were dead. "We're movin' out fast," Lieutenant Price called. "Leave everything but your weapons and ammo. No packs, no food, no bullshit."

A lot of guys were hurt, so we flat out ran through the jungle. The NVA had already withdrawn, and we evacuated casualties to a small clearing so choppers could get in and medevac them out. Captain had me and some other guys inspect the perimeter to make sure the Viet Cong were really gone.

We moved through the tall elephant grass, totally on edge, and for the first time in months I forgot about the rats and boot rot and mosquito bites on my body and how bad I stunk. All of my senses were on high alert, so much so that Stone's heavy breathing to my left was getting on my nerves. I really wanted a cigarette. It's amazing where your mind goes when you're literally under the gun like that. What were folks back home doing right then? Watching *Bonanza,* munching popcorn and complaining about their taxes, while we piled up KIAs and choppers took them away.

We made our way along the ridge heading up toward Hill 886. Everything seemed quiet and I found myself thinking maybe the NVA really had cleared the area. We continued moving up and I stopped to take a breath. The first cracking sound confused me. I thought a tree limb must have snapped off nearby, but then the air filled with one long, steady stream of automatic weapon fire. I heard the whooshing and exploding of RPGs being fired, then mortars hitting in front of us. I hit the dirt and pressed myself low in the tall grass. Glancing to the left, I saw Stone hugging the ground. Nobody to my right and nowhere to take cover.

When the gunfire slowed, I heard a couple of our guys screaming, "Medic!" I froze at first, wanting to go help, but wanting to stay put even more. I peeked over at Stone who made a heads down motion with his hand. Ahead I saw movement, or at least I thought I did, so I fired off a full magazine with my M16 pointed in that general direction. I wiped the sweat from my eyes and waited for the smoke to clear. Stone jerked and dropped his gun. His hand went to his hip, which was covered in blood. "Motherfucker," he groaned through clenched teeth, rivulets of sweat mingling with the bits of jungle grass on his muddy, brown face. I flipped to my next magazine and fired blindly ahead for a few seconds, then snaked my way over to Stone. Without thinking too much, I got up on my knees and pressed his hand over the wound to try to staunch the bleeding.

"Stay cool, man," I said. "It ain't bad. We gotta hang tight for a few minutes until Doc gets here."

As I fished into the pouch on my flak jacket for some gauze, I thought about being on patrol with Stone and another guy we called Speedy about a month back. There had been a firefight, and we came across a wounded gook who couldn't have been but 16 or 17 years old. His hip was half gone and he was bleeding out. When we came upon him, his eyes grew big and he looked longingly at his weapon, which was maybe 10 feet away. It might as well have been a mile for all he could move. I thought about whether to get him a medic or let him bleed out when Stone pulled his combat knife, stepped forward and sliced the kid's throat easy as a melon at a Fourth of July picnic. I looked away, but the gurgling sound from that guy's neck stuck with me for days.

I grabbed some gauze and helped Stone press it on the wound. The NVA must have been within throwing distance because VC grenades were falling all over our position. One landed right where I had been a minute before, skipped and settled a foot and a half from us. At that instant, time seemed to slow. Should I try to grab it and throw it back? If I do, will Stone bleed out? If I don't, will it go off anyway? Or maybe it's a dud?

I laid down on top of Stone, kicked my right foot wildly and felt the contact with the grenade. I tried to pray, but like an actor forgetting his lines, the words wouldn't come. I breathed in Stone's acrid sweat, raw earthiness, and the metallic scent of war. Voices yelled, "Pull back!" but they sounded far away, like they were coming from the other end of a long tunnel. I was so tired, so doggone tired.

I thought of that magical dance with Allison only a couple months earlier. Her lips felt so soft against mine. Her neck so tender when I nuzzled it. And the way being with her filled me up. It took away any thought of past or future pain. Was she thinking of me at that moment? If I died, would she remember me fondly, or would I just be that guy Johnny who came back in a box from Vietnam?

Then a supernova of light hit my retinas, and thunderous sound blew out my eardrums. Heat seared my body and pain cut into me. Some blissful mercy sent my world into blackness.

o o o

One thing I can say for certain about the United States Military—it has good drugs. No, the best drugs. Really strong shit. I vaguely remember waking up in a tent hospital in Saigon. But mostly those memories are a blur of faces and sounds and the odor of industrial soap. My mind's clearer about the next hospital, the one in Japan, where they took my leg and kept me wicked doped up. Those pretty, petite nurses, with long, glossy, black hair, speaking no English, smiling, and giving me sponge baths in my gauzy morphine haze. Then, somehow, I ended up at the naval hospital in Philly. They backed off the good dope and brought me back to an "I'm-so-screwed" reality.

"How we doing today, soldier?"

The question came from a matronly nurse named Carol, or Karen, or something like that.

I opted for honesty rather than phony suck-it-up cheerfulness. "Shitty."

This drew a scowl. "No need for vulgarities, soldier. There's many brave men here much worse off than you, so count your blessings."

"Sorry," I said half-heartedly.

"The doctor will be in shortly," she said. "Have some more ice chips. Remember, one at a time."

She placed a Dixie cup in my left hand. I brought it to my lips and took one of the wet chips into my parched mouth. If my tongue hadn't been so dry, it would have sung out in gratitude. I closed my eyes, nodding off. Ethereal dreams of Allison and apples played in my mind. Time passed. Soldiers groaned. Nurses did their best to comfort. Some lived. Some died. Eventually, a dark-skinned guy in a pristine white lab coat and thick glasses came in and talked in low tones to the guy in the bed next to me. I knew from the nurses that the man in the bed was an army grunt who somehow survived an encounter with a Bouncing Betty. I'd tried talking to him, but he just moaned, like wind gusting through an old barn.

I closed my eyes. A hand nudged my left shoulder. "PFC Andrews? I'm Doctor Nasser. How are you feeling today?"

"Like a truck ran over me, then stopped, and backed up

over me again."

The doctor smirked, then pushed his glasses up with an index finger. "An accurate description, I'm afraid." He paused, running his fingers through his thick, black hair. "As you know, we had to do corrective surgery on the amputation you received in Saigon. We tried to save the knee, but between the damage and the infection..." He let the sentence drift off like cigarette smoke in a stiff breeze. "You also suffered significant internal injuries, and we almost lost you from a systemic infection when you arrived here. Your kidneys nearly shut down completely. But you're stronger than you think. Your fever is down, your blood pressure has stabilized, and I think you've pulled out of it."

"Why am I so sick? I tried eating chicken broth, but threw it up. Same for the Jell-O. The goddamned puking hurt as much as getting blown up in the first place."

"That's an unfortunate effect of the antibiotics we have you on. Some people experience extreme nausea. It will pass." He looked at his watch, then glanced at his clipboard. "On the positive side, the breaks in your right arm are already healing nicely. Same for your clavicle. Although there was some debate among the surgical team, we opted to do our best to screw and pin the bones in your left leg together rather than amputate. Our hope is that someday you may walk again. And—" The doctor's sentence was cut off by a wail from the room across the hall. "Excuse me."

And like my leg, the one I used to hold to do a jackknife off the bridge at Sherwood Pond, the man in the white coat was gone.

o o o

The heat is so oppressive. My body is lathered in sweat. If I squatted, which I can't with this 80-pound pack on my back, sweat would wring out from my saturated underwear.

I want to move, I have to move, but I can't. My boots are filled with lead. All I can do is scream...

"Jonathon. Jonathon—wake up."

I open my eyes, cheeks damp with tears, to see my Mom's face a foot above me. Her eyes are frightened, concern etched deeply into the grooves in her face. I think to myself, My God, how she's aged. Did I do this to her?

"You were having another nightmare," she said. She ran her fingers gingerly through the hair that had regrown on my head.

In another room in the house I hear the rhythmic beat of the unstable washing machine as it sloshed through its cycles. Tick-clomp. Tick-clomp. That must be the noise that mingled with my dream.

"You're covered in sweat," she continued. "How late were you out?"

"Sorry, Mom." I wiped my face with my tee shirt and tried to ignore the pounding in my head. "Not sure what time I got home."

"You look awful. Is your leg hurting you?" she took my hand in hers. "Do you need me to get you a pain pill?"

I hated myself for the worry in her voice. I also wondered what she really saw when looking at me. What did she and my father say to each other when alone in their room at night? My parents had to be able to see right through me. Especially Mom, who could always detect a lie before I even told it. They had to see how broken I was. See what I'd done over there. See what I'd become. When would they turn away in disgust?

"No thanks, Mom. No pills today unless I really need 'em. Give me a minute and I'll meet you in the kitchen."

She stood, still holding my hand. "I'll pour you a coffee. Want some scrambled eggs and biscuits?"

"Sure, that sounds great. Thanks, Mom."

She left, closing the door to my new bedroom, which used to be the family dining room. My father and Uncle Ken closed it off and put in the door once they knew for certain I'd be coming back home. My former bedroom was upstairs. Uncle Ken owned a custom furniture shop and built a ramp so I could get in and out of the house fairly easily. But there was no way to get this 180 pounds up those stairs in a chair.

Out the window I could see the sun just making its way over the horizon, casting a pink glow over the orchards. Late October, my favorite time of year. The harvest was over and the cider press would be churning away. Soon enough it'd be deer hunting season. Almost Halloween. I could really scare the bejesus out of the local kids this year if I wanted to.

I fought the urge to go back to sleep, threw off my covers, and tried not to look at my stump. Like iron to a magnet, though, I couldn't resist. There it was, a human ham. No longer the pulpy meat it had been when I was in Japan, it now looked like a Virginia ham with one end battered and deep fried. The left leg was there, but it too looked much the worse for wear. Stippled and off color, speckled with dents and valleys, its primary use was occasionally for leverage, but at a steep cost. The resulting pain was hardly worth it.

I skootched to the side of my bed and did the upper body exercises the physical therapists in Philly had taught me to do before the day's gymnastics. Basically, this entailed swinging my arms in circles, then flailing left and right. No easy feat with my brain aching like it was. Once my muscles and joints were warmed up, I pulled my 48-pound wheelchair, now life companion, over, set the brake, and with a practiced combination of shifting, pressing, contorting and shit luck, I transferred into the cold leather seat. I reversed right, then two rolls forward brought me to the bureau Uncle Ken had made especially for me. It was the right height for a guy my size in a chair, and the drawers were made with some special casters so they slid out easily. It was made of a beautiful cherry wood. Inside, I found a clean sweatshirt and some chinos, which were easier to put on than dungarees. Even so, getting dressed was a generally unpleasant undertaking. At the hospital I had nurses to help, but I had to do it myself in the real world.

Twenty minutes later, I splashed some cold water on my face, brushed the sweaters off my teeth and wheeled myself into the kitchen, prepared for another day of sitting. Mom bustled around the kitchen in her apron. The smell of bacon almost brought a smile to my face. I heard the front door open and turned to see my Uncle Ken coming in.

Ken is an all-around large man. He's about six-four. In high school, he played center on the football team and weighed about 240. He'd definitely put on 40 or 50 more pounds since then. Although his bushy hair was graying, it was always tucked neatly under a Stihl chainsaw cap, and his feral beard generally contained a few leftovers from his last meal. But he was so humble and friendly, you just couldn't help but warm up to the guy.

"Hey, Johnny," he said, swiping his size 14 boots on the welcome rug.

"Uncle Ken. What brings you here?"

"Your mom promised me breakfast, and it's been almost two hours since my last meal." He grinned through whiskers in need of trimming. "Plus, I was hoping to have a word with you."

"I'm pretty busy." I looked at my wrist where a watch would be if I wore one. "But I suppose I can make time."

"C'mon, knucklehead." We proceeded to put away a half dozen eggs, a pound of bacon, and the best biscuits north of Georgia.

"Betty," Uncle Ken said as he did his best to wipe biscuit

crumbs from his beard. "I believe that might have been the best breakfast I've ever had. To repay you, I'm going to take this lazy scoundrel off your hands for a few hours."

Mom sent a worried look my way, but didn't say anything. "Anytime," she said, then continued with her never-ending cleaning. Ken finished another cup of coffee while I got a heavy flannel shirt from my room. We then went outside to his truck. Unlike my parents or Rick, he didn't offer to push my chair or help me get into the truck. He just waited patiently for me to muscle my way in, then folded the chair and put it in the bed.

I knew he had something in mind, but Ken was a quiet man. We rode in silence, which was fine with me. I was beginning to feel the effects of the Demerol I'd taken before we left, protecting me softly like a warm blanket fresh out of the dryer. We drove lazily through town, past the library and the Shell station, turning left on 12B towards Shelburne. Eventually he pulled onto the road leading to his shop, then we parked in front.

"What's the plan?" I asked after he didn't make a move.

"I wanted to talk to you and get you out of that house. Give your poor mother a break."

A few snappy remarks came to mind, but I let them slide. Ken was a good guy, and I knew what he meant.

"You been home, what, three months now?"

"About that."

He stared out the windshield at the shop. "So, what are your plans, Johnny? You just going to go out every night and party your life away?"

I started to object, but he cut me off.

"Now, don't try bullshitting me. I was young once, and I've still got friends who tell me you pretty much drink whiskey and smoke dope with your pals until you pass out most nights. I can see it in your bloodshot eyes this morning, so let's just be straight."

I shifted in the seat. I couldn't even get out and fucking walk away. Goddamned cripple. My eyes started to burn, so I closed them and rubbed them with my hands.

"Well?"

"Maybe I've been drinking a bit much, but you would too, if you were me. It's hard, Ken. Harder than you can imagine. Sorry, but I can't walk. I can't drive. I can't dance with a girl. I can't get a real job. I can't help out at the farm."

"I know it's hard. But you know what John Wayne said? 'Sorry don't get the job done.'"

We sat in silence for a minute or two. Cars whizzed by behind us, and I knew it was about time for Ken to get to work. "I'm thinking I can still help at the orchard, ordering stuff, working the stand. Maybe I'll take some classes and learn how to keep the books."

"All good ideas." He pulled a cigarette out of his pocket and offered me one. I declined, and he lit his with his favorite Zippo. "I'd also like you to think about coming to work for me."

"Really?" I almost laughed. "Doing what, exactly?" I looked carefully at his face, but he was dead serious.

Ken exhaled a big gust of smoke and said, "C'mon. I'll show you."

He got my chair and I wrangled myself into it. Rather than going in the front door of the shop, which had five steps, he walked around the left side of the building. Once I turned the corner, I saw him walk up a short ramp. I wanted to ask if he'd done this just for me. He pulled out his keys to open a door that hadn't been there before. He turned and said, "Come on."

The ramp only had to incline about a foot and a half, so it was easy to get up. The door was fitted with some sort of lock and release mechanism so it could be locked open, then released with the push of a button on the inside. Ken had obviously put some thought into this.

The shop smelled like sawdust and pine, and always triggered nice memories of coming here as a kid. Ken was a fine carpenter, capable of building anything from a picnic bench to reproductions of antique Queen Anne furniture. Over the years he'd made me wooden puzzles, sailboats, cribbage boards, and a miniature rocking chair that my mom still had in my old room.

Around the shop were various pieces of equipment—table saws, band saws, drill presses, lathes, planers. There was a wood storage room, and a front desk with a phone and file cabinet for taking orders. I figured that must be what he had in mind. I heard something creaking behind me and turned one wheel to spin around. Ken was pulling a handle connected to two small ropes, attached to a kind of platform that rose up maybe eight or ten inches.

On the opposite side of the ropes was a short ramp. "C'mere," he grunted after putting the object in front of the lathe. I rolled over, wondering what the hell Uncle Kenny had been smoking. "Go up the ramp on the left side, then spin yourself so you are in front of the lathe. Put on your brake so you don't go falling off and gettin' me sued or killed by your mother."

Tentatively, I rolled over and up the short ramp. The platform was probably five feet by five feet, so there was room enough to pivot and lock myself in place.

"Move forward six more inches," he directed. "Good, stop there. Now reach to the right, then left."

I did as I was told. I'd taken wood shop in high school, so I was vaguely familiar with most of the machines. It took some stretching, but my arms were long enough so I could manipulate the chuck, the headstock and the tail stock, and easily hit the start and stop buttons.

"Good. That's good. I figure this is the most difficult for you to reach. Most of the other equipment should be a breeze."

"You want me to operate the lathe? And the table saw? Are you kidding?"

He gave me a simple answer. "No."

He told me how he'd built the ramp using pine for weight and maple for strength. The wheels underneath were on a spring system, so when weight was on the platform it wouldn't move. But without weight on it, it could easily be rolled from machine to machine.

He removed his hat, ran a hand through his hair. "I'll have to do some cleaning up, and we can rearrange things as you gain experience so it goes easier for you. But I think we're in good enough shape for now. What do you think?"

I ran my hands across the heavy metal of the wood lathe. I was glad I'd taken the Demerol, or else I might burst into tears like a baby.

The world had turned so dark since I'd come home. Ugly thoughts constantly ping-ponged inside my skull. Mom putting me on the prayer tree at church. Mrs. Woodson telling me if I had enough faith, Jesus would surely heal me. That look crossing strangers' faces when they first noticed the creepy guy in the chair. Shock followed by repulsion followed by pity followed by let me look at anything else. Except the kids, curious and pointing, "Mommy, what's wrong with him?"

Ken wanted me to work. Not just answer the phone and fill out paperwork, but actually use my hands to build something.

"When can I start?"

o o o

As the sander stopped, I ran my fingers over the cool surface of the wood. The smooth, silky feeling gave me incredible satisfaction. I brushed the sawdust from my hands, arms, and legs. The 48-inch round tabletop on the sawhorses in front of me had been sanded five times now and should be ready for spraying. An ember of pride grew in my chest.

I'd made this. I'd also made the four legs, but working the lathe was relatively easy. Sanding, not so much. But cutting a perfect circle out of an expensive plank of hard wood, then planing and gently chiseling, routing, and sanding to make this beautiful top—that was something.

Uncle Ken had started me on the easy work, which was understandable. A guy with his talent should be making fine cabinetry and custom desks while somebody else cranked out picnic tables and Adirondack chairs. That somebody was me, and I was happy to do it. While my first picnic table might be good enough to put out by the apple stand, it wasn't good enough for a paying customer. However, after five more, I'd gotten the hang of how to do it, and in half the time it took me to make that first one. Adirondack chairs aren't all that more complex, but there's a lot more parts and sanding to be done. So, first I learned the small side tables that go with them, then I started making chairs from Ken's template pieces. I can't say I never screwed up, but experience helps cover the occasional mistakes.

Simple bookcases followed by more complicated shelving units with detail work came next. Then Ken had entrusted me to make this oak bistro table for a rich lady from the city, and I felt a jolt of pride like I hadn't felt since I'd graduated from basic training.

I put the tabletop into my wagon and pulled it over to the spray booth. Ken was out measuring up some kitchen cabinets, so I went over to my workbench and took out the parts to my side project.

A few weeks before, I was out at O'Brien's with Rick, having a beer or three. Since I started with Ken, I'd cut way back on the hard liquor and weed, but I still needed to get out from time to time to throw a few back with my friends. The first time I saw Allison glide into the bar, my heart did that flip floppy thing it always did in her presence. She was home from the University of Buffalo on Christmas break, and she looked better than ever in her tight pants and sweater. Her hair was longer and wavier, and she didn't seem to be wearing any makeup, which she didn't need in the first place. She scooted right over to give me a hug and kiss. Nothing romantic, mind you. The hug was awkward, and she turned her head when I went for a smooch.

"You're looking great," she said, stepping back. "I like you with longer hair."

I thanked her, and then asked about her semester before any further discussion of my appearance dragged on. That was a road I didn't want to go down.

"It was great. College is much cooler than high school. Most of the professors are groovy. They even let us call them by their first names. And classes are much mellower, with open discussions and thought experiments, rather than old Mrs. Crandle expecting us to regurgitate the same crap she memorized 20 years ago. That shit is past. The world is different now."

She wore a dreamy look, and I tried hard not to dwell on the distance between us. "Regurgitate. You really do sound like a college chick now!" I was hoping for a laugh, but Allison just looked like she wanted to say something but didn't. "How long you home for?" I continued.

"Another week, then I'm going skiing with some friends in Vermont. Mount Snow..." her sentence trailed off as she considered my wheelchair.

"Sure," I tried to break the awkwardness. "I've heard

that's a great mountain. Should be fun."

She grabbed a chair and sat next to me. We chatted about her classes and her roommate and how her family was doing. She asked about me, but didn't request any war stories, which I was grateful for. Ninety percent of the people I ran into wanted to hear how I lost my leg, and anything else gory I could throw in about the war. Allison seemed genuinely happy that I was working at the shop with Ken. She got up to get a glass of wine and then went over to the jukebox. As she leaned forward to study the selections, I studied her sweet curves and nearly burst with horniness. As "Light My Fire" started to play, she turned and smiled at me. She looks like a rock star, I thought. Then I had an idea. A great idea.

I talked with Ken the next day. After a bit of searching through some catalogues, he helped me find a build-your-own-guitar kit. The pieces came precut and already bent and carved into the right shapes, so mostly it involved a little screwing, a lot of gluing, and some finishing sanding. But it did what I wanted, which was to teach me about the way a guitar is built.

Rick and I went to the library and found a copy of *The Luthier's Handbook*, which covered everything I needed to know about the correct woods, shapes, balance, and action. I ordered some seasoned rosewood, mahogany, and spruce from Sam's Lumber in Chenango, and began my special project.

The neck was finished and bolted to the body and it was time to glue the face in place. But before I did that, I took out the wood burner, put on a flat tip, and plugged it in. I was nervous about this part, but it was key to my plan.

On the inside of the guitar back, right under where the sound hole would be, I wrote **MORRIS** in calligraphy with a pencil. The S was the trickiest letter, but that's why I did it in pencil, so I could erase it and do it again. Now that the penciled letters were perfect, it was time to go over them with the wood burner, branding the name forever.

Taking a deep breath, I touched the hot tip to the letter M and very carefully began to char the wood. The burnt-sugar odor of the scorched rosewood filled my nose, but I stayed focused on moving at a steady pace. Ten minutes later, I put the hot tool down and studied my work. The bottom of the "I" was a little long on one side, but there was nothing to be done about that now. At a glance, no one would ever notice. I wiped the sweat off my forehead and readied myself to glue down the face of the guitar.

o o o

A couple months later, the guitar was finished. Allison was home for spring break. I'd written her a few letters, and although she wasn't very quick in writing back, I understood she was busy with her classes. She told me when she'd be back home, though, and said it would be great to get together.

My problem was how to arrange it. Although I'd heard of vehicles being modified so chair users could drive them with hand controls, I didn't have that kind of dough. I wanted to ask her out for a nice dinner, maybe Century Inn or the Adirondack Café, but they didn't have ramps, and who knew how tight the seating was. I knew I didn't want to be the focus of everyone's attention in the place when I was trying to have a good time with Allison. Rick suggested I just invite her over to my parents' house for dinner, since it was practical and accessible. But how romantic was that? Let's have dinner with my mom. Maybe she'll tell you how much I hated broccoli when I was a kid, or that I wet the bed until I was six.

I did mention my dilemma to Uncle Ken, who came up

with a good solution. He even offered to help with my plan, which I took him up on. The day after Allison was home, I called, and she agreed to pick me up in her father's Buick. I sensed reluctance, but I convinced her she was strong enough to fold my chair and get it in and out of the trunk. If not, my master plan would go right down the toilet.

Allison showed up about a half hour late on Tuesday evening, dressed in a short, neon-green skirt, nearly making my dad's eyes pop out. She had the legs of a model, so she looked great, but my folks weren't accustomed to seeing that much skin. But the real kicker was her earrings. They were made of thick copper wire bent into the shape of a peace sign and hammered thin. Allison was very proud of them and told us all about how some hippie friends at college made them. I could tell both of my parents were thinking she was not only a slut, but a hippie, war-protesting slut. They managed not to say anything and painted on fake smiles while I did my best to hurry us out of there. My dad followed us out and put my chair in her trunk so Allison didn't have to. He tapped on the passenger window before we left and said, "Just call if you have any trouble."

"Sure thing, Pop," I said. "See you later."

Allison turned the Buick around and headed out toward town. "I don't think your mom and dad liked me very much."

"I wouldn't say that. They're just a little old fashioned. Squares. And they're worried about me. They can't help that."

"If you say so." She turned on the radio and tuned into WQBK, Albany's home of rock-n-roll. Cream's "Sunshine of Your Love" played. She told me to take the wheel, which I did reluctantly, while she fished in her purse to pull out a joint and pushed in the lighter. "Here," she said, handing me the joint. "Spark it up."

We smoked the doobie, which did help with my nervousness. She kept turning to talk and look at me while she drove, and I prepared to lean over and take the wheel, but I managed to get her to drive us to Uncle Ken's shop without incident.

"I thought you said we were going out for dinner?"

"It's a little unusual, I know." I hoped Uncle Ken had done what he said he would, or I was screwed. "Please just trust me."

She gave me a look like I was a door-to-door insurance man, then hopped out to open the trunk and wrestled my chair out. I sighed. A real man would never let his girl do the heavy lifting, I thought. A lot of banging and swearing came from the trunk, but eventually, she managed to flop my chair onto the pavement.

"Just stand it up and push outwards on the handles. It will lock into place," I instructed. A second later, she was by my open door with the chair. Allison was not exuding happiness by any stretch of the imagination. I led the way to the shop's side entrance and opened the door.

"Ladies first," I said with a big smile. Allison, still looking perplexed, stepped into the shop. I followed her inside, hit the door release, and stared in momentary shock.

"Oh my God," she said. "I can't believe this!"

Uncle Ken had outdone himself. Somehow, he'd moved the drill press and table saw, creating a clear spot in the shop. The floor was swept, and there was a card table covered in a checkered tablecloth, complete with a bottle of wine and a six-pack of Rolling Rock on ice. A chair was in place for Allison, with an open spot opposite for me. To one side of the table was a small bench with a takeout bag of food. The table had been set, with a lit candle in the center. The florescent light at the front of the shop was the only light on. So, all things considered, it was unexpectedly romantic.

"Come on," I reached out and squeezed her hand. "Let's

sit and have a drink before dinner."

It might have been the weed, but she smiled and wiped at her eyes for a second. Maybe the evening wouldn't be a total flop. We sat down and I poured her some wine and cracked myself a beer.

Since we were later than expected, the food was more lukewarm than hot, but we were both hungry and it definitely hit the spot.

Over dinner, Allison told me more about college, about classes and partying, and how much she was digging going to concerts with her new friends. Already this year she'd seen Jefferson Airplane and a band named The Grateful Dead, who I'd never heard of.

"Do they have any songs on the radio?"

"I don't think so," she said. "Only commercial musicians make it on the radio. The Dead aren't mainstream. They're out of sight. More like underground music. Their sound is very trippy. Very San Francisco. You definitely should get their album. You'll love it."

We finished our food and I was on my third beer. She had almost polished off the wine, so I figured now was as good a time as any for my gift.

"Will you do me a favor?" I asked.

"That depends." There wasn't much playfulness in her voice. Had time made her more on edge, or was it me? Was there a spark between us, or was she simply doing a good deed, humoring the crippled guy?

I looked away and took a deep breath. Take it easy, man. "Excuse me for a minute." I rolled back and over to my work bench. Reaching underneath, I pulled out the guitar case, put it on my lap, and said, "Now close your eyes."

"Why?"

"Because I asked you to." My voice was a little sharper than I intended. Taking a deep breath, I tried to calm myself.

"I promise nothing bad is going to happen."

I rolled back over to the table and saw she had actually kept her eyes closed. I took a second to soak in her beauty. Just in case this didn't go well, I wanted to savor this moment. I bit down on my nervousness and said, "Okay, you can open them now."

She did, and a puzzled look crossed her face.

"I know you love music, and I wanted to give you something, so here." I leaned forward and put the guitar case in her lap.

"Is this really what I think it is?"

I grinned. "Go ahead, take a look."

Allison slid her fingertips slowly across the top of the black case. It seemed as if she'd come to some decision. She flipped the latch and opened the case. Inside, on a cushion of green velvet, was the guitar. Allison's eyes went wide. My heart swelled with pride as she slowly ran one finger around the pick guard, which I'd made into a funky M shape with a coping saw, a razor blade, and a lot of sanding. The face of the guitar was a gorgeous reddish maple color, with so many coats of lacquer and polish her face reflected like a mirror. To me, that face was the one thing in this world more beautiful than the guitar.

"Johnny," she said. "Johnny, this is too much."

"Look in the sound hole."

She bent forward, still not taking the guitar from the case, to peep in the hole.

"Morris," she read. Then her eyes brightened as she looked up and smiled at me. "Morris."

"Remember?" I asked. "Right before I shipped off. We were dancing to the Doors down at O'Brien's and you said you wanted to name your first kid Morris."

She laughed then, and the sound made me feel like I could leap out of my wheelchair.

"I can't believe you remembered that." She strummed the steel strings with her fingernails. The sound resonated through the shop.

"There's a harmonica kind of thing in that compartment under the neck. It's a tuning pipe. I did the best I could, but I'm sure you'll have a better ear than me."

"How did you get the name on the inside of the guitar?"

"I used a pencil and wood burner before I put the face on it."

"Before you... You... You made this? Are you shitting me? You made this guitar?"

"I did." I soaked up her surprise like a welcome burst of sunshine. I'd put my heart and soul into this guitar for her and built something beautiful.

"I can't believe it." She looked down and shook her head slightly. "You made this. How? How long did it take you?"

"About a hundred hours. Give or take. The bending of the sides is a very slow process, as is the carving of the neck. It's made of American mahogany, and I did it all by hand. It's an inch and three quarters wide, since I wasn't sure how long your fingers are." I cut myself off. The details interested me, but they wouldn't matter to Allison.

"Johnny..." She looked serious as she tried to find words. "Thank you, but I can't accept this. You made this. It took you like a million hours. How can I keep it?"

"It's yours." I rolled forward a foot and took her warm hands in mine. "I made it for you."

I waited until she looked up at me and imagined I could stare into those eyes forever. "It's been hard since I got back. Real hard. My uncle was nice enough to give me a job and show me the ropes. Building this guitar for you, it was like a goal for me. It gave me a purpose, and I enjoyed doing it. I hope you'll accept it and learn to play. That'd make me very happy."

She leaned forward, almost toppling the guitar and case to the floor, taking my face in her hands. She kissed me. Her lips were softer than the rain, and the lingering taste of wine made every hormone in my body do backflips. Allison pulled away, giving me a killer smile. She stood, lifting the guitar with one hand and putting the case on her chair with the other. With a short spin, she plopped herself on my lap. I wrapped my arms around her as she strummed lightly, and prayed the moment would never end.

ATTACHMENTS

"Imagine no possessions
I wonder if you can
No need for greed or hunger
A brotherhood of man."
– "Imagine" by John Lennon

Allison recognized the guy across the room from the peace sign patch on the knee of his dungarees. He had a vague resemblance to Paul McCartney on the White Album poster with his scraggly, sexy beard. Not a dead ringer, but with the right mix of beer and wine and pot and mushrooms, he could definitely be Paul's brother. He caught her looking and sent her a dreamy smile. Despite his beard, she saw a dimple on one cheek that was cute as hell. She smiled back, and he weaved his way around the mass of bodies at the party to join her.

"Hi," he said over the Kinks blasting on the stereo. He stopped two feet in front of her, beamed a 100-watt smile, and opened his arms for a hug. Without hesitation, she stepped into his arms, feeling his strength embrace her as she breathed in his scent, an intoxicating mixture of patchouli and earthiness and weed and maybe even a touch of cinnamon, although that might have been her imagination, or the mushrooms, playing tricks on her.

He stepped back, placing a finger to his forehead as if deep in thought. "Piss on Nixon," he said. "Am I right?" She blushed as she smiled at him. He was referring to the sign she'd been carrying at the protest that afternoon.

"Yes, you are," she said, then mimicked his finger to forehead gesture. "And you, you were 'Don't kill babies,' right?"

"Close," he said. "'Drop acid, not bombs.' A little cliché, I know, but I was short on time and I reused it from the rally in Albany two weeks ago."

"That's cool," she replied. "Recycling. That's cool." She looked for a second into his eyes, which were a little bloodshot, but a vibrant blue with tiny specks of green in the irises. His gaze was too intense, though, so she had to look away.

"What's your name?"

"Allison, but I prefer Allie. And you?"

"Call me Ocean."

Allie started to giggle, but he didn't. "Ocean? That's your name?"

"It's not the name the cogs who raised me labeled me, but my Zen name. It's a good expression of who I am. I'm constant and fluid and relaxing and sometimes unpredictable."

"Cool." She looked into the empty plastic cup in her hand, struggling to think of something clever to say. She'd never heard of a Zen name, but she liked the concept. She felt something pull inside her, wanting to know more about this guy.

"You a UB student?"

"Nope." He brushed a stray hair behind her ear with a gentle finger. "Too much concrete for me. I'm on a truth quest, and when I heard about the protest, I felt the need to be here."

"A truth quest? What's that?"

"It's something I learned from a shaman in Mexico." The way he pronounced Mexico like 'meh-heco' gave him a genuine-deal vibe. "Truth comes from authentic people, not from textbooks. I can see that you are also a seeker. Come," he said as he took her hand. "Let's share more wine."

A few hours and many glasses of wine later, they were stumbling, arm in arm, across the quad toward her dorm. Ocean had produced a couple of purple capsules from his shirt pocket while "White Rabbit" was playing on the hi-fi at the party, and now they were both chatting and giggling like school kids on a field trip. When Ocean said that a big fat joint would really round out his buzz, Allie whispered that she had some killer stuff from Panama back in her dorm and off they went.

Allison left Ocean by the emergency exit of Silliman Hall, or just Silly as everybody called it. "Hang out here and have a smoke. I need to go sign in and then I'll come let you in." Before she left, he grabbed her arm, pulling her into an embrace. They kissed, soft and gentle, bathed in the moonlight of a crisp autumn night.

"Five minutes," she said, jogging towards the front entrance.

"Make it four!" he called after her.

Still giggling, Allie attempted to get herself under control before entering Silly. Since it was after midnight, the door was locked. Mrs. Fulton, the dorm supervisor, commonly referred to as 'the old gray mare,' scowled and let her in.

"Have you been drinking, Miss King?"

What a stupid question, Allie thought. It's the weekend on a college campus in Buffalo, New York. Tricky Dick was in the White House, and American soldiers were napalming innocent Vietnamese families. The only thing sane people could do was dull the pain a little. "Just one glass of wine," Allie answered. "But I really do have to go to the bathroom. Have a nice evening." Allie scampered up the steps to the third floor, then checked her room.

Linda, thank the Lord, had gone home for the weekend to visit her creepy boyfriend. His name was Raymond Crutcher, and he bore a striking resemblance to Norman Bates in the movie *Psycho*. But all that mattered now was Linda wasn't around. Allie headed to the other stairwell, descended to the first floor, and let Ocean in.

"Jesus, I thought you'd never get here!"

"Shush!" she said in a loud whisper. "You'll get us in trouble."

"What trouble?" His voice echoed through the stairwell. "It's Saturday night!"

Needing to shut him up, she pulled his face toward her and kissed him. He tasted of wine and menthol from his cigarettes. "Not another word until we're in my room—got it?" She kissed him again so he wouldn't talk. He must have understood because he nodded. She took his hand and pulled him up the stairs.

At the third floor, she opened the door a few inches and peeked down the hallway. If Katie Alongi or Cheryl Gregor knew there was a man in the dorm, they'd throw a conniption fit. But, of course, those two prudes had probably said their prayers and gone to bed hours ago. Light shined under several hallway doors, and quiet music and muffled voices could be detected, but they should be fine.

"Is the coast clear?" he asked with a laugh.

She elbowed him. "Shushhh."

She took his hand and jogged down the hall to her room. She pulled him inside and locked the door. She hit the light switch and they both cringed while their eyes adjusted. He hooked an arm around her waist and pulled her into him. He kissed her, harder this time, and she felt his hand reaching up under her shirt. She stopped the roaming hand with one arm and pushed back with the other.

"Hold your horses there, big fella. Take it easy. This isn't a race."

He released her with a sheepish smile, then pressed his palms together and bowed.

"Come. Sit." She went to her record player, bypassed *Sgt. Pepper's* and started *Cosmo's Factory* by Creedence Clearwater Revival. One good thing about her roommate was that her older brother worked at a record store, so Linda had a totally choice album collection. Once the music was on, she adjusted the volume low, then turned on her desk lamp and put a tie-dye scarf over it. She flicked off the overhead light and turned towards Ocean. "Better?"

"Much," he said.

She opened her bottom drawer, lifted up her economics book, pulled out a bag of weed and a half-full bottle of Boone's Farm strawberry wine. Ocean's eyes grew big, and even in the dim light his smile shone like a beacon.

As she sat down on her bed next to him, he fished in his shirt pocket and pulled out a wood pipe.

"Mind if we use this? I got it two summers ago when I was in Montana—Navaho country. I crashed for a while with these Indians, and one of them hand carved this for me. It's birch—one of their sacred trees."

She accepted the pipe and turned it over in her hands. It looked exactly like one she'd seen at Crazy Eddie's Head Shop in downtown Buffalo, but she kept that to herself. She put it down between them and handed him the wine. Laying the Creedence album cover on her lap, she took a bud from her stash. As she broke it apart and started pulling out the seeds and stems, she asked where he was from.

"I was born in Saint Nowheresville, Minnesota, but split as soon as I could. Me and a friend thumbed our way to California, which is really where it's at. I crashed with some hippies in the Haight, and that's where I learned to meditate on the truths."

"The truths?"

"Buddhism and the eight-fold path. The four noble truths. The middle way to cease all suffering." He unscrewed the top of the wine and took a slug from the bottle. "It changed my world. You really should read up on it. Find a teacher. I'm positive you'll dig it."

"Hmmmm... Sounds interesting."

Growing up, Allie's family were Congregationalists. Her dad sang in the choir and her mom taught Sunday school until Allie was in eighth grade. While she didn't love church, she didn't mind it either. It was nice to think that Jesus, or God, or the Holy Spirit—she'd always had trouble with the concept of the trinity—cared and was watching over her. Then, during what could only be called a midlife breakdown, the Kings started attending a small Pentecostal church in Edwinton. While her mother seemed to relish the fire and brimstone, it totally turned Allie off. This whole self-righteous, God-created-you-only-to-damn-you thing just rang a little too much like man-made oppression to her ears.

In time, she began to think that commie, Marx, or was it Lenin, had it right. Religion is the opiate of the masses.

She filled the bowl and handed it to Ocean, expecting him to ramble on about Buddhism bullshit. But he was busy scanning her room and his eye landed on the picture of Johnny above her desk. It was a photo of him dressed in his fatigues, an M16 in his arms, a big helicopter and dense jungle in the background. He'd sent it with his first letter while over there.

"What's with the homage to the baby killer?"

She took his lighter and lit the bowl, dragging a long hit and holding it in as she passed the pipe to him. She exhaled, coughed a little, and said, "He's not a baby killer. He's an old friend. He's a good guy."

"By good guy, you mean he uses a flame thrower to torch Vietnamese villages, or tosses hand grenades into bunkers where innocent grandmas and children are just trying to stay alive for another day?"

Her guts stiffened up like quick-set plaster stirred a little too long. Last summer, shortly before she returned to school, she told Johnny that she couldn't be his girl. They were just too different, and she had plans. Plans like traveling and visiting exotic places. Places you couldn't get to in a wheel-chair. She wasn't ready yet, but some day she wanted to marry and have kids. She wanted a husband her kids could throw a ball with. Sled with. Ride bikes with. Go fishing with. It wasn't kind to either of them to think Johnny might be that guy. And then there was the whole war thing, a topic they'd danced around all summer. But even so, who was this guy to presume anything about Johnny?

"He got drafted," she lied. "Four months into his tour he got one leg blown off, and the other was busted all to shit."

She looked away as Ocean took a toke and she made herself not tear up. She wasn't sure why she still kept the picture of Johnny up on her wall. It certainly didn't fit in with her politics or beliefs, and since they had no future, why try to hold on? Still, deep in her heart, she knew he was a good guy.

The war was a horrible, tragic mistake. And despite what everybody claimed, most of the US soldiers were probably guys just like Johnny. Good guys fighting for a bad cause.

"Karma," he was saying before bogarting another hit.

"Johnny's in a wheelchair now," she went on. "He's learned to work with wood. I've seen some wicked neat tables and bookcases he's made by hand. He even made me this totally fab guitar."

He exhaled a huge plume of blue smoke. "Really? Is it here?"

She took another hit and handed the pipe back to Ocean. While he smoked, she moved some stuff from under her bed and pulled out the guitar case. She sat down and opened it up with reverence, admiring the beautifully shiny red surface. Johnny had put so much of himself into this guitar. So much love.

Ocean tried passing her the pipe, but she shook her head no. "Do you play?" he asked.

"Not really." She strummed the strings with one fingernail. "I got a book and learned the basic chords, and even practiced a bit. But I just don't have a talent for it. Still, I like the sound, and it's relaxing sometimes to just sit and mess around."

He put down the pipe and held out his arms. "Mind if I give it a go?"

"Do you play?" She took the guitar from the hard case, carefully handing it to him.

"I try. The way I figure it, the music is already out there in the universe. It's mostly a matter of tuning in to the right frequency so you can pull it into your fingers."

Ocean plunked a few chords, then played what Allison knew was a pentatonic scale. He wasn't Neil Young, but he obviously knew how to play. She took a few sips of wine while he started strumming an open G chord, then C, then she recognized the melody. In a scratchy voice that was surprisingly fitting to the original, he started to sing softly.

"How many roads must a man walk down,
Before you call him a man?
How many seas must a white dove sail,
Before she sleeps in the sand?
Yes, and how many times must a cannonball fly,
Before they are forever banned?
The answer my friend, is blowin' in the wind
The answer is blowin' in the wind..."

She couldn't help but smile. This was obviously a kind man, trying just like her to figure things out. She picked up the pipe and refilled the bowl as he finished the song. They both smoked some more, and he sang another tune she didn't know. Then he played a silly version of "Henry the Eighth" which busted both of them up laughing. She put the guitar away in its case, and he tossed it on Linda's bed.

They finished the bowl, then the wine, then he kissed her tenderly on the lips. "Sorry 'bout your army friend," he said softly. "We suffer in this life because of our attachments. Attachments to material things, and to ideals. And the universe is always trying to teach us the futility of these attachments. We all need..."

Allie wasn't in the mood for a philosophical discussion. Between the weed and all the wine and the pills, she was interested more in release than salvation. She grabbed him by the beard and pulled his face to where she could kiss him.

"Ouch," he groaned when she let go. He caressed her cheek with a feathery touch, then ran his fingers through the strands of her hair. The coarse hairs of his beard tickled as he kissed her chin and jawline.

This time, she didn't push his hand away as it caressed the bare skin of her belly and made its way to her breast. Her skin tingled at his touch, and a jolt of electricity ran through her pelvis when he pinched her aroused nipple.

She kissed him again, then pulled off her shirt and tossed it to the floor. He did the same. They had sex while the record player crackled and popped in the grooves at album's end. Curled into Ocean's embrace, Allie fell asleep as he talked on and on, something about how a man should never be the hero of his own story.

The sun was fairly high in her window when she managed to pull herself from sleep. The first thing she noticed was the pain in her bladder. She had to go to the bathroom something fierce. The second thing she noticed was that she was naked. And thirdly, Ocean was gone. That was probably best, she thought, as she pulled on a bathrobe and made her way to the bathroom for a much-needed pee and teeth brushing.

She definitely needed a shower, but it was getting late and she wanted to tidy up the room and get some breakfast before the dining hall stopped serving. Linda would be back that afternoon, and they had an agreement about keeping the room fairly neat.

Allie put her robe away and got a pair of fresh underwear from her bureau. She was used to not wearing a bra, so she slipped on a clean sweater and some pea-green corduroy pants. After putting on her shoes, she scooped up her dirty clothes from the floor and Linda's bed, and something seemed off. Something niggled at the far reaches of her brain.

Allie glanced around the room. The Creedence album was sitting on top of the turntable. She removed the tie-dye scarf from her desk light and turned it off. Her bed was a mess, but that wasn't it.

There was an impression on Linda's bed, but no guitar. She felt fairly certain, despite the dope and fuzziness in her brain, that she'd put Johnny's guitar back in its case and on Linda's bed before she and Ocean started fooling around last night. She stepped forward and felt the empty bedspread. Yes, it was there last night. She dropped to the floor and looked under her bed.

It wasn't there. She looked under Linda's bed. It wasn't there.

Sweat broke out on her forehead as she frantically searched her closet, then Linda's closet, then under the beds again. A dorm room isn't that big, and while a part of her wanted to believe Ocean had put the guitar someplace, wretched reality knew the truth. Ocean—she didn't even know the bastard's real name—had stolen her guitar. Johnny's guitar. The guitar he'd spent a hundred hours on. For her.

Tears welled as she muffled sobs with her hands, biting down on her palm to hide a scream. What had she done? A chorus of, "How could I?" broke through her wails, like glass pinging onto tile. How could she be so irresponsible? How could she have done this to Johnny? She looked down and saw the empty Boone's Farm bottle on the floor. Which made her think of her weed.

A quick glance around the room revealed nothing. Closing her eyes, she saw the weed, the pipe, the lighter, on the bedside table last night. On top of the Creedence album. Nothing there now. She looked under her pillow, in the bedding, in her bureau drawers, and in her desk. Under the bed. In her boots. Nothing.

The pounding drumbeat in her temples was unbearable. Shame, it hammered. Shame. You should be ashamed.

Allison wept.

CAPTAIN JACK'S

"Many times I've lied and many times I've listened
I've wondered how much there is to know
Many dreams come true, and some have silver linings
I live for my dreams, and a pocket full of gold"
  – "Over The Hills and Far Away" by Led Zeppelin

The assholes arrived a half hour into my shift.

"Danny," Reggie, the cook with the big afro that drove the manager nuts, called out. "When you get a sec, grab a box of burgers from the walk-in."

The walk-in freezer was located in a storage room by the back entrance. Since the dinner rush hadn't started yet, I slipped outside for a few drags off a Marlboro first. A beat-up VW bus clanged into the parking lot, Zeppelin blasting out the windows. It nearly clipped my '64 Dart, known affectionately as the 'turd' to my friends. While the unfortunate paint job might remind you of something the dog left in the back lot, it was still my most treasured possession.

The van sported Michigan plates and the rear bumper was attached by something I'd bet a hundred bucks was nothing more than a bent wire hanger. The music died, abruptly halting a Jimmy Page guitar solo. Three people spilled out of the bus. "Suck my dick," said a girl who looked to be maybe 20, while the two older guys she'd arrived with busted out laughing.

The girl had dirty blonde, shoulder-length hair and wore a tee shirt and tight jeans, although she didn't have much of an ass to fill them out. Despite the cool weather, she wore flip flops and didn't have a jacket. The guy in the passenger seat had on jeans with holes in both knees and a jean jacket

with a big confederate flag patch sewn on the back. I immediately thought of him as denim dude. He had greasy red hair
parted in the middle. He put a skinny arm around the
shoulder of the girl while they waited for the driver to join
them. I pinched off the burning end of my cig and put the
unsmoked half in my pocket for later, then grabbed a box of
frozen burgers from the freezer.

"Thanks, man." The cook was also enjoying a smoke, but
in the kitchen. Logan, the manager, would have a shit fit if he
saw him. But Reggie was keeping one eye on the back door,
and Logan probably wouldn't show until dinner service was
in full swing.

I took a second to glance over at Lily, the dishwasher.
She's only 16, a little nerdy, but still kind of cute. I've been
trying to be friendly, but so far, it's not working. No doubt
her parents told her to stay away from guys like me.

Jane and Gwen were waitresses. At the moment, Gwen
was dumping one half-full bottle of ketchup into another,
making a full bottle to put out on the tables. No doubt this
was Logan's idea, believing a full bottle of ketchup, no matter
how old, looked better to customers. Jane was out serving,
and a third waitress, Maddy, was late. She had something
like five kids at home and a husband who was sometimes
there, sometimes not. But she was friendly, and good when it
came to tipping out.

Jane bustled through the swinging doors with a dirty
plate and a yellow order slip. She clipped the slip into the
new order wheel. "I need a cheeseburger, fries, tuna salad no
fries, and an order of wings. Danny, bus number 7 and make
sure 3 has water."

I grabbed an empty bus tub and banged through the
swinging doors into the dining room. The change in atmosphere was like stepping into an episode of the *Twilight
Zone*. The kitchen was hot and loud. Waitresses barked

orders and cooks hollered that food was up. The grill and fryer sizzled, and the dishwasher scraped plates while the machine rumbled and boiled. Meanwhile, the dining room was like another reality. It was cool with low murmuring at each of the 24 tables. Some kind of mellow, synthetic music piped through speakers in the ceiling. The paneled walls and carpet kept things quieter.

Heading over to the bus station, I grabbed a pitcher of ice water. At table 3, the man was sticking to his Jim Beam on the rocks, while his wife, who had bright red lipstick on her teeth, smiled wide and asked for more water. Meanwhile, the trio from the parking lot had seated themselves at table 13. The girl and denim dude had taken one side of the table while the driver, who had black curly hair and a matching beard, sat opposite them.

"Boy," one of the guys said.

I picked up the tub and turned toward them. All three lit up smokes, but it was denim dude who spoke. With his jacket off, I noticed a crude homemade swastika tattoo on his forearm. "Hey boy, git us a new ashtray."

Did this shitbag really just call me boy? Twice? I briefly considered smashing his face with the bus tub, but I really needed this job. The guy glared at me, then with the tips of his dirty fingernails flipped the glass ashtray off their table onto the floor. He and the girl, who looked younger now that I was closer, broke out in laughter, while the bearded guy just grinned and shook his head. I stood and watched as the ashtray tumbled then bounced, dumping a small mound of gray ash and three or four butts on the gold carpet. I have to admit, it shocked me even more than him calling me 'boy.' Then I really got pissed. I briefly considered braining him with a full bottle of ketchup, but just muttered, "Motherfuck-er," and hustled through the swinging doors back into the kitchen.

Jane was prepping a milkshake and must have noticed the steam shooting out of my ears. "Danny—is there a problem?"

"The red-headed cocksucker at number 13 just dumped the ashtray on the carpet. He asked me for a new one, then he intentionally knocked the dirty ashtray off the table. It was all I could do not to punch him out."

"You made the right choice," Jane said, putting a hand on my shoulder. "I'll get them a new ashtray and water. You grab the vacuum from the coat closet. There's an outlet by table 10. Just keep your mouth shut and clean it up."

I found the vacuum and quickly sucked up the mess on the carpet. The trio went silent, watching, while I tried to figure out how I could accidentally spill a bowl of boiling soup on the asshole's head. Winding up the vacuum's cord, I noticed a cluster of pimples on the girl's chin and downgraded her to maybe ninth or tenth grade. Denim dude smoked and studied the menu. The bearded guy tried to look down Jane's blouse as she poured their waters.

"Can I get you guys anything from the bar?" Jane asked.

"A pitcher of Miller and three glasses," bearded guy said.

"I'm going to need to see your ID, sweetie," Jane addressed the girl.

"I, uh, don't have my driver's license on me," she stammered.

"Sorry," Jane said. "Two glasses then."

"Fuck that," denim dude spat out. "She's 19—I'll vouch for her."

"Hun, you can vouch all you want," Jane put her order pad back in her pocket. "No ID, no alcohol."

I waited for Jane to go before following her back toward the kitchen. Denim dude uttered "Frigid cunt," loud enough for everyone in the restaurant to go silent. I paused. Jane kept walking, so I followed her lead. This was only my second month in this job, but I'd never witnessed such dicky behavior. Who did these fuckers think they were?

More people arrived and things got busy, so I didn't wonder for long. A little girl at table 19 smeared ketchup from her fries all over the tablecloth. I changed it out for a new one. Glancing at table 13, I wasn't surprised to see the girl drinking beer from denim dude's glass. The bearded guy seemed to be entertaining them with a tale about his adventures in Montana, from the little I could overhear. I watched as denim dude took all three of their steak knives, and the full bottle of ketchup, and slipped them into the girl's purse. He then ran a hand up her skinny thigh until it was about buried in her crotch. She pushed his hand away.

Maddy almost collided with me as she carried out a tray full of drinks right as I was heading into the kitchen with about 40 pounds of dirty plates and silverware. "Sorry, Maddy!" Maddy just swished out of the way like a practiced bullfighter and smiled as she continued on to table 8.

Back in the kitchen, I deposited the heavy tub and saw Lily struggling to keep up. "You need me to take this trash out?"

She turned, looking more determined than frazzled. "Yes, please." She tucked an errant hair behind her ear and almost worked up to a Mona Lisa smile. I took a minute to pile the plates so Lily could rinse them. Picking up the trash can, I hoped she would take a second to admire my biceps, but no go. She was focused on loading dishes.

The sun was down and the cool night air was a welcome change from the heat of the kitchen. I hoisted the heavy garbage can and unloaded its contents into the dumpster. After putting the empty can down, I stood and stretched my back and shoulders. I pulled the half-smoked Marlboro from my pocket and lit it, enjoying a long draw before exhaling into the clear night. The stars were just starting to reveal themselves.

A couple years back, I'd joined the Boy Scouts. It was pretty lame, so I only lasted a few months. I wanted to try camping, go hunting, and maybe shoot something. But all we did was haul a ton of heavy shit up a mountain and eat half-cold Dinty Moore Beef Stew in the can. Anyway, there was one kid, Jeff Wurtz, who knew all the constellations. He'd point out the Big and Little Dipper, the Bear, the Archer, but none of it stuck. To me, the stars were just thousands and thousands of other suns, so far away, so unknowable they really could have been gods. Taking another drag, I listened to the noise and rhythm of the kitchen. The night was quiet and I could hear Lily unloading plates, the dishwasher running, and Reggie barking that an order was up.

There were maybe a dozen cars in this lot. They were mostly bar customers. Restaurant goers generally parked on the other side of the building. The Captain Jack's sign was lit up to try and attract cars driving by on Route 41. When I'd asked Logan in my interview about the name, he said the restaurant was founded in 1899 by a former sea captain. Back then all they served was seafood. Seafood? In Pickering-ton-fucking-Ohio? Whatever.

I stepped over to the turd and removed a leaf from the rear window. Taking another step, I looked at the asshole's VW bus. Just like I figured, the rear bumper was secured by a rusty coat hanger. The bus had a layer of grime all over it, and enough dings and dents to qualify it for a demolition derby.

I peeked through the driver's window. A blue-and-white high school graduation tassel hung from the rearview mir-ror, along with a feathered roach clip. The vinyl seats and dashboard were sunbaked and full of rips and tears. *Led Zeppelin III* protruded from the under-the-dash eight-track player.

Without thinking, I tried the driver's door. It was locked. I stepped back and looked around. In my head I heard denim dude saying, "Hey Boy... Frigid cunt..." over and over again. I remembered the pleasure on denim dude's face as he knocked the ashtray to the floor.

How long had I been out here? I still had an inch of cigarette, so not more than two or three minutes. One of the bar customers had backed out of their parking spot and was heading out to the road. Otherwise, no one was around.

I flipped the butt to the pavement and walked around to the passenger side. Bingo, the double door opened. I rustled through the crap in the back seat. The most noticeable thing, aside from the stink of old sweaty clothes, was a black guitar case. It was a little scuffed up, but otherwise looked in good condition. There were some empty booze bottles and Burger King wrappers, a muddy pair of clodhoppers, some tic-tacs, a flowery bra, a shoebox full of eight-track tapes, and something wrapped up tightly in a towel.

A quick check showed the parking lot was still quiet. I unwrapped the towel to find a ceramic figurine. It was about six inches high and featured a mother cradling a baby. I couldn't be sure, but it kind of reminded me of these figurines Grampa Lee had brought back from Germany after the war. They were called Hummels, or something like that, and were valuable, according to Gramma. She'd sold them a while back. She got a monthly government check, but it was never enough.

I quickly re-wrapped the figurine and grabbed the guitar case. Shutting the VW door with my foot, I fished my keys from my front pocket and hustled toward the turd.

I fumbled to get the key into the trunk of the Dart. I was breaking out into a sweat, alert for any movement in the parking lot. Headlights swept over the row of cars, briefly illuminating me as a car pulled into the recently vacated spot.

Stay cool, man. Stay cool.

The reluctant key went in and I popped the trunk, tossing the guitar and statue inside with an echoing twang. I slammed the trunk shut, stepped over to the dumpster to grab the garbage can, and hustled back to the kitchen. Cool, I told myself. Everything's cool.

The first thing I noticed was Reggie had put on a hairnet. The second thing I saw was Logan eyeing Lily, although it was hard to tell if he was checking out her butt or calculating how fast she was working.

As I put in a new trash bag, Logan turned and said, "Where you been?"

Although the trash can made it obvious in my mind, this doughy guy with a bowl haircut was my boss. "Just taking the trash out to the dumpster."

"Isn't that her job?" Logan nodded his head toward Lily, who was pushing a full load of dishes into the washer.

"She was swamped and I had a minute."

"You have a smoke, too?"

Shit. What had Logan seen? I liked this job. Everybody was friendly, and nobody grilled me about school or my family or my private life. Work hard, get paid, go home. Simple. I hoped I hadn't screwed it up. Maddy, God bless her, tossed me a lifeline.

"Danny, we need refills on the water pitchers ASAP. And there's a spill by the little boy at table 14."

"Excuse me," I said. Before I made it through the swinging doors, Logan said, "Smoke on your break time, not my time."

I refilled the pitchers with fresh water and ice, cleared the dishes off 19 and 6 and 3. Over at 13 they had finished their food, but were still drinking and smoking. The bearded guy stood and walked over. "Hey man. Where's the baño?"

"Hunh?"

Bearded guy smiled like he was the Lone Ranger talking down to Tonto. "The can? The john? The bathroom?"

"Down that hall," I pointed. "To the left." If he followed my directions, the dorkster would end up in a closet.

"Gracias," he said with a smirk.

I grabbed the full tub and some silverware. Blondie was making out with denim dude, right in front of everyone. Total skank. A quick survey of the kitchen revealed no sign of Logan. I put down the tub and started scraping plates for Lily.

"Busy night, hunh?"

"Yeah." She rinsed a load of plates with the hose sprayer.

Stalling, I stacked the dirty plates and separated out the dirty silverware. "You go for your license yet?"

"My dad says I can't until I'm 17. And my grades improve."

"That sucks." I put the empty bus tub with the others and went over to refill the dining room silverware tray. "What does improve mean?"

"Nothing but A's and B's." Lily closed the dishwasher door and pushed the green button, unleashing about a hundred decibels of pumping waterpower into the air.

"You strike me as one of the smart kids," I said, based entirely on nothing. It did get a little smile from her, though.

"Yeah, right. Tell that to my trig teacher."

Trig? I almost laughed. I was struggling with basic algebra in the class full of jocks and potheads and derelicts. Lily was probably working to save money to attend some fancy college. Working wasn't really an option for me. Without cash, I'd have no car, no gas, no insurance. No smokes or treating my little bro to pizza on a Saturday night.

I imagined Lily in her big white house, her mom driving a station wagon with a golden retriever sticking its head out the open window. Like another *Twilight Zone* episode. I tried to imagine how Lily would react to my world. The three of us crammed into that tiny one-bedroom apartment, sleeping on the pull-out couch. Gramma in front of the TV, pissing herself every time she has a coughing fit. No phone, so the bill collectors can't hound us.

Our chat was interrupted when a fuming Jane came bursting in through the swinging doors. Cheeks flushed, she spit fire. "Reggie, run into the back parking lot and look for two dirt balls and a blonde girl. They just chewed and screwed."

Reggie was in the process of dumping a basket of fries onto fresh plates. Carol jumped in. "Reg—go. I got this." Reggie took off like an Olympic sprinter, heading to the back parking lot. I dropped the silverware and followed, just in time to see the taillights of the VW van heading south on Route 41. "That was them."

Reggie turned and eyed me. "You know 'em?"

"Naw," I said defensively. "I saw them pull in. A VW van with Michigan plates. Those were the assholes who dumped the ashtray in the dining room."

Reggie pulled off his hairnet and scratched his scalp. "Sometimes you win, sometimes you lose." He took out a pack of Camels and offered me one.

"I better get back," I said. "Logan already bagged me once."

Reggie just gave me a look and nodded, which made me wonder if maybe he'd seen something instead of Logan. But Reggie was cool. He'd never say anything.

Lily stood at the kitchen door. Her white apron was wet and splattered with various sauces and juices, but she still looked good. "What's 'chewed and screwed'?" she asked.

I almost burst out laughing. This girl could learn a thing or two from me and my friends. "It's when people take off without paying their check."

Her eyes went wide. "People do that?"

"Probably not too often here," I said. "But those dirtbags were just the type to try it."

"Did you or Reggie get their license plate number?"

"Naw." I shook my head and considered, just for a second, telling her about my earlier acquisitions. But girls like Lily saw the world as black and white, right or wrong. She wasn't capable of seeing stealing the way I did, as a form of balance.

The next 15 minutes or so involved Jane explaining to Logan what happened, followed by Logan bitching and moaning that we weren't on the ball. We weren't team players. We should all keep a constant look out for this kind of shit. He actually made Jane go with him to the office, all while Maddy and Gwen were still swamped with customers, to call the police and file a report so he could claim the $23 on the restaurant's insurance.

Aside from a brief shouting match between Gwen, who was complaining that Carol was taking too long on her surf and turf order, and Carol snapping that she wasn't able to make the fucking beef cook any faster, the rest of the night was reasonably uneventful. So far, that seemed to be one of the positives of restaurant work—time went by fast during the rush. One minute it was 6:30 and you were working your ass off. Then, before you knew it, the dining room was empty and it was nearly 10:00.

As things slowed down, I took another shot at softening Lily up. Not only was she busy with the dishes and glasses and silverware, but at the end of the night, there were serving trays and bread baskets and creamers and butter dishes. Several pots sat in the big double sink, one of which was chili that had been cooking all day.

I went over and filled the pans with hot, soapy water. The first one I tackled was the burnt chili, which was a real bitch. I checked the dining room and saw there were only two tables left, so I returned to the big sink and did a few more pots for Lily.

"Thank you," she said after I'd finished.

"No problem," I answered. "Glad to be of service."

I grabbed an empty bus tub and headed out to the dining room, all the while mentally kicking my own ass. 'Glad to be of service'? What an idiotic thing to say. Who am I? Alfred the butler? What the hell was I thinking? I might as well tattoo 'dork' across my forehead.

"Danny, when you finish busing that table," Jane said. "Could you put out all new tablecloths and fresh ashtrays?"

"Sure thing."

Back in the kitchen, Lily was taking off her apron and putting it in the dirty laundry, finished for the night.

"You need a lift home?" I asked.

"Mom's already here," she said as she pulled her purse from under one of the counters. "But thanks." She punched out, then skipped out the back door.

I looked around, didn't see anything needing to be done, so I also punched out. Stepping out back, I had a smoke and waited for the waitresses to finish up and tip me out. Maddy was first, giving me $10.50 and apologizing that it wasn't more, even though it wasn't bad for a Thursday night. I wandered back into the kitchen where Gwen handed me eight bucks and maybe another buck and a half in change.

Jane clocked out and said, "Thanks for all your help tonight." She looked tired. "Join me in the bar."

I tentatively followed her into the bar, wondering what Logan might say if he saw me there. Jane must have read my mind. "Don't worry," she said. "He's upstairs counting and recounting the night's take. He won't be down until the bar closes."

There were still a handful of people in the bar—an old

couple at one table and three guys at another arguing about football and how the Bengals might fare the rest of the season. I took a seat next to Jane at the bar.

"Couple of Buds, Henry," she said.

Henry, who was balding and had a huge beer gut, nodded and grabbed two pint glasses.

"Jane," I said in little more than a whisper. "I'm only 17."

"And honest and hardworking and adorable," she said.

Henry put our beers on coasters in front of them. Jane tried to hand the barkeep a five, but he waved it away.

"You're the tops, Henry," she said, then picked up her beer. "Cheers."

I took my pint and clinked glasses with her. "Cheers." I took a long drink. The beer was crisp and cold and foamy—absolutely perfect after a long night's work. That first swallow was quickly followed by another. "Not a bad crowd for a Thursday," I said, trying to make conversation.

Except for the assholes who skipped out on their check," she answered sharply. "Those fuckers don't realize what it costs me. No tip, a lecture from Logan, and then I'm not there to finish up the tables I'd been serving, so I lost that tip money, too."

"Gwen and Maddy didn't give you the money for the tables you served?"

She fake laughed, then took a long sip of beer. "That's not how it works, honey. We're all trying to scratch out a living here."

"That sucks."

"That's life," she said. "You want another?"

"I should probably get going," I said. "School tomorrow."

"Corrupting a minor," she smiled. "Not my first time." She fished in her pocket and handed me $12. "Wish I could give you more."

"Keep it," I said. "I appreciate the beer."

"My God, you really are an angel," she said, shoving the money into my hand. "If that Lily has any sense at all, she'll latch onto you like a tick on a hound dog."

"Uh, thanks," I said, pocketing the money. "You having another beer?"

"You change your mind?"

"Stay here. I'll be back in a second."

"Honey, I ain't going anywhere anytime soon." She pushed her empty glass forward and Henry took it to the tap to refill it.

I jogged to the now empty kitchen, through the back door, and out to the turd. I opened the trunk and retrieved the figurine.

"Here." I handed the towel to Jane, who put down her beer and eyed it suspiciously.

She unwrapped it slowly and her eyes grew big as she saw what it was. Jane's hair was a medium-length dark brown, and while she was like thirty, she still had a nice figure. And in a weird way, she kinda sorta looked like the mother figure in the Hummel. I had no idea if she had any kids or not, but hoped she'd still like it.

"Umm," Jane cleared her throat. "And where did you get this? Not the type of thing I'd expect a young man to just have in his car."

I cleared my throat as well, considering how to respond. "Can we just say I found it, and the assholes who lost it won't miss it?"

She turned the figurine in her hand, inspecting it. When she looked at the bottom, a devious smile crossed her face. "Guess you're no angel after all."

She re-wrapped the figurine carefully, then leaned over and kissed me softly on the cheek.

"Thanks," she said. "Now go home before we both get into trouble."

IDLE TALK

*"Some people call me the space cowboy, yeah
Some call me the gangster of love
Some people call me Maurice
'Cause I speak of the pompatus of love"*
– "The Joker" by the Steve Miller Band

I stared, dumbfounded, at the grizzled old man in the sweat-stained Cleveland Indians cap. "Are you serious?"

He scratched his four-or-five-day beard and smiled. "I think 40 is more'n fair.

"But it's a Martin, in mint condition!" I exclaimed. "It's got to be worth a couple hundred."

"It ain't no Martin." He pointed his finger at the plastic thinggee under the sound hole of the beautiful cherry-colored guitar. "Somebody cut this pick guard in the shape of an M. My guess, it was Morris, as the name painted inside says. A Martin has a thicker neck, and has the word 'Martin' on the headstock."

I hated to admit it, but the old guy sounded pretty sure of himself. "All of them?"

"Son, I must have bought and sold a dozen or more Martins in my time. Every one had the name up at the top."

I took a moment to look disgusted and scanned all the crap in the pawn shop. Knee-high red leather cowboy boots. A couple of 10-speeds and an old Huffy. A beat up set of golf clubs, lots of records and eight-track tapes, and a long surfboard propped up in one corner. In Youngstown, fucking Ohio—a damn surfboard.

"But do you hear the sound of this baby?" I plucked one string, then another. The mellow sound filled the cluttered space. "It's fantastic. A friend of mine said it was the best sounding guitar he's ever played."

Without missing a beat, the old guy put something back in the jewelry cabinet and said, "Good. Sell it to him."

The tires on the Impala were as bald as Telly Savalas, and my rent was almost two weeks late. I needed some cash. "How about a hundred? I'm sure you can get one twenty, maybe even one fifty for it."

He lifted his cap and scratched his buzz-cut head. "I believe this here guitar is handmade. It's nice, but completely replaceable. Maybe somebody'll want it. Maybe not. I'll give you fifty bucks. That's my last offer. Take it or walk."

I left Al's Pawn Shop with five crisp tens in my wallet. As I walked to my car, the door to Fatima's Fashions swung open. I nearly collided with a raven-haired bombshell in painted-on jeans and a bright yellow tube-top.

"Ex-cuse me, foxy."

I laid on my most charming smile, careful not to show too many teeth since, being slightly crooked and a little on the yellow side, they're not my finest feature. She flipped me the middle finger and walked right by as I admired the fine contours of her jeans. No sweat, I thought, and continued on my way. But before I reached the Impala, I came across such an odd sight, I thought I might be on *Candid Camera*. Two old geezers were crawling around on the sidewalk like infants.

It was a man and a woman. Everything about them was ancient. Their gray hair, wrinkled skin, even their clothes looked like something from 1930s Hollywood. On their hands and knees, they were running their fingers along the pavement, like they were feeling around for something. Then I noticed the white canes they'd laid on the sidewalk near them.

A part of me, I'm not happy to admit, thought about

sparking up a Winston, leaning back and enjoying the show. But the old lady kinda reminded me of my nana, so the better part of me won out.

"Everything okay?"

When the old woman turned to me, I could tell right away she was blind. She had that unnatural look in her eyes most blind people have. The old guy's eyes didn't look like that, but they didn't look quite right, either. Kind of bulgy and yellowed, like they were painted with a fine shellac.

"Could you help us?" the woman asked. "Please. My wedding ring slipped off. I'm not as big as I was when I first put it on." Her right hand moved to her left to show the ring wasn't where it belonged on her finger. "I know it's around here somewhere."

"Sure," I said, thinking maybe a little reward money might be in my future. "How do you know it fell off here?"

"I was reaching into my pocketbook for a tissue." The woman continued tracing her fingertips along the concrete. "When I pulled it out, I heard the ring hit the sidewalk. It must have rolled or settled somewhere." Her voice cracked. "It's a family heirloom." That last bit, I have to admit, got to me.

"Sure thing." I scanned the sidewalk in their vicinity, then glanced back the way I had come, checking the ground, not seeing anything but some wisps of grass struggling to grow through the cracks.

I walked behind them, searching all the while, then looked on the other side of the man, who had made his way to the wall of the pizza joint that butted up against the sidewalk. I walked slowly 10 feet or so, eyes roving from side to side like a pendulum, but I only saw a pull tab and a few cigarette butts. I checked the crack where the brick wall met the sidewalk, then on and around the step that led to the door. No luck.

I wandered over to the curb, then the street, where a bunch of teenagers cruised by in a jacked-up Camaro, Steppenwolf's "Born to be Wild" drifting out the windows. I used the toe of my sneaker to move a clump of yellowed leaves and a flattened Mountain Dew can. Something shiny caught my eye.

"Found it!"

Once the two geezers retrieved their canes and got to their feet, which was no easy task at their age, they thanked me so much, I was embarrassed.

"Now," the woman said, "you must join us for lunch."

Hey, free food is good food, I figured. Over the next hour and a half, I managed to get down four slices of greasy pepperoni pizza, two Miller High Lifes, and got acquainted with Barbara and Clarence Dodwell.

Barbara had been born blind, but Clarence lost most of his sight at around age 20 from some retinal disease. Clarence was in school for accounting at the time, and a friend of a friend introduced him to Barbara.

"He took me to a dance at the Methodist church, and at first I refused to go out on the floor because I'd never danced before," Barbara said. "Glenn Miller was playing, and Clarence managed to get me out there, put his arm around me, and the rest of the world just disappeared." When I saw a little sunbeam in her smile as she remembered that first dance, I had to smile, too.

Eventually they married, and after what seemed like hundreds of rejections, Clarence found an assistant accountant position at Jacobs and Clark in Youngstown. Apparently, the man who hired him had an uncle who lost his sight fighting the Krauts in WWI, so he had a soft spot for the disabled. He hired Clarence on probation for 90 days, and once he proved himself both capable and reliable, he began a 41-year career with the firm.

They were nice old geezers, so after lunch I offered them a lift home. At first, they said no, but it didn't take much convincing to make them change their minds. They only lived about a mile away, in a little two-bedroom ranch on Spring Street. It was surprisingly well-kept. Honestly, I didn't think two blind people could have maintained a home.

"It's only about 200 yards from the bus stop," Barbara said. "Convenient to downtown."

I'm not a bad guy, mind you, but I've never considered myself a do-gooder, either. But as I dropped them off and refused their offer to come in for a glass of lemonade, I told them to give me a shout if they ever needed help with anything. It was just an idle statement, really, just something you say to folks out of politeness. They both said they would, then old Clarence asked for my phone number.

"You want me to write it down for you?" I asked. Then I thought, what good would that do? The old guy couldn't even see his own nose.

"No," he said with a smile. "I'm a numbers man. I'll remember it."

A week later, about the time the Dodwells were fading from my not-so-great memory, the phone rang.

"Clarence here," he said. "I don't suppose you'd mind coming over to help cut down a big old forsythia bush in the backyard."

At the time, I was watching a rerun of *Hogan's Heroes* on the shitty black-and-white TV that came with the garage apartment, moving the antenna around to try to get a stable picture.

"Sure," I answered, my brain scrambling. "My friend Ralph's probably got a saw."

"Oh, I've got a good saw," Clarence said. "And a wheel-barrow and work gloves. Mostly I could use your muscles. Barbara will cook us something good once we've finished."

So, the following Sunday I was over at the Dodwells helping Clarence take down and cut up a dying bush near his vegetable garden in the backyard. Tomatoes, peppers, zucchini, and a couple other veggies I couldn't identify grew in rows. He said he wanted to expand the garden, so I asked if he had a shovel, which he did, and I spent a good hour digging up the roots to the bush. He was a chatty old guy, a Cincinnati Reds fan, listening faithfully to the games on his radio. He regaled me with tales of former Reds he admired, especially a guy named Ted Kluszewski, with biceps so big he used to have to cut off the sleeves of his uniform so he could fit into it. And Joe Nuxhall, now the Reds announcer, who, at 15, was the youngest player ever to pitch a professional game.

That made me think. At 24, I was spending my days chasing skirts and getting loaded down at the Wagon Wheel, while that 15-year-old was playing professional baseball. Some guys just have all the luck.

After I got the roots in the garbage and bundled up the branches of the bush so the trash guys could haul them off, Barbara served up a damned tasty pot roast with the works—roasted potatoes, carrots, and celery. They even had a cold six-pack of Miller in the fridge, which I thought was mighty considerate of them.

Barbara told me how she played piano at the school for the blind as a little girl. Their hands met as they reached out towards each other. I sat, awed by the way they sometimes finished each other's sentences, and how, through their shared love of music and gardening, they seemed to enjoy every inch of each other. When Clarence sometimes started a story, "That reminds me of the time..." Barbara was quick to interrupt. "No, dear," she would say with a loving tap on Clarence's arm, "what really happened was..."

A couple of weeks later, the Dodwells invited me over

again, this time to help replace a gasket in their toilet that was causing it to run. Clarence knew what to do, which is good because I didn't have a clue. He told me to shut off the water and drain the tank, then take out this thing called a flapper, which we brought to the hardware store for a replacement. I put the new one back in, and there you have it. No more leak.

Our efforts were rewarded with chili over spaghetti covered with cheddar cheese, which is how Barbara said her family always made it. Most of the chili I ate was made by a guy named Hormel and came from a can, so that was like heaven to me.

We got into a groove where I'd come by on Sunday afternoons and help them with this or that and then we'd have dinner together. Despite her blindness, Barbara knew every inch of her kitchen and her cooking put my poor momma's to shame. Brisket, enchiladas, chicken parm—she put out some of the best grub I've ever eaten.

One weekend, Barbara and Clarence went to visit Barbara's sister, Maggie, down near Columbus. I looked around my place, the odors of stale beer and gym socks filling the air. I took in the empty beer cans, the old pizza boxes, the stupid happy and sad clown faces that came on the wall with the garage apartment, then the growing mountain of dirty laundry.

"Jeff, my boy," I said to the dumpy apartment. "Today is the day. Ten hut! Let's whip this rathole into shape!"

I proceeded to fill up three Hefty bags: one with trash, one with returnables, and one with laundry. I dumped the trash in the bins by the garage and tossed the other two bags in the back seat of the Impala. With two dollars and thirty-five cents in change from returning the bottles and cans at the QuickMart, I headed over to Suds-n-Duds. I ignored the 'Don't Overload Washers' sign above the Speed Queens and crammed all my clothes into one of the washers, fed in my quarters, and took a load off in a hard plastic chair.

There were two other customers in the laundromat. A pockmarked old guy was passed out with a pint of Jim Beam held in one hand, sitting below a 'One Day at a Time' bumper sticker on the wall. And an older woman, maybe 35, was folding laundry on one of the cigarette-burned tables. Her hair was frosted all silvery, and the jeans she wore seemed a size or two too small for her ass. I had to look away as she folded her granny-panties.

I lit up a cigarette and daydreamed about Theresa, a curvy blonde girl I went with for a few months a while back. She used to do my laundry for me sometimes at her parents' place, not when they were around, obviously. Part of me felt guilty about it, us fooling around while my dirty laundry did its thing in her parents' machine. But being with her was like killing two birds with one stone, so to speak. Nice while it lasted.

The following Sunday, Barbara and Clarence had me get a sock out of their vacuum cleaner, which I'm sure either one of them could have done easy enough. I wasn't really in the mood to go over, but it's the least I could do. They were so nice. If I didn't, I'd feel guilty.

Barbara served up a spread of roast chicken with asparagus and mashed potatoes. As usual, there were some cold Millers in the fridge. The evening was winding down. Old Clarence was smoking his pipe, the cherry-scented smoke a perfect complement to the mellow evening. Barbara told me about the first time she cooked a turkey and left the neck and gizzard and heart inside.

"I had no idea that stuff was in there," she laughed. "It's funny now, but I felt just awful then."

"Like the time you cooked my Florsheims?" Clarence asked.

"That wasn't my fault, you silly old man," she declared. "You're the dodo who put his shoes in the oven in the first place."

I went and got another beer for me and a whiskey sour for Clarence while he told the story of stepping into a nasty puddle on his way home from work one day. He washed his shoes off in the kitchen sink, then figured he'd just put them in the rack in the oven, out of the way, to dry overnight. Barbara had said they were having soup for dinner, so there was no need to use the oven.

"But she changed her mind without telling me," he grinned. "She decided to have chicken pot pies instead, so she turned the oven on to preheat it without checking first."

"Who checks an oven first? Especially when they live with a man who wouldn't know how to cook an egg if his life depended on it? When I'm gone, he'll be stuck with Grape Nuts and cold cheese sandwiches, I swear."

I don't have a million old stories to share, so I usually just filled them in on the gossip at my job during our Sunday dinners.

"Anything happening on the romance front with you, Jeffrey?" Barbara asked, not for the first time.

"Maybe," I lied. "I got the phone number of this really cute red-haired girl named Penny at a party last night."

"That's great," Barbara said, while Clarence nodded his approval.

Feeling a little antsy at the mention of romance, I offered to clear the dishes, then beat it out of there and made my way home.

The weeks rolled by and I got more and more involved in their lives. I helped Barbara take down her drapes and wash them. She ironed them. Who irons drapes? Then I rehung them. I took Clarence to the podiatrist and helped weed the gardens, which felt good, real good, the sun on my back, my hands working in the rich black soil.

There came a Sunday in October when the sun was shining extra bright and all the trees were flaunting their colors like proud red and orange and gold peacocks. Folks' lawns were smattered with fallen leaves and would soon be in need of a raking. I showed up at Barbara and Clarence's in the late afternoon. We hadn't actually made plans, but our Sunday get-togethers were pretty routine by now. So, I just made my way over, ready to feel good all over because they would be glad, as usual, to see me.

I parked my freshly washed Impala and made my way up to the front porch. I rang the bell. No response, so I rang again. Still no movement from inside. I opened the storm door, gave the locked wooden door a good knock and listened, but didn't hear anything.

Just as I was thinking they must have gone out, I figured I'd check out back before I took off. As I came around the side of the house, I heard soft voices. There was Clarence with his old pipe and his whiskey sour, talking with Barbara in her housedress and apron. They were sitting at a small table on the back porch, enjoying the late afternoon sunshine.

"I am just at a loss for anything else to have him do."

"You'll come up with something," Barbara replied. "It makes him feel good to think he's helping."

"He's a nice kid, don't get me wrong. But he really should be spending time with people his own age, going to discotheques or whatever young people do these days."

"I really don't think he has any friends, aside from those people he works with. And they never seem to socialize outside of work. If only we knew someone with an eligible daughter." Barbara's voice trailed off.

I'd heard enough. Up front, I stomped on some zinnias I'd planted a few months back. I hopped into the Impala, removed *Strange Days* from the tape deck, and tossed it on top of the shoebox where I keep my eight-tracks. I hit the ignition and slipped in the bootleg Stone's concert tape I'd lifted from Theresa's younger brother's room. Mick Jagger, unquestionably the best singer in America, belted, *"I'm just a fella, with a one-track mind..."*

I felt a cold burn in the center of my chest, like a huge block of ice was pressed against it. *No friends. Feel sorry for him.* My lungs squeezed tight; I was breathing too fast. Easy does it, man. Just take it easy.

I turned the volume up on the car stereo so loud the bass notes vibrated the coins I kept in my can holder. An old lady across the street gave me the stink eye, but I didn't care. The music was like a big pencil eraser pressing into each of my ears, rubbing out that icy pain in my brain that wanted me to cry. I searched in the ashtray, but found only stale butts. No big deal.

I joined in with Mick, seeing myself onstage, all bright lights and horny chicks galore, braless and grooving and eager for the after-party. We sang, *"But it was just my imagination... runnin' away with me..."* Revving the gas, I released the clutch on the beat and burned a few hundred miles off my new tires.

They could be replaced.

Q AND A

"Johnny made a record, went straight up to number one
Suddenly everyone loved to hear him sing his song
Watching the world go by, surprising it goes so fast
Johnny looked around him and said, 'Hey, I made the big-time at
last.'"
– "Shooting Star" by Bad Company

I'm Tim 'Mister Morning' Martell, and this is the Mighty 800, WLPL. This morning, we are very fortunate to be joined by Mike Hammer, lead vocalist and guitarist for Stone Toad, a folksy, sometimes punkish rock band that's breaking onto the music scene. They just released their second album, *Permanent Damage*, and are winding their way across the good old USA, sharing their sound with hundreds of adoring fans. But before I get onto plugging their show, welcome to the city of brotherly love, Mike.

MH: Thanks a lot. Good to be here. Early, though.

TM: You do look a little tired. Two burned holes in an Army blanket, my mom used to say.

MH: Was your mom in the Army?

TM: No (laugh) it's just an expression. Your eyes are, well, let's just say you could use some Visine.

MH: You make a habit of criticizing your guests?

TM: Of course not! Let's move on. Did you and the rest of the band stay in the city last night?

MH: Sort of. We're all up at the Holiday Inn, but we hit a couple of clubs, don't ask me which. I think one was called Elans'—something like that.

TM: One of our more notorious gentlemen's clubs. Moving on—

MH: I 'bout fell in love with this one stripper, Chrystal her name was. Huge (beep) and an (beep) that would make a priest want to (beep) like a jackrabbit.

TM: Well, Mike, despite the hour, this is still radio, and we don't want to wear out the censor's kill switch.

MH: More like the city of sisterly love, all I'm sayin'. Some damn fine ladies.

TM: Tell me about the band's origins. You grew up in Carterstown, Georgia, if my information is correct.

MH: Yup. Small town, nothing to do but get stoned and make noise. We started out playing in my friend Blizz's basement. He had some drums, I had a crappy guitar my parents bought from the Service Merchandise catalogue. Witham got a bass somehow, and Rich used to just keep the beer flowing until we convinced him to try the keyboard. Later we added Loser on rhythm.

TM: Your first band was named the Little Rascals—is that correct?

MH: We went through lots of names early on. We played a

talent show at Crappytown High under the name 'Little Rascals' because they wouldn't let us use the name we really wanted, Pig (beep). But we sounded like (beep) back then. Growing pains, ya know. Every band needs to make a lot of noise before they're ready for prime time.

TM: I hear you (loud cymbal sound). How did you guys arrive on the name Stone Toad?

MH: We were all on a backpacking trip. Red River Gorge, in Kentucky. Ever been there? What a trip.

TM: Not much of a backpacker myself. Unless it's down to IHOP for their endless pancakes! (laugh track)

MH: I bet they lock the doors when they see you coming. Can you say, Jabba the Hutt?

TM: Not only an aspiring musician, but also a comedian (ducks quacking). Back to the band's name.

MH: Yeah. Right. So, we were backpacking in this totally awesome gorge. We were tossing back a few beers and grillin' up some steaks, when we ran into a couple of dudes from New Mexico who offered to trade us some mushrooms for a piece of steak.

TM: Steak and mushrooms? Talk about roughing it!

MH: Magic mushrooms there, Bozo, not shitake. Anyhow, we all feast, and we're sitting around the fire, just trippin' to the flames, ya know? Me and Blizz gotta take a whiz, so we step away from the fire, when Blizz all of a sudden sort of freaks out. 'Look at this (beep) man!' Maybe it was the shrooms, but

I look over and don't see nothing. 'There,' Blizz says, pointing a finger. Not five feet from us is this huge, gargantuan toad. I'm talking like one of them African toads. Eyes as big as ping-pong balls, just staring at us. I said like wow or some (beep) like that, when Blizz says 'It ain't movin'. I think it's made of stone.' I said, 'It ain't stone. You're stoned,' and then we both started crackin' up. We finish (beep)ing, and just start jabberin' on about toads and bein' stoned and eventually decided that Stone Toad would make a great band name.

TM: Ah, a story I can hear you telling your grandkids someday. (laugh track)

MH: You (beep)ing with me?

TM: Just keeping it light, mi amigo. Right now, it's 7:08, and time for a check on the traffic. We'll be right back with Mike Hammer, lead vocalist and guitarist for Stone Toad.

TM: Welcome back to WLPL, the Mighty 800 on your AM dial. We're here with Mike Hammer of Stone Toad, who will be jamming out at the Philly Fillmore tonight. They will be doing songs from their latest album, *Permanent Damage*. How is the album selling, Mike?

MH: Not bad, from what I understand. Our manager is this (beep) from New York, and aside from his accent, he seems like a pretty good guy. The way I figure, if the checks don't bounce, we're doing okay.

TM: Now I hear there's a story behind the song 'Midnight Blues.' The song was recorded live, and I believe there was some excitement leading up to the show. Tell us about that.

74

MH: Can I get some more coffee? (beep)ing early, man. (pause) Thanks.

TM: Sorry, Mike. Can't smoke in here.

MH: (exhaling) So, yeah. We were playing a show in Columbus, no, Youngstown, Ohio. Our manager, Marty, made a deal with some dudes to record certain songs for the album, although we ended up only using the one. Anyway, we pull into Youngstown, and as usual, we go out and get a little lubricated before the show. We get a couple rooms at the Super 8, and I think I was watching a ball game when all of a sudden there's screamin' and hollerin' like Charlie Manson is on the loose in the adjoining room. Me and Blizz rush over and find Witham's psycho girlfriend, who was supposed to be back in Atlanta but decided to surprise him, totally going all wackadoodle on this naked red-headed chick Witham must have been boning a minute earlier. Blizz gets in between the naked girl and Linda Blair there, and I helped her scurry into our room. I told her I'd get her clothes for her, but she was crying and wanted a hug, and ya know, so I didn't rush off until I heard (beep) breaking next door. By the time I got there the crazy (beep) had broken my (beep)ing Olson over Witham's head and was swinging the neck and broken body around like Reggie Jackson at a home run derby.

TM: (laughing) Oh, the crazy life of a rock star. So, what did you do?

MH: Blizz finally got the crazy (beep) in a headlock, although she still managed to get Witham right in the (beep) with a right foot. (beep) should kick for the (beep)ing Falcons. By then Marty had shown up and managed to get rid of the looney tune while Loser was helping Witham get the blood off his face. But now we were in a real fix. My friggin' Olson was all busted to (beep), and we had a show in like three hours. So Rich and I head out to look for a music store. But we can't find nothing, and time is gettin' away from us. Finally, we pull into this pawn shop somewhere. We go in, and they've got a few acoustics, but most of them were pure crap. The guy's got a nice Martin, but you could see glue and (beep) around where the neck meets the body, so that's no go.

TM: You must have been sweating bullets about then, am I right?

MH: (pause) So, I try this cherry-colored number, a no-name guitar. It's got a funky M-shaped pick guard, and the name MORRIS printed inside the body beneath the sound hole, so I guess some cat named Morris hand-made it. The thing's in good condition, and once I got it tuned up, the sound was pretty good. Great action. As I said, time was ticking, so I bought it. I think I paid about a hundred and fifty, which seems like a rip off, but once I put on new strings, that guitar had a really sweet, mellow sound. I used it on 'Midnight Blues' that night, as well as on a couple others, but that's the one that made it onto the album.

TM: Do you still play it?

MH: Nope. Some (beep)head stole it that night after the show. We have a couple of guys travel with us to help set up the shows, but Marty usually hires a few locals to help with the grunt work. They work cheap, no bennies, you know. I think one of them lifted it while we were partying after the show, but I can't prove nothin'.

TM: Wowza—what a story. Does that make 'Midnight Blues' a little more special to you and the band?

MH: Did you really just say 'wowza'? What's up with that, man?

TM: It's eleven past the hour, time for weather with Jillian. We'll be back for more adventures with Stone Toad after this break.

TM: Welcome back to WLPL, the Mighty 800 on your AM dial. We're joined today by Mike Hammer of Stone Toad. The band will be rocking the house at the Philly Fillmore tonight at eight o'clock. Tell me, Mike, who were some of your musical influences? When I listened to parts of *Permanent Damage*, I thought I could hear some Byrds, maybe a little Roy Orbison there.

MH: Roy Orbison? Man, are you high? (beep) sake, my mother listens to Roy (beep)ing Orbison.

TM: Again, Mr. Hammer, please watch your language. And for your information, Roy Orbison has revolutionized music over the last two plus decades. 'Only the Lonely.' 'Crying.' 'Pretty Woman.' I could go on.

MH: (beep) sake, please don't. Whenever he comes on the radio, I do feel like crying. I'll give you that. But, that annoying (beep)ing twang, both in his voice, and in his music, it goes through me like (beep) through a goose.

TM: The Big O had over twenty Top 40 Billboard hits before you were potty trained, I'll have you know.

MH: Even then he gave me the (beep)s.

TM: You long-haired ignoramus. 'Blue Bayou.' 'Mystery Girl.' 'Running Scared.' Roy Orbison has more talent in his left hand than your band has cumulatively.

MH: Oh, cumulatively. Somebody's showin' off their community college degree. Too bad you never took a class in music appreciation, or you would know to turn your precious Roy Whinerson albums into ashtrays.

TM: If I gave a roomful of monkeys cowbells and ukuleles, they'd have more melody than you and your talentless, stoner freak show.

(sounds of scuffling, followed by two minutes of radio silence)

This is WLPL, the Mighty 800 on your AM dial. I'm Jillian Hart, and we'll have a short commercial break while we sort out some technical difficulties in the studio.

HITCHING

Carry on my wayward son,
There'll be peace when you are done
Lay your weary head to rest
Don't you cry no more."
– "Carry On Wayward Son" by Kansas

"Sorry I'm not going further." Gravel crunched as the guy named Ed pulled the big gas-guzzling Cadillac into the breakdown lane of I-91. He put out a doughy hand, the hand of an accountant or human resource specialist or any variety of generic paper pusher.

Matt Blackwell took the outstretched hand in his calloused hand. "Thanks for the lift," he said, then opened the passenger door and slipped out, moving to the rear to retrieve his things.

"Good luck to you."

Matt stepped away from the Caddy as it moved forward onto the exit ramp. He shucked off his jacket and tied it to his pack. He stretched before hoisting on the heavy backpack. Fishing in his shirt pocket, he counted his Winstons and frowned. Only four left. He lit one, taking a long drag.

He didn't like being on the highway. Cops were on the highway, and he'd much rather not encounter any boys in blue. But he was maybe 10 miles northeast of Bennington, and there wasn't much traffic. Hopefully, he'd catch a ride before too long. He coughed, spat an ugly gray glob into the gravel, picked up his guitar, and started walking.

He read somewhere that Vermont had more cows than people. True or not, that idea pleased him. While he knew there were good people out there—people who ran into burning buildings to save others, people who fed the homeless or adopted a dozen African orphans—he hadn't run across too many of them.

"I'm an asshole magnet." He spoke aloud to the highway, then thought that might make a good punk band name.

The two strips of gray highway before him were surrounded by thick forests of trees and hills. Every few minutes, a truck or car would drive by. Matt turned and stuck out a thumb. Above him, the sky was a turquoise blue, reminding him of home. Or what used to be home. More clouds here in the Northeast. In books and movies, kids would lie back in the tall grass, staring upward and seeing ponies and castles and dragons in the clouds. All Matt saw were wisps of dreams breaking up and scattering.

A silver sedan slowed enough that he could see the two middle-aged women in the front seat, then sped up as it drove by. Matt tried to remember what day it was. There was a newspaper in the diner somewhere in New York about a week ago, the *Albany Gazette*, maybe, dated August 10, 1981. He'd glanced over a story about the baseball strike finally being over. Then, last night he'd played a few songs at an open mic night in a bar outside of Springfield. *Good Times*, the place was called. Probably named after that TV show with Jimmie Walker, the guy who will forever be known by his catchphrase, "dyn-o-mite!" Probably have it on his gravestone some day, if he wasn't dead already. Matt didn't have the opportunity to keep up with celebrity news, but knew they died fairly often from fame overdose.

He thought last night was Wednesday, so today would be Thursday. At the half-full, hole-in-the-wall bar, he'd sat by himself sipping on Knickerbocker drafts until it was his turn to perform. He did a reasonable version of "Dust in the Wind," then returned to his table.

Two girls asked if they could join him. One was taller, with soft brown eyes and coppery red hair. Her name was Annie, a psychology major at a local college. She had beautiful skin, a captivating smile—the type that could catch the interest of any guy she wanted. Martha, her cohort, was about five feet tall, with the figure of a cinder block. Her hair was coffee-colored and hopelessly curly, but she struck Matt as authentic in her blue flannel shirt and jeans.

"You play well," Martha said. "Nice voice. First time here?"

Matt nodded. The girls both had beers of their own, which meant, at least for the moment, they wouldn't expect him to treat them. After an awkward pause, he said, "You two going to perform?"

Annie laughed. "I never get that drunk. Martha has a great voice, though." She ran a hand through her hair, strands slipping through long fingers while she grinned at him.

"I sing sometimes," Martha said. "Can't play and sing at the same time, though. Not enough brain cells to manage both."

Matt smiled. He liked people who could poke fun at themselves. After some small talk, Annie seemed bored and joined a table of frat boys with dumpy pants and backwards ball caps. Martha was called up to perform. She drained her beer and strode to the stage.

"As usual," she began. "My band is parked out back in the limo getting wasted, so I'll be performing acapella tonight." She closed her eyes, took two deep breaths, and then started singing in a soft voice that steadily grew stronger and more confident.

It took a minute, but soon, Matt recognized the tune as "The Tennessee Waltz." Martha snapped her fingers on one hand and tapped the floor with her foot to keep time. Annie was right, Martha's voice was exceptional, especially in a place like this.

Martha came back to his table with a pitcher of beer, and he liked her even more. He asked her about herself, and she told him about how most of her friends were in college, but that just wasn't for her. She worked in a factory making stereo speakers, which Matt thought sounded pretty cool. Martha and Annie had been friends since middle school. They shared an apartment, and since both of them were slobs, that worked out fine.

When it was his turn to sing again, he asked her to join him to sing Neil Young's "Old Man," and they received the most applause of the night. Martha asked where he was staying. She insisted he crash at their place when he told her he planned to pitch his tent behind the Mobil station down the road. Matt thought he might get lucky, then grew anxious because he didn't have any rubbers. He needn't have worried. Martha gave him a blanket and a pillow and parked him for the night on the couch.

She shook him awake around 6:00 a.m. "Rise and shine. I leave for work in a half hour, and Annie will have a fit if you're still here when she wakes up."

He wiped the sleep from his eyes. "Any chance I can grab a shower?"

"Make it quick." She moved into the kitchen and the coffee pot started gurgling.

Ten minutes later, he was clean and dressed and slugging down a cup of java. Martha made him an everything bagel with cream cheese, which at that moment was the most delicious thing he'd ever eaten. She dropped him by the highway, gave him her phone number, and told him to call when he got to Boston. He promised he would. A half hour later, he caught a ride with the fat guy in the Cadillac.

Four 18-wheelers, six cars, and two vans passed him by.

He smoked another cigarette. Two down, two to go. He thought about the '72 Pinto he'd started out in, abandoned somewhere in Colorado with a broken timing chain. Stupid to think that shitbox would last for long on a road trip.

The sound of tires on pavement came from behind him. He turned and put out a thumb, then scowled as the blur of the sedan solidified into the gray and green of a Vermont state trooper. A quick glance around revealed woods on either side of the highway, and nothing else. No roads, no paths, no trails. And with all his gear, running would be one step below stupid. Matt Blackwell stood there and prepared to face his fate.

The cop drove past him, and for a fraction of a second Matt thought he might keep going. But he pulled into the breakdown lane, then backed up the 100 yards or so until he parked 10 feet from him. The door opened, and Matt took a deep breath.

"Afternoon," the cop said, adjusting his hat as he approached Matt. "Car trouble? I didn't see a vehicle south of here."

The statie wasn't tall, maybe five nine or so, but was very broad in the chest. Maybe 35 or so years old. Hard to tell with buzz cut, clean shaven white guys in uniform. He didn't give off a threatening vibe, but neither had the cop in Kentucky before kicking the shit out of Matt in an abandoned rest area.

"No, sir."

"Where you headed?"

"Boston," Matt answered. "I've got a cousin there."

"Boston?" The cop almost smirked. "This is Vermont, and you're headed north."

Matt paused, glanced at the Trooper, and then took a deep breath. "The guy I caught a ride with this morning came this way. Dropped me off a couple miles back. Now I can say I've been to Vermont."

"You aware it's illegal to hitchhike on an interstate highway?"

Matt hesitated. "Yes, sir."

The cop tilted his head slightly, watching him. Matt counted the heartbeats pounding in his head. "You got any drugs or weapons on you?"

"Just this." Matt reached into his pocket and pulled out his Buck knife.

It was a five-inch lock blade with a wood and brass handle his foster dad gave him for his twelfth birthday. He opened his palm to show the cop, who reached forward and took the knife. He opened the blade with a *click*, then tested the sharpness with his thumb.

The cop closed the blade and said, "I'm going to hold on to this for now. You can't be on this highway. I'll give you a lift to the next exit."

Matt was stunned. "Cool." He warily put his gear and himself in the back seat of the cruiser.

The cop started the vehicle and slowly eased back onto the highway. He whistled some tune Matt couldn't recognize as they picked up speed.

"What kind of guitar you got there?" The cop glanced back at him in the rearview mirror.

Matt reflexively looked out the door's window, not wanting the cop to see the blood draining from his face. "It's an acoustic. Nothing special."

"Where'd you get it?"

Fuck, Matt thought. Fuck, fuck, fuck. He had to stay cool, answer the cop. The truth was he'd stolen the guitar from a shitty warm-up band that was playing in some ramshackle theater back in Youngstown.

Matt had been washing dishes for some quick cash at a pub called Crawlies, staying on the couch of these two guys,

Todd and CJ. He did that every month or so—he'd find an under-the-table gig, save some dough, and move along. Todd, a stoner former football jock, said the theater was looking for guys to move equipment for the band. They'd pay a hundred bucks for a night's work. Plus, they'd get to see the show for free. Matt said he was in.

The night came, but they hardly got to enjoy the show because they were humping heavy amps and lights and mixers and cases of soda and God knows what all, out of the trucks on stage, then back again, for each of the three bands. At the end of the night, this creepy bald dude gave them each a 50-dollar bill. A couple of the guys complained. But Baldy, next to this seven-foot, 400-pound goon, said they only paid $100 if the show sold out, and it didn't. "Take it or leave it," Baldy said with a grin that made Matt want to knock his pretty teeth out.

He took the cash, then snuck back to the trucks and the van where the musical instruments were stored. As luck would have it, the van wasn't locked, and he became the proud owner of this no-name, but sweet-sounding guitar. He left his Yamaha, which had a crack in the body anyway, at Todd and CJ's before he took off again.

"I got it for my fifteenth birthday," he said. "Back in Colorado."

"That where you come from? Colorado?"

"Yes, sir," he lied.

"Where abouts?"

What was with this cop? Matt had spent a week in Durango, so he went with that.

"Durango. Ever been there?"

"No," the cop said.

"You're not missing much. Kind of resembles here. Maybe a little more mountainous."

"How old are you?"

"Twenty," he answered.

Did this cop think he was a runaway or something? Fortunately, they turned onto an exit ramp, then turned left and crossed the highway. A quarter-mile or so down the road, the cop pulled into a gas station next to a strip mall with a video store, a Dunkin' Donuts, a hair salon, and something called Market Basket.

"I'm going to drop you here. You should be able to catch a ride with someone heading south. Down in Springfield, you want to catch a ride east on the Mass Pike, or possibly Route 2, either of which will take you to Boston."

Matt thanked the cop and got out. The fresh air hit his lungs like he'd just been let out of a choke hold. Then the cop got out of the car.

"Almost forgot." He held out the Buck knife.

A little surprised, Matt accepted it and thanked the cop again.

"Stay out of trouble, hear?"

He nodded and held his breath until the cop got back in the vehicle and drove away. Smoking a much-needed cigarette, he looked around. Besides a few cars at the Dunkin' Donuts and in front of the Market Basket, not much action here. Matt walked around the side of the strip mall and saw two large dumpsters. He stashed his pack and guitar behind one of them and went back to the store to buy a fresh pack of smokes. An old lady with a long white braid was struggling to get a box out of the back of her dusty pickup truck.

"Can I help you?"

She looked up and took a second to focus on him through her thick-lensed glasses. "If you don't mind, I'd appreciate that." Her voice reminded Matt of Mrs. Fielding, the librarian back at South Street Elementary, and that made him smile.

He grabbed the box, which was heavier than he'd expected, and said, "Lead the way."

The old lady in her corduroy shirt and work boots strode to the front door of the store and opened it for him. "Just put it here." She indicated a counter.

A guy in a store uniform looked up from his paperwork and gave Matt a suspicious stare. "Morning, Shirley. Just a sec and I'll get your check."

She turned to look at Matt. "Thank you, young man."

"No problem," he answered, then made his way to the cashier's line to grab a pack of Winstons. He had retrieved his belongings and was making his way over to the gas station where he figured he stood the best chance of bumming a ride, when he heard the old lady's engine grinding. She let out an impressive stream of curses, then a sporadic clicking sounded from beneath the truck. He glanced over. She had her head against the steering wheel like she was going to cry.

"It's your starter," he said as he approached.

She looked up, her eyes struggling to focus on him. "What?"

"When you try to start it and it clicks like that. Usually means the starter is going."

"It did it at Hannaford's this morning, but on the second try it worked." She turned the key, but all that happened was *click, click, click, click.* "Shit."

"Is it a standard or automatic?" he asked.

"My Frank would never own an automatic," she replied.

"Good. You ever pop a clutch?"

She smiled at him. "Not for 40 years or more. But I'm game. Do you..." Her voice wavered.

"It's slightly downhill toward the road. If you put it in reverse, I'll push you backwards. Hold in the clutch until you're going good, then let it out quick. The engine will probably complain, but just depress the clutch again and let it catch. Then you'll be on your way."

"Well, I'm not so sure..."

"C'mon," he encouraged her. "Give it a try."

As Matt put down his pack and guitar, a middle-aged man wearing a Dire Straits tee shirt approached the door.

"Excuse me," Matt said. "Can you give me a hand? This lady's starter is dead."

Wordlessly, the man came over and put a shoulder to the grill of the truck. Matt grabbed the bumper and pulled alongside the driver's side. The truck started moving. "Now," he called.

The truck bucked to a stop, coughed, then roared as she depressed the clutch and hit the gas. She smiled like a kid with a cooler full of ice cream sandwiches.

He walked back to grab his stuff when she pulled back up next to him. "You need a lift somewhere?"

"Sure," he said. "Mind if I put my stuff in the back?"

Matt stowed his guitar and backpack on the floor at the tail of the truck between two heavy boxes so they wouldn't move around. He got into the passenger seat and put out his hand. "I'm Matt."

She took his hand in hers and gave it a firm, surprisingly strong shake. "I'm Shirley. Shirley Vogel. Where you head-ed?"

He told her he started out in New Mexico and was making his way across the country. This was his first day in Vermont, so he'd just go wherever she was going. She had another delivery to make in Putney, then in Hartland. After that, she'd be heading home to White River Junction.

"How far is that?" he asked.

"Eighty miles, give or take. It's on the New Hampshire border."

All around the highway was green, and he could tell they were rising in elevation. "Not many signs of civilization," he said.

"That's the way we like it," Shirley answered. "Burlington, Montpelier, Rutland—those are the big cities. The ski mountains get lots of tourists in the winter, but the rest of us are just scattered about. Up in the Northeast Kingdom, you can drive for an hour and never see a sign of a single human being."

"How about where you live? River Junction?"

"White River Junction. Used to be a trading town, so there's people, stores and shops downtown by the highway. But just outside is mostly farms, some artists, and folks who keep to themselves."

"What are you delivering?" he asked. "It was heavy, and that was a grocery store back there. I assume it's not artwork."

Shirley grinned. "We keep bees, as well as apple trees and some sugar maples. I'm delivering fresh native honey. Best in Vermont."

While they drove, Shirley told him about how she inherited some money after her father died. She and her husband, Frank, bought the 15 acres and old farmhouse outside White River Junction and made a go of it.

"It was hard work, establishing the bees, harvesting the syrup, planting the orchard, the vegetables, the canning. We both worked our tushes to the bone, especially with Elizabeth." Shirley's voice trailed off, like she'd left a thought incomplete.

"Elizabeth?" he asked.

"Our daughter. She's 34. She's a sweet girl. Most folks would say she's a little off. But a heart made of gold, and a good worker."

"Off?" Matt said. "How's that, if you don't mind me asking?"

Shirley paused, pushed her glasses back up her nose. "Elizabeth was always a fussy baby. Not colicky, exactly, but things bothered her. She didn't like how socks felt on her feet, so she'd cry. She'd sit and stare at nothing for what seemed like hours on end. She didn't like when people, especially strangers, talked to her or touched her in any way. By the time she got to school, she screamed at teachers. Hit the other kids. Eventually, Frank and I decided to keep her home. Frank used to work at IBM up in Essex Junction. He was good at teaching her math and history and reading. She loves puzzles, and she's really good at them." Shirley put on her blinker and passed another pickup pulling a horse trailer.

"But enough about that. Tell me about yourself. Aren't you about 20 years late for hitchhiking your way across the country? Aren't your folks worried about you?"

Matt usually evaded personal questions, but Shirley seemed like she genuinely cared. She'd offered him a ride, after all, when most people wouldn't even consider helping a guy like him.

"My mom died in a car accident when I was 10." Technically, this was true. Matt didn't feel the need to add that she was wasted on Quaaludes and cheap tequila at the time. "My father hit the road years before that, so me and my older brother went into foster care. We lived with this family, the Reeses, until Jerome got into trouble. He went to juvie and I went to this other family, the Beals, in Silver City. They were a lot nicer than the Reeses, but when I turned 18 and the checks from the state stopped coming, they told me I had to move along."

He quickly covered moving in with his friend Nick's family, working at the warehouse in Aztec, then buying the Pinto and deciding to travel across the country and just experience life for a bit. He managed to find jobs, usually washing dishes or pumping gas, here and there to earn money before moving on.

Shirley listened, nodded, and only asked an occasional

question. "You're having quite an adventure," she said after he'd mentioned starting out in Springfield that morning. "Most people wouldn't have the courage to just set out like that."

"Or stupidity," he said with a grin. Shirley laughed.

They exited the highway and drove down a winding road past a trailer park and several farms with dairy cows to Barbari's Country Store. Shirley put the emergency brake on and shifted the truck into neutral to keep the engine running.

"You want me to bring the honey in while you watch the truck?" he asked.

"I don't know what it's like where you come from," she said as she got out. "But in Vermont we don't worry about such things."

Matt grabbed a case of honey and carried it in for her. He stepped back outside for a smoke while Shirley and the lady in charge of the store gabbed about how her zucchinis and tomatoes were doing, and whether or not Luke and Laura would really get married on *General Hospital.*

Matt drew hard on his cigarette, enjoying the pleasant lightheadedness as the smoke permeated his brain. The afternoon had brought in some clouds and a slight breeze. At first, his surroundings seemed almost perfectly quiet. There was Shirley's truck idling, but no other cars or horns or people. No lawn mowers or loud music or chain saws. But underneath that peaceful stillness, a little symphony of clicking and chirping and chitting played. Birds were easy to identify, but those other sounds, they must be insects. So many insects and sounds he didn't even have words to describe them.

The sounds seemed to disappear as a car approached from the North. It was cruising along, music blaring through the open windows. The car, a primer-gray Nova, slowed, but didn't pull into the store. Matt took another drag on his butt, and the teenaged driver and his pal just stared like he was a two-headed goat before hitting the gas and heading on their way.

The bell on the store's door rang as Shirley exited. Matt dropped his butt on the pavement and ground it out with his boot. They continued on for a half hour or so before making another delivery in Hartland. Back in the truck, Shirley looked at the gas gauge and scowled. "Less than a quarter tank."

"I saw a station back where we got off the highway," Matt said.

"Yes, I know, but aren't you supposed to turn off your engine when filling up? Can't the gas fumes explode?"

Matt grinned. "Only in the movies. I'll get out and pump for you. It'll be fine. I promise."

"You know a lot about cars and trucks?"

"A little," he said. "Me and my friends back home didn't have much money, so we all helped each other work on our beaters."

"What are beaters?"

"Our broken-down cars. Nobody I knew had a nice one, and beaters is a word we used. Beater, shitbox—you know." As they wound their way to the gas station, a thought popped into his head. "Is your husband good with engines?"

"Not anymore," Shirley said. "He died three years ago come September. It was on the third, a Sunday. We were watching *60 Minutes*."

"Sorry," Matt said. He fiddled with a hangnail until Shirley spared him from the awkward silence.

"Why do you ask?"

"I'm 90 percent sure you need a new starter. I was thinking if there's an auto parts store where you live, you can save a lot of dineros buying the starter and putting it in yourself."

"Can you put it in?" she asked.

"Sure, if you've got the right tools. A socket and wrench set are probably all you need."

"My Frank was a world-class putterer. He left a whole chest in the garage full of tools. I'd be shocked if he didn't have what you need."

"I've got nothing else on my calendar," Matt said.

And so it was decided. They filled up Shirley's truck without it exploding, and got a new starter for the truck in White River Junction for $78 plus tax.

The late summer sky was growing overcast as they pulled into the long gravel driveway to the house where Shirley and her daughter lived. On either side of the driveway were large vegetable gardens. Matt noticed rows of corn and tomatoes and peppers, plus a bunch of stuff he couldn't easily identify. The house was exactly what you would picture an old New England farmhouse would look like. A simple, squarish, faded white clapboard building with a front porch and four windows, one in each quadrant of the front of the house. They parked by a barn-type building maybe 20 feet from the house.

"Are your husband's tools in the garage here?"

"Don't worry about that now. Come in and bring your stuff. Elizabeth will show you to the guest room. I'll throw some chicken on the grill and boil up some corn for supper."

Matt rarely, if ever, refused the offer of a meal. "Thank you for your kindness. Anything I can do to help?"

"Just take a load off for now. You like beer? I've got some in the fridge."

They stepped through the side door. "Boots go over there." When Shirley took off her boots and placed them on a plastic tray, Matt did the same.

The entryway led to a kitchen that was clean and tidy and resembled something from a 1950s movie. The gas stove was a giant white thing that looked like it was made of cast iron. Same for the refrigerator. Aside from the Mr. Coffee, there weren't any modern appliances. No microwave and no dishwasher. In front of the window, a plant grew in a pot suspended from an old iron hook. A needlepoint picture that read "God Bless Our Home" hung on the wall by the table. The linoleum floor was clean but worn and certainly wasn't level.

"How old is this place?"

"About 100 years old, built around 1880, we think. Back then people just bought property and built a house on it. They didn't concern themselves with records." Shirley had removed some chicken from the refrigerator and hollered into the next room, "Elizabeth, please come here. We have a visitor."

Shirley set about rubbing salt and pepper into the chicken and put a big pot of water on the stove to boil. Matt just stood there with his guitar and pack, not sure what to do, when a thundering came from above, making the whole house shake.

"Jiminy Crow, that girl walks like a damn elephant," Shirley muttered. A moment later, a stocky woman with long mousey-brown hair came into the kitchen. She was about five-foot-four, solid, with big shoulders and arms. She wore faded jeans and a tan chamois shirt buttoned to the top.

"Elizabeth, this is Matt. He'll be staying here tonight. Now say hello."

Elizabeth stared at something on the floor. "Hello."

"Hi. I'm Matt. Pleased to meet you."

"Show Matt where the guest room and bathroom are, then please pick six ears of sweet corn."

Wordlessly, Elizabeth turned and walked through a dining room and then up a set of stairs. He followed. The bathroom was right at the top of the staircase, so Elizabeth pointed at it without speaking, then turned down a hall lined with framed family photographs. Just beyond were doors to the left and right. Elizabeth pointed to the one on the left.

"This is the guest room," she said, still avoiding his eyes. She then pointed at the other door. "This is my room. Keep out."

"Thanks." Matt sidled past her with his things and dropped them on the bed, which was covered with a patch-work comforter. When he turned back to Elizabeth, she was already clomping down the stairs, presumably to go get fresh corn.

After a quick visit to the bathroom, Matt returned to the kitchen where Shirley had a beer in each hand. She handed him one, said, "Cheers," and took a long swallow. He did likewise.

"What can I do to help?"

Shirley was back by the stove peeling potatoes. "You can give Elizabeth a hand shucking corn on the porch. You know how to shuck corn?"

"No problem," he said as he headed outside. There were four high back wooden chairs on the porch and Elizabeth was in one of them. She had a beautiful cob of corn in her lap and was shucking another into a basket.

"Can I help?" he asked.

"I don't care."

He took the seat next to her, lifted one of the ears from the porch floor, and got to work. "It's beautiful here," he said, trying to make conversation. "You like it here?"

"Yes."

"Have you ever lived anywhere else?"

"No." Elizabeth finished her second ear and reached down for a third.

"You like the yellow or the white corn better?"

Elizabeth didn't answer but focused on picking hairs

from the ear of corn she was holding. He finished his ear and bent to get another.

"Why are you here?" She kept picking hairs, not looking at him.

"Your mom gave me a lift, and she's having trouble with the truck. Starter's dying, I believe. She asked if I could fix it, which I'll do tomorrow."

"A lift from where?" She bent and picked up the last ear of corn, ripping the husk off as aggressively as a hunter he'd once seen in Kentucky skinning a rabbit.

"Not sure, exactly. By a store north of Bennington. I helped her get the truck going, and she offered to give me a ride."

"Where's your car?"

"I don't have a car. I've been hitchhiking across the country."

Elizabeth finally turned to look at him, her eyes bugging out of her head. "A hitchhiker?" She stood, held the four ears of corn in one arm while balling her other hand into a tight fist. "My dad said we should never pick up hitchhikers. They're psychos and murderers."

With that, she scampered back into the house. A moment later, Matt heard voices raised in the kitchen. He reached down and took a long pull off his beer. Then, he finished with his corn. Inside the house, Elizabeth ranted about killers and rapists while Shirley tried to calm her down.

Matt took out a cigarette and lit it. He left his two ears of corn on the chair and walked away from the house. The day had cooled as dusk crept along. Back in Silver City, it was still late afternoon and undoubtedly hot as a campfire skillet.

Back when he lived with the Beals, they had taken in two other foster kids. Tina, who was 13 and must have come from a really bad home. She was mean as a rattlesnake with a toothache, as Mrs. Beal used to say. And Joey, who reminded him a little of Elizabeth. Joey kept to himself and was very quiet. One thing about him was that he'd never look you in the eye. Tina had held his face in her hands and tried to make him look at her straight on once. Joey totally flipped out and had a meltdown. Matt and Mr. Beal had to peel him off Tina or else he might have killed her. But most of the time Joey was a good kid. He was friendly, and loved any kind of animal, especially the Beals' cocker spaniel, Nellie. He enjoyed playing with her far more than he did any of the kids in the neighborhood.

The porch door opened with a squeak. "Matt? You done with that corn? Need another beer?"

"Corn's on the chair." Elizabeth's outburst put him on edge. She was troubled, and the last thing he needed was trouble. "I'm just having a smoke. Be there in a minute."

The table was set when he reentered the kitchen. He put his empty beer next to Shirley's three empties on the counter and cautiously asked Elizabeth where he should sit.

"This is my seat," she said, putting a glass of milk at one spot.

"Elizabeth," Shirley spoke with the firmness of a mother at the end of her rope.

"You sit there," Elizabeth pointed to the seat across from her. "Mom sits here." She indicated the chair beside her.

Matt put his beer down and took a seat. Shirley placed a plate piled with food in front of him. He unfolded his napkin and put it in his lap, as Mrs. Beal had instructed him civilized people do. He waited to eat in case these were grace-sayers. When Elizabeth attacked her food like a starved coyote dining on an antelope, he figured probably not.

"Don't wait," Shirley said. She sat before her own plate of food and took a slice of butter with her knife. "Dig in."

Matt hadn't eaten anything since the bagel that morning. The food smelled delicious, and tasted even better. The chicken was seasoned with a smoky rub and grilled to perfection, and you didn't get fresher corn.

"Great potatoes," he said between bites. "Are those onion bits in them?"

Shirley smiled, pleased with the compliment.

"I taste cumin in the chicken rub," he continued. "Salt and pepper. Anything else?"

"Chili powder, and of course, garlic. You like to cook?"

"Being a nomad, I don't do much. But I've worked in a lot of restaurants. I enjoy learning how the cooks make their specialties taste so good."

Shirley took a long drink of beer. "Maybe that's how you'll end up after your cross-country adventure, as a cook or a chef."

Matt nodded as he ate. Glancing up, he noticed that Elizabeth was looking at him.

"Are you Mexican?" she asked.

Out of the corner of his vision he saw Shirley rolling her eyes, but she didn't interject.

"Why do you ask?"

"I've seen Mexican people on TV." She pushed something around on her plate with her fork. "They speak Spanish. You look like them."

"Well, you're right. I'm half-Mexican. My mother came from Juarez, which is just south of El Paso. Her name was Liliana Jimenez, and my real name is Mateo Alejandro Blackwell. But everybody just calls me Matt."

"Why did you come to Vermont?" Elizabeth asked.

"I just sort of ended up here. Like I said, I've been catching rides to come across the country." He intentionally avoided the term "hitchhiking," afraid it might set her off again. "This morning I was in Springfield, Massachusetts, and now I'm here in White River Junction."

"Aren't you scared of riding with strangers?" Elizabeth

stabbed at an already-eaten corn cob with her fork. "Aren't you worried some crazy person will kill you?"

Matt took a swallow of beer and contemplated his response. It was obvious Elizabeth had both a fascination with and fear of death and hitchhiking. Lord only knows what her father told her as a kid.

"There have been a few uncomfortable rides," he said. "But most people are pretty nice. Some folks are lonely and just looking for someone to talk to as they drive. It gives me an opportunity to learn about some of the places I've been, the type of work people do, the weather and so on."

"What do you mean, uncomfortable?"

Shirley had taken their plates away and brought him a fresh beer while she busied herself with the dishes.

"Well, for instance," he said, leaning back in his chair. "I was in Indiana and this old man picked me up. He insisted I put my stuff in the back seat and sit up front with him, which was no big deal. We drove for a bit, just chatting. Then he reached over and put his hand on my leg."

"Why would he do that?" Elizabeth asked.

"I don't know, but I didn't like it."

"What'd you do?"

In truth, he'd taken out his Buck knife and told the old pervert to pull over and let him out before he cut the guy's hand off. But he said, "I told him to keep his hands to himself, and to pull over or else I might throw up in his car."

"Good thinking," Shirley chimed in over the water running in the sink.

Without losing a beat, Elizabeth continued questioning him. "Do you like Vermont better than Mexico?"

"I come from New Mexico, and I've only been here one day. But so far I like it. It's very different from where I come from."

"Are there bees and maple trees in New Mexico?"

"Bees, yes," he said. "No maple trees, though. We have more cactuses than trees. And scorpions and rattlesnakes and green chilies. In New Mexico we put green chilies on everything."

"Are green chilies hot, Mom?"

"Yes, they are," Shirley said, drying a pot with a dish towel before putting it away. "They don't grow around here, but you'd probably like them."

Matt helped clear the dishes. Afterwards, he went to his room and read a tattered paperback he'd picked up at a bus station before falling into a deep sleep.

The following morning, Matt woke to what he thought were cops breaking his door down with a sledgehammer. It was just Elizabeth delivering a message that breakfast was on the table. After brushing his teeth and slipping into some clean clothes, he went downstairs and was hit with the fragrant aroma of fresh ground coffee.

"It's Green Mountain Roasters," Shirley informed him. "I think it's the best."

She put a plate of scrambled eggs and toast in front of him. "Take your time. Here's the keys to the truck. Tools are in the garage. Elizabeth and I need to tend to the bees before it heats up out there and they get cranky."

Before he had a chance to respond, Shirley was out the door calling to Elizabeth. Matt sipped his coffee. He wondered at a woman who had to be in her sixties and put down seven beers last night to his four, chipper than a prairie dog in heat this morning.

Shirley's husband did have a good selection of tools, including a five-ton hydraulic jack and a creeper, which made working under the truck much easier. One bolt holding the starter in was rusted solid, but Old Frank had three cans of WD-40 tucked away on a shelf. A few squirts did the trick. Matt had the new starter installed in about an hour and a half. When he got in the truck again, he said a quick prayer, pushed in the clutch, and let out a sigh of relief when the engine turned over once and roared to life.

He put everything back where he found it, and left the old starter in the box of the new one in the truck bed. Some stores took them back for rebuilding, but he'd leave that decision up to Shirley. He'd discovered several jugs of washer fluid, so he refilled the truck's reserve, then checked the oil and brake fluid, which were fine.

After washing up at the kitchen sink, he wandered outside to take a look around. The day was a little cloudy, but when the sun came through, it made him feel all was right with the world. The air was full of the sounds of birds and insects and smelled, well, very green. Earthy, he supposed. New Mexico was so dry and arid, except for the occasional smell of somebody cooking tamales or maybe diesel exhaust fumes, there wasn't a whole lot to stimulate the olfactory gland, if that's what it's called. But here, the air smelled both full of nature and clean.

Matt walked around the vegetable garden, which he estimated was about 100 feet long and 50 feet wide. It was the largest home veggie garden he'd ever seen, and all the corn, tomatoes, peppers, cabbages and what not seemed to be doing well. Apparently, there wasn't drought in Vermont. He walked behind the house and found another smaller garden, jammed full of large, thorny raspberry bushes. He carefully picked a berry the size of a grape, popped it into his mouth, and then wandered further. He paused by two white crosses stuck in the ground. Frank? A family pet? His thoughts were distracted when a couple of bees flew too close to his face, so he moved on.

As he got closer to a section of the property lined with rows of medium-sized trees, he saw they were apple trees. Some of the apples were red, but most were still green. As he walked down one row, he heard Elizabeth telling Shirley something was too big. He rounded a corner and discovered a large tree adjacent to the orchard had fallen across the rows of trees, crushing most of one apple tree and part of another.

"Whoa! What happened?"

"That damned maple came down night before last." Shirley said. Her face was sweaty as she pushed her glasses back up her nose.

"Doesn't look good," he said.

"No, it doesn't."

He paused. "Truck's done at least. Everything's working fine now. I left the old starter in the bed. Maybe you can bring it back to the store for rebuilding."

"Yes. Thanks."

"Ray Kaminski can probably do it," Elizabeth said, still eyeing the downed tree.

"And charge me an arm and a leg," Shirley said. She turned to Matt. "You ever run a chain saw?"

He shrugged. "Once or twice."

Shirley threw her hands up, then laughed. "Silly me. I don't suppose you have much need to chop down cactus."

"Actually, I helped a guy chop up a couple trees that fell down after a bad rainstorm in Illinois. He had the bigger chain saw, and I used the little one to cut off all the branches. I don't imagine what I did is much different from what you need here."

Shirley shook her head. "I can't have you chopping your hand off on my account."

Elizabeth stood, observing the conversation.

"Your husband had a chain saw? Somewhere in the garage?"

"Hasn't been run in years. It's too much for me, and Elizabeth has always been afraid of them." She wiped sweat from her brow with her shirt sleeve. "Besides, I don't think we have any two-cycle oil. I remember Frank telling me you needed that to start the damned thing."

"How about I take a look? Can't hurt."

Shirley kicked at a rock on the ground. "I suppose..."

"It's near the big bag of fertilizer, behind the tiller." Elizabeth perked up, like she enjoyed being helpful.

Fifteen minutes later, Matt unscrewed the fuel cap on the chainsaw in the gravel driveway. Elizabeth helped him find the gas and oil, then told him how her dad used to pour equal amounts into the chainsaw, then shake it around to mix it in. He remembered to depress the safety, then gave the starter cable a pull. The engine coughed once but didn't catch. Elizabeth hurried into the house.

A dozen more pulls proved fruitless, although it fired a few times and seemed like it wanted to start. His arm felt like rubber, so he put the saw down and went into the house for water.

Shirley busied about making sandwiches and serving home-canned peaches. "Any luck?"

"Almost," he said. "I'm going to take the spark plug out and clean it. Maybe that will do the trick."

"Wash up and have some food first."

Matt accepted the roast beef sandwich and glass of ice water, and joined the women at the kitchen table to eat. Elizabeth demolished her food in about 60 seconds, while Shirley listened to a talk show about gardening on the radio.

After lunch, Matt checked the chain guard, then primed the carburetor. There was a choke lever, so he tried moving it 90 degrees before pulling the starter. This time, the engine ran for a few seconds. He moved the choke lever a few degrees more and tried again. With an ear-splitting roar, the chainsaw leaped to life. He checked that the chain wasn't moving, then fiddled with the choke until the engine sounded right. He killed it and put it down on the driveway.

Shirley clapped as she and Elizabeth came out of the house. "You did it."

"So far, so good," he said. "Let's go tackle that tree."

Shirley pushed her glasses up, concern etched on her face. "I know I don't have to tell you how dangerous a chainsaw can be, Matt. You're a smart young man. You be careful, now."

Matt nodded. These were nice people. He wanted to be helpful.

"Start by just trimming off the branches, a few at a time. Elizabeth can help clear them away with the tractor. Once that's done, cut the trunk in lengths. Two feet or so, starting at the top where it's narrower. We'll use that for firewood. If you get tired, or it's too much for you—stop. The last thing I want is you getting hurt."

During his last experience with a chainsaw, the old-timer named Skip insisted he wear safety goggles to protect his eyes. There hadn't been any goggles in the garage, so Matt retrieved his $2.99 gas station sunglasses from his pack upstairs. He headed for the orchard while Shirley and Elizabeth set out towards the gardens.

The tree wasn't completely severed at the base. It was big and heavy and barely trembled when he kicked it solidly with his boot. Near the bottom, the limbs were almost as thick as trees themselves, six or more inches in diameter. He decided to start at the top where the branches were thinner, more pliable, while he adjusted to the saw.

The saw's wail drowned the noise around him. After only a few minutes, the muscles in his arms protested from the vibrations. The top branches cut easily, and he moved with confidence further down the tree. A short while later, he killed the chainsaw and put it down, shaking out his arms and hands. He dragged the severed limbs into a pile before resting while he had a smoke.

As he went at the tree again, his mind wandered back to old Skip in Illinois. Matt was working at a taco shop near the university in Carbondale. The old guy, who was only in his fifties but looked more like 80, chatted him up after ordering his usual lunchtime special. Skip was fighting for the army in Vietnam long before "the goddamn mess," as he called the war, officially started. Still imagining the VC were out to get him when he returned stateside, he holed up in a cabin outside the Shawnee National Forest. Making furniture in his wood shop, drinking, and complaining that "Uncle Sam gave me goddamned cancer."

Skip was self-medicating with Jack Daniel's and home-grown marijuana. He invited Matt to hang around anytime he liked. One day, he took the old guy up on the offer and ended up staying a few weeks, helping him out here and there. The cancer was deep in Skip's lungs, and between that and all the pot he smoked, the cranky bastard could barely breathe. But he showed Matt his workshop, with all his various power tools. And how to use a chain saw. Matt helped him chop up fallen trees on his property after a wind-storm. He split and stacked them to season for firewood. When Matt decided it was time to move on, Skip gave him a hundred bucks, which he initially refused.

"Look, son"—Skip tucked the bills in Matt's flannel shirt pocket—"I'll be dead by this time next year, and my asshole brother will inherit all I have left. I'd much rather you had it."

"Thanks." Matt had a fairly good stash of money, but another hundred was more than welcome.

"Oh, and here." After a coughing spell that sounded like he was vomiting out his guts, Skip took a toke off the doobie in the ashtray on the kitchen table, opened the freezer, and handed Matt a sandwich bag packed with weed. "A little bit of Illinois' best to remember me by."

Matt accepted the pot. He sold it the next day to some guys at a bar in Carbondale for another 50 bucks. Two rides later, he was on his way to Indianapolis.

Without warning, the chainsaw bounced off the limb Matt was cutting, like it had been kicked by a mule. Matt let go of the trigger and snapped his attention back to the saw in front of him. Unconsciously backpedaling, he tripped and landed on his ass, then smacked his shoulder hard against a severed limb. In what was probably a second, but seemed like an hour, the saw finally stopped and he put it down.

"Aw, shit," he spoke aloud. A tremor passed through his body as adrenaline and the realization of what could have happened possessed him. "You stupid shit," he scolded himself. He'd been daydreaming, which is something no one should ever do when operating a chainsaw. Skip taught him that. He must have hit a knot in the tree and was lucky he'd managed to control the saw before he did some serious damage.

Matt got up slowly, massaging his butt and checking his shoulder for blood. Everything seemed to be in place. He walked back to the house for a break. Elizabeth and Shirley filled a half dozen baskets with fresh vegetables. Elizabeth carried them to the cellar.

"Whatcha doing with those?" he asked.

"Farmer's market is tomorrow. It's cool in the basement, so we keep the veggies there until morning," Elizabeth answered.

"Grab a case of honey and one of syrup while you're down there," Shirley hollered to Elizabeth.

Matt took a drink from the garden hose. He shook his head as Elizabeth carried the cases up the stairs and outside to the truck. She was strong as an ox.

"How's it going?" Shirley asked. "I see you still have all

your limbs."

"Going fine," he said. "It's tiring on the arms, so I'm just taking a short break."

"Take as long as you like. You okay with spaghetti for dinner?"

"I love spaghetti." In truth, Matt was getting hungry, and hoped spaghetti also meant meatballs and a red sauce. "I better get back to it."

Matt worked for two more hours, taking breaks that didn't relieve the cramps in his arms. He knew he was probably squeezing the saw too hard, but he didn't want any mishaps. By the time he quit, he'd made a pile of branches the size of an Econoline van. He put his sunglasses in his pocket and walked back toward the house.

"Elizabeth!" Matt jerked away when Elizabeth stepped in front of him from behind an apple tree. "You surprised the shit out of me."

"I was watching in case you cut your arm off."

The two walked from the orchard toward the house. Matt remembered to take off his boots before he walked into the kitchen, then went to the sink to wash up. His stomach growled when he smelled sauce simmering on the stove.

"Elizabeth, go upstairs and wash up before supper," Shirley said while she stirred the spaghetti. "Matt, help yourself to a beer in the fridge. Grab me a fresh one while you're at it."

The spaghetti Shirley dished up didn't come with meatballs, but the sauce was full of chopped beef and pork and hit the spot. There was also a big bowl of salad, all ingredients picked from their garden that afternoon.

That evening, when they sat in the living room, Shirley drank beer and watched *Jeopardy!* and *Wheel of Fortune* while Elizabeth worked on a 500-piece jigsaw puzzle. The puzzle was a picture of a bunch of marbles on a black tray.

The edges could be worked out from the black pieces, but the marble pieces all looked pretty much the same to Matt. Elizabeth was patient and methodical, though, humming to herself and slowly making the connections.

Matt stepped out on the porch for a smoke. Sitting there, watching the dusk turn to night, he reflected on the random path that led him to this unlikely place. Shirley liked him. That he knew. Even Elizabeth seemed to accept he wasn't a psycho killer after all. The way she smiled when they talked, and the way she came to the orchard to make sure he hadn't permanently disfigured himself with the chain saw, told him she enjoyed having someone new to talk to. He knew her loneliness. He had the same lonely ache in his belly. Yes, he always had people in his life, but he had no connections. No family, no girlfriend, no best friend. He tried to convince himself he liked being a loner, and for the most part he did. But being here, with people to talk to, eat with, and share stories with? A place to work where he was needed, appreciated even. *A body could get used to this.* He *could get used to this.*

Matt jerked awake in the dark as Elizabeth pounded on his door. "What?"

She opened the door. "It's Saturday. Farmer's market day. If you're coming, you better get up."

Matt wolfed down a bowl of oatmeal and a cup of coffee before heading out to where Shirley and Elizabeth were finishing loading the truck. Around him the world was covered in a fine dew, the birds were active and chirping, and the truck bed brimmed with baskets of vegetables, boxes of honey, folding chairs, and a couple tables.

"How long have you two been up?"

"An hour or so," Shirley said as Elizabeth scooted over and made room for him on the front seat. She reversed the truck. "If you hadn't fixed this baby," she slapped the dash, "we'd be stuck here for who knows how long."

"No problem," was all he could think to say.

They drove in the quiet morning past other farms and woods. Then a section with more modern houses appeared, where bikes and swing sets littered the yards. Then into White River Junction, past the automotive store, a Grand Union and Wendy's. Just beyond the business section of town, Shirley cut right on a dirt path into an acre or so of grassy field. A couple dozen other people were there in the pre-dawn, quietly setting up tables and chairs, unpacking farm goods, pastries, and homemade crafts to sell. Shirley and Elizabeth unloaded the truck and set up without speaking. Matt took comfort in their easy rhythm.

"Can I help?" When Matt spoke, Shirley only grunted, so he helped Elizabeth set up the two tables.

Then they loaded the tables with baskets of produce, displaying one basket of each vegetable with extras in the truck under a tarp. He also carried over a box of honey and one of maple syrup. Shirley took out a jar of each and put them next to a cup with plastic spoons so potential customers could sample them.

Once the sun was up, shoppers started walking by, the questions always the same. "These are local?" "Organic?" "What's the price of the corn?" Shirley smiled, patiently answering. Elizabeth, scowling, sat next to her mother.

Matt smelled coffee brewing at a vendor down the way. "Anybody for java?"

"That would be nice," Shirley tucked a few dollars from a man who bought a dozen ears of corn into her money pouch.

Elizabeth picked at a fingernail. "I don't like coffee."

Matt took off toward the booth where the guy selling coffee also had deep-fried donuts and hot chocolate. He bought Elizabeth a cup of the latter, then got coffee for himself and Shirley.

The morning passed by, the sun getting higher in the deep blue autumn sky, and the day grew warmer. Matt removed his flannel shirt and collected his friends' empty cups. On his way to the trash bin, he checked out the other vendors' tables, set up in two parallel rows. A few sold vegetables, so Shirley and Elizabeth had competition. Others were selling freshly butchered chickens, lamb and beef out of big red coolers.

"Here," a woman said, holding out a bite of meat on a toothpick, "try this." But when Matt got closer to the woman's table and peeked into the cooler that sat there, the dead animals inside looked about the size of housecats.

"What is it?" he asked warily as the woman proffered the meat.

"Rabbit." She was a friendly, innocuous looking woman with a '50s beehive hairdo. "Smoked, with just a little salt and pepper. Give it a try."

He cautiously accepted the morsel, which turned out to be gamey, but pretty good. He thanked the woman, whose smile faded when Matt failed to buy one of her cat-sized bunnies.

The energy on the field had picked up since they arrived at dawn. Someone was actively recruiting customers to take a look at his wood carvings, and another his paintings on thin panels of wood. One guy was selling tubes of something wrapped in waxed paper, which puzzled Matt until he walked closer and saw they contained butter. "Salted and unsalted," the guy said as he smeared some on a piece of bread and handed it to Matt.

People still made their own butter in the late twentieth century? "Delicious," he said as he wiped away an errant breadcrumb.

"Got cheese, too." The guy handed Matt a slice. "Cheddar. This one's about six months old."

Matt ate the cheese, sharp and tangy. Nothing like the stuff he used to top those tacos with back at the place where he met Skip. He left the table with a pound of it wrapped in brown paper.

A few tables further down, a girl about his age sat by a beat-up Datsun B210. The rusty rear quarter panels were patched up with green duct tape. Music came from the open windows, something with acoustic guitars and bongos he didn't recognize. Shiny earrings, bracelets and necklaces, some made of silver and turquoise, were spread out on a card table next to the girl. Upon closer inspection, the girl was quite attractive, in that crunchy, granola kind of way. Her light brown hair, parted down the middle, fell a few inches below her shoulders. Her eyes were big and brown and lit up when she smiled at him. Her earrings were large silver hoops, like some of the ones she was selling. Without a bra under her pale-yellow tank top, it was difficult for him to look away.

"Hola, señor. Quiera comprar mis cosas?"

Matt's grin matched hers. "You speak Spanish?"

She laughed and shook her head. "No entiendo de Espanol! I remember about seven words from the Spanish I took in middle school, so please don't make me feel stupid."

"Most of the Spanish I know are swear words, so let's stick to English."

The girl wore several rings. A butterfly tattoo fluttered on her forearm. "Deal." With another radiant smile, she crossed one leg over the other, ruffling her long skirt and revealing a very shapely calf. A shapely calf that hadn't been shaved in a while.

"Who you listening to? I like the way the percussion works with the guitars."

"I know, right? It's *Lamb's Bread*. My girlfriend Carla is playing the bongos. She plays the higher notes. A guy named

Michael plays the bigger, bassier, African drum."

"She's fantastic," Matt replied, trying to hide his disappointment. His momentary daydream of a date with this beauty dissipated like a too-short, but much-needed summer breeze.

"Not when she's stoned and practicing at two in the morning," she said with a delicious laugh.

They talked about the band, how hard it was to get gigs that weren't in dive bars, and how the unnamed hippie chick had gotten into making jewelry. "I make pretty good money at music festivals, Dead shows—that kind of thing. Not so much at flea markets or farmer's markets, but I keep showing up. You never know when you'll catch a break, right?"

"Right." Matt smiled, then turned to look over her wares, picking up an earring here, a bracelet there, glancing occasionally at the seller. He missed female companionship more than he wanted to admit.

After a few more minutes of chatting about bands and shows, he picked up a thin silver bracelet with a turquoise-colored stone. "How much?"

"Five," the girl said.

He paid. Before he moved along, he took one more hopeful look at the girl.

The market broke up promptly at noon. They loaded up the truck, then Shirley counted her profits. "A hundred twenty-eight," she said, waving a wad of cash in the air. "We're gonna splurge at the Grand Union on the way home."

"I bought some cheddar," Matt said as they loaded into the truck. "How about I make you two dinner tonight?"

Back home, Matt took a large cast-iron skillet and sautéed garlic and onions, then added ground beef, beans, canned green chilies, and a few diced tomatoes. "This'll take a while," he said, before covering the pan and setting it on low to slow-cook.

As he worked, he glanced out the window and saw the fading gardens, the hills in the background and a bright blue sky marbled with scattered clouds. Images of the hippie chick jeweler at the farmer's market danced in his head. Maybe there were other girls around here, he thought, girls that were available. He just needed to get out and explore. He stirred his beef and bean mix, the steam rising and releasing its spicy fragrance into the air.

Yeah, maybe there was hope here.

Matt spent the next few hours cutting more of the downed tree. Elizabeth helped him take all the small limbs and branches to a dumping ground at the back of the property, then waited while he cut the bigger branches into two-foot lengths. They stacked the smaller of these pieces between two large maple trees, leaving the rest in a pile to split later.

Back in the house, Matt showered, then returned to his cooking. Shirley was very interested in what he was doing, and of course plied him with a fresh beer the minute he finished the one he was drinking. She got some corn, which he had her boil in the husk, then grill. While he grated the fresh cheddar and assembled burritos, he had her mix ingredients to make a spicy cheese sauce. He shucked the cooked corn and coated it liberally with the sauce, then squeezed a lime over the platter to make what he called Mexican street corn.

As he put the food on the table, he felt a spark of pride. *Orgulloso*, his mother used to tell him. The dishes all looked good, probably as good as anything he'd get back home. Shirley lit a candle and put it in the center of the table.

"How do you say bon appetite in Spanish?" Shirley asked.

"*Buen provecho*," Matt answered, then picked up a burrito and took a bite.

Not a fan of change, Elizabeth was initially skeptical of

the food he put on the table. Shirley said it would be awesome—she promised—and eventually Elizabeth's appetite overcame her trepidation.

Two minutes later, face covered in goo like a child's, she announced, "This is the best corn I've ever had!"

Shirley complimented his cooking a half dozen times. She refused to let him clean up after dinner, so he went into the living room with Elizabeth. She was about done with the marble puzzle, with just a Rorschach blotch of empty space in the center to finish. He sat across from her at the card table where she worked and he pretended to help.

When he was growing up, the television or radio was always on, a constant din of background noise. Spanish music always floated in the air. All the neighbors listened to the radio or records like a never-ending dance party.

Yeah, the quiet here was really different, nice.

The next morning, when Matt got up Shirley had already gone into town to do some errands. Elizabeth told him she needed to tend to the bees and water the gardens, but then she could help him move and stack wood if he needed her to.

"Thanks," he said. "That would be great." He reached into his pocket and took out the bracelet he'd bought from the hippie chick at the farmer's market. "Here, I bought this for you. I don't think it's real turquoise, but lots of jewelry from where I come from is made of turquoise and looks like this."

"Wow!" Elizabeth was genuinely pleased. "I really like it."

"The chain is really thin, so you might want to be careful."

But Elizabeth was set on putting the bracelet on, and gave a rare smile once she clasped it.

Matt ate his breakfast and watched as Elizabeth fondled and admired her new bracelet. She kept glancing at him with happiness etched on her face, which made him feel good.

After downing a big mug of coffee, he headed out to the orchard. His plan was to cut up the serious portion of the tree. These were thicker pieces that took more time and wore on his hands and arms. Just before lunch, he cut the last piece. A bit of stump still remained, but he figured he could deal with that another day. For now, he'd have Elizabeth help him haul the pieces over to where the woodpile was and he'd split it up to season. Lunch consisted of sandwiches and sliced apples. The McIntoshes were ripe in the orchard, and Shirley had already picked several baskets full.

Matt found Frank's axe in the garage next to a five-pound sledgehammer. Elizabeth informed him that her dad often had to hammer the axe through the tough wood to get it to split apart, so Matt took her advice and grabbed the sledge. Indeed, still being pretty green, the wood didn't split easily, especially the first cut on the bigger pieces. Those definitely required hammering. Then, with a little luck and a lot of force, the smaller pieces would split with just the big axe.

"How come your dad never invested in one of those hydraulic splitters?" Matt asked.

"I don't know what that is." She fiddled with the bracelet on her wrist. "My dad was really strong. He liked splitting wood. He used to make four tall rows for burning in the winter."

Matt imagined Frank in this very place, chopping and splitting cord after cord of wood. And honestly, the work felt good. He felt manly, doing a job men had been doing for thousands of years to provide heat come wintertime. The pounding of the sledge on the worn axe head was both monotonous and therapeutic, cleansing of a sort. All frustration and anxiety and hurt and sorrow in a body could be channeled into the hammering and splitting.

By late afternoon, Matt's muscles were complaining. It was a good kind of soreness, but he knew he had better call it quits before he was unable to brush his teeth tomorrow. Inside the house, Shirley handed him a cold beer and asked if he liked pork chops for dinner. He took a long pull off the cold beer and said, "Love 'em," although they weren't his favorite.

Matt showered and the effort of shampooing his hair convinced him to take a couple Tylenols before dinner. Shirley's pork chops had a hot rub on them, which he thought she might have done for him. They were a little tough, but he washed them down with Labatt Blue and dug into the fresh salad and bread.

Retiring to the living room while Shirley did the dishes, Elizabeth started a new 500-piece puzzle, this one featuring a pyramid of cupcakes with various colored frostings and a solid blue background. After dumping the pieces into a pile, Elizabeth immediately started sorting the all-blue pieces, separating out the pieces with a flat side. Matt was helping when Elizabeth asked, "How come you never play your guitar?"

"Well, I wouldn't say I never play it," he said. "I just haven't played it since I've been here. Which is what—five or six days?"

"How many songs do you know?"

"Hmmm... Not sure. I know parts, or the main rhythm of probably a hundred songs or so. I probably know 50 fairly well."

"Who taught you?"

"Mostly I taught myself," he said. "When I was 15, I traded a car stereo I had to a kid for a crappy acoustic with nylon strings he had but never played." Matt deliberately left out the part about how he stole the Pioneer car stereo out of a Monte Carlo in order to trade it for the guitar he wanted. "I got a pitch pipe and a book from the library to learn about fingering and chords, then I listened to the radio and practiced a lot."

"What does 'acoustic' mean? Why are nylon strings crappy?"

"An acoustic means a wooden, hollow body guitar, as opposed to an electric guitar. The sound comes from the strings vibrating and is magnified through the body of the guitar. Nylon strings aren't crappy, but metal strings sound crisper, louder, resonate better, and are just nicer in my opinion. They are also a lot tougher on your fingers. It takes a while to build up callouses."

"Why don't you play your guitar now?"

Matt finished his beer. "Want to meet me on the porch in a few minutes? I need to hit the bathroom and then tune up."

"Sure!"

"Mom, Matt's gonna play his guitar on the porch."

The ladies were seated and waiting for him when Matt arrived with his case. He removed his guitar and showed Elizabeth the pitch pipe. "If you blow into the E6 tube, that's the same as the top string on my guitar."

Elizabeth blew into the pitch pipe with all her might, making a horrible sound that caused her mother to shriek and cover her ears with her hands.

"Gently," Matt said. "You aren't putting out a fire."

Elizabeth blew the note more reasonably, and he showed her how moving the tuning peg made the pitch of the string go up and down. Then he settled the tune where he wanted it and asked Elizabeth to play the next note, which corresponded to the A string. Once the tuning was done, he showed her some basic chords.

"Are you ever going to play something?" she asked.

"Elizabeth!" Shirley cautioned.

Matt laughed, strummed a few G chords, and then started picking the low E string and moved into "Ring of Fire," always a crowd pleaser. As he sang he saw both of the ladies' faces light up, and as he picked out the ending they both clapped with delight. Inside his chest, he felt that ember of pride, *orgulloso*, coming to life. With barely a pause, he moved into the Beatles with "Rocky Raccoon" and "I Wanna Hold Your Hand." Matt covered a couple of Dylan songs, "Take it Easy," then ended with "Puff the Magic Dragon" which Shirley, now on her fifth beer or so, sang along with.

"I think that's it for tonight," Matt said as he put his guitar back in its case.

"Awww, one more," Elizabeth pleaded. "Please! Just one more song."

"It's getting late," Shirley said, twisting the top off another beer and handing it to Matt. "And you are smelling a little ripe, young lady. You definitely need a shower before bed."

Elizabeth scowled. Matt imagined she'd been making that same face for 30 years now when her mother told her it was time for bed. He sipped the cold beer and took his guitar back out. "Tell you what. I'll try playing a song I've been working on for a year or more. It's called 'Buckets of Rain' by Bob Dylan, and the fingering is very difficult."

"I don't know that song," Elizabeth said.

Shirley cracked another beer for herself. "Just shush and listen."

Matt changed the tuning of several strings on his guitar, fingering notes on the higher strings and matching the tone to the lower strings. Around them the night had cooled, the moon was bright, and all the crickets and bugs were playing their own symphony.

Matt started playing, flubbed a note, stopped, and started up again. Once his fingers started doing what they inherently knew to do, the rhythm of the song flowing within him, he sang, "Buckets of rain, buckets of tears. Got all them buckets comin' out of my ears. Buckets of moonbeams in my hand.

You've got all the love, honey-baby, I can stand..."

Once again, the ladies clapped when he finished playing. He put his guitar away, took a sip of beer, and soaked in the night as a wave of exhaustion slowly overtook him. "I'm bushed."

Elizabeth thanked him and said he was the best guitar player she had ever met. He smiled and thanked her back as she went inside for the night.

"You've had a long day," Shirley said. "Before we head in, I want to thank you for all the work you've done around here. You've been a huge help and I want you to know that I—that we—really appreciate it."

"My pleasure," he said honestly. "You and Elizabeth are good people, and I think you have a great life here. I can understand why you and your husband decided to chuck the rat race and give this place a go."

"You've never spent a winter here," she said with a laugh. "It starts to snow in November and doesn't stop until April, sometimes May. But it's peaceful and it suits us."

They both sat in the stillness and drank their beers. Shirley stood up and extended a hand. "You get yourself upstairs and get some sleep. Leave the bottles. I'll take care of things here."

He accepted her hand and she pulled him to a stand. He picked up his guitar, said good night, and trudged up the stairs to his bedroom. Elizabeth was in the shower, so he pulled off his jeans and shirt and rested on the bed for a minute. He'd pee and brush his teeth once Elizabeth was finished.

Matt took approximately six seconds to fall asleep. In his mind he dreamed of climbing a tall, wooded mountain. The trail was steep and even in his dream he was exhausted. Each step took momentous effort, and when he used nearby trees and plants to help pull himself up, his shoulders ached from the effort.

From somewhere nearby, he heard a cry, then a scrab-bling of sorts. He paused his climbing, attempting to get his bearings and identify the sounds—and then it was on him. A beast of some sort knocked him down and was on top of him, teeth gleaming as the animal went for his throat.

Matt cried out, both in his dream and in the reality of the guest room bed of the Vogel house. His eyes snapped open and the fogginess of sleep cleared quickly in the light of the bedside lamp. There was a monster on him, but, no, it wasn't a monster. It was a human, a strong human straddling him and trying to bite, no, kiss his face.

"Elizabeth?!"

"Kiss me," she whispered.

Matt shook off his gauzy sleepiness. "Elizabeth. Stop!" Her hair was still wet from the shower and smelled like roses. Her fulsome, naked breasts pressed into his chest.

"What are you doing?" He probably shouted, but he wasn't sure.

"I want you to kiss me."

He tried to push Elizabeth away, but not before Shirley knocked on the door, then barged in.

When Elizabeth turned and saw her mother, she started pounding Matt's chest. She wailed and shrieked like a trapped wild animal.

Shirley yanked the quilt off the bed and wrapped it around her naked daughter. Then she pulled Elizabeth off Matt and propelled her daughter to her own bedroom. Matt, dressed only in boxers, struggling to take in what had happened, sat on the edge of the bed. He put his feet on the floor, glad to have something solid beneath him. What the hell had just happened? Why would Elizabeth...

Shirley closed Elizabeth in her bedroom, then marched into the guest room. "It's time for you to go."

"I was just—"

She held up her hands to cut off his flailing explanation. Her nostrils flared as she tried to control her rage. "Elizabeth's no more than a child," she hissed.

"I was asleep! She just—"

"If you're not gone by 7:00 a.m., I'll call Sheriff Ballinger. He doesn't take kindly to drifters." She slammed the door behind her when she left. A picture of an old state fair fell from the wall and hit the floor, cracking the frame. He heard her go back into Elizabeth's room but couldn't make out their words.

What the fuck just happened? What was Elizabeth thinking? Why would she attack him like that?

As the questions tumbled in his mind, Matt got himself dressed and quietly rolled his clothes and returned his belongings to his backpack. He heard Shirley go to her bedroom and shut the door. The house was quiet, but, for Matt at least, it would never return to the peaceful place it had been a half hour ago.

He waited. He had plenty of experience waiting. For the next foster home. The next car to pick him up out on the highway. Why did things always end so ugly? He tried to slow his breath, to shut down his racing thoughts, then retrieved the pocket US Atlas from his backpack. Interstate 89 cut through White River Junction, heading north all the way up past Burlington, and southeast into New Hampshire and beyond. He tucked the map away and put his Buck knife in the front pocket of his jeans.

After an hour he put on his jacket, hoisted the pack over his sore shoulders, and picked up his guitar. He glanced around the room for anything he'd missed. There was nothing.

He crept down the stairs in his stocking feet and set his things on the porch while he put on his boots. He considered leaving a note but decided not to. This was his life, after all. An endless series of partings, most of them unwanted and unwarranted as far as he could tell. Explanations didn't matter. The only thing he knew how to do was to keep on moving on.

It took him about an hour to hike to where the highway crossed the road, to White River Junction's stores and restaurants. He made his way to the lot behind Wendy's. He decided not to set up his tent. He would just crawl into his sleeping bag to crash under the stars for a few hours. In the morning he'd catch a ride going east and see where the cosmos would take him.

Despite the exhaustion weighing him down, sleep didn't come. He stared into the night sky, more and more stars becoming apparent as his eyes grew accustomed to the dark, their light the solemn echo of a distant past.

He closed his eyes and conjured up an image of his mother from a snapshot of her, Jerome and himself holding hands when Matt was about five. Back when home was a solid thing he could rely on. He tried to focus on the image of his mother, but the memory of her face, her eyes, her curly hair, had begun fading long ago. The pixels had spread and blurred, and she just wasn't clear to him anymore.

The image he tried to conjure went dark as he fought back the tears.

Crying won't help you, he told himself. Praying won't do you no good. Somewhere out there, he'd find a place where he fit. He'd find a place where he belonged.

NASHUA

"Who's gonna tell you, it's too late?
Who's gonna tell ya, things aren't so great?
You can't go on, thinking nothing's wrong
Who's gonna drive you home, tonight?"
– "Drive" by The Cars

Anya Weber smiled when she saw the Welcome Duck. It happened every time she approached her apartment door and saw the cartoonish white duck painted on a wooden plank. She thought of her mother who gave her the silly thing, and that made her happy and sad at the same time.

She unlocked the door and with a hip-check, knocked it open. She stepped into the living room, the denim-covered futon to the right, a 19" TV on top of an empty milk crate to the left. Three of the four walls were covered in that horrible, dark brown paneling that was popular in the '50s. Anya had painted the lone plaster wall a color called Tropical Pineapple to brighten the room, but the contrast made the paneling look even more bleak.

"Honey, I'm home." Anya stepped into the kitchen filled with the scent of her roommate Charlotte's sandalwood candle, and *The Best of Bread* playing from the boom box on the top of the fridge. Her roomie really needed to update her cassette collection.

"In here," Charlotte called. "Getting ready. Be there in a jiff."

The apartment kitchen was long and narrow and hazardous when more than one person cooked at the same time. They also shared a bathroom, so Anya and Charlotte staggered their schedules, trying to keep out of each other's way.

"We have a photographer." Charlotte joined Anya as she sorted the mail on the counter. "Nathan and I signed the contract today, so we're set to go."

Anya scowled at the cable and electric bills, both in her name. Both her responsibility next month after Charlotte moved out. "Still time to back out," Anya joked.

"You stop that," Charlotte said, holding one of her dangling earrings. "Do these go with my shirt?"

"You wouldn't be the first runaway bride." Anya tossed the bills back down and glanced at Charlotte. "They look great. The blue highlights your eyes and the silver matches your belt."

The soon-to-be Mrs. Nathan Larson couldn't look more American pie in her tight jeans, white button-down, and black espadrilles. Anya went into the bathroom to freshen up before tackling the first difficult question of the night—what to wear? The guys were supposed to get here at six, then the four of them would head down to the Porthole Pub, assuming Marc showed up on time. Punctuality wasn't Marc's forte.

Charlotte poked her head through Anya's door. "Looking good. Want to split a wine cooler with me?"

"Sure."

Anya went back and forth in her mind half a dozen times before settling on her rust-colored boots, her black jeans, and the peach-colored blouse. It could use an ironing, but a few slaps of the palm and voila! It's presentable. As if Marc would notice anyway.

She kicked her work clothes into the corner. She'd pick everything up tomorrow. At the kitchen table with Charlotte, she said, "So, you got the photographer, the caterer, the venue, and the DJ. You're at the finish line. Congratulations."

"Not exactly. There are still plenty of Ts to cross." Charlotte picked up her wine glass and held it out.

Anya clinked glasses with hers. "Happy Friday." Before the glass reached Anya's lips, Charlotte plowed full-speed ahead. Anya glanced around their cozy little kitchen while Charlotte droned on. The coasters that came from Hampton Beach. The cooking utensils all hung in a row. The microwave Charlotte would take with her when she left, unless some generous family member bought her a new one as a wedding gift. One could always hope.

She'd miss this place. She didn't have any leads on a replacement roommate, and she couldn't swing the rent by herself. She talked to Marc about moving in. They had been going out for six and a half months, after all. But he was too invested in staying with his guy friends, Derek and Timmy. The three stooges, as Charlotte liked to call them. They weren't all that bad, except when they drank too much, which they did a lot of the time.

"... I just don't know how it's all going to get done."

"You've still got plenty of time," Anya said. When she saw the look on Charlotte's face, as if she had opened a smelly old container of cottage cheese, she knew she'd said the wrong thing.

"Jesus," Charlotte snapped. "You sound just like Nathan. This stuff doesn't just happen, you know."

Three sharp knocks came from the front door before Anya could reply.

"Hello?"

When she heard Nathan's voice, Charlotte called out, "In here, hon. Grab yourself a beer."

"I'll start with water, thanks. Hey, Anya. Hey, babe." Nathan was over six feet tall, with coffee brown hair and the polished look of a community theater supporting actor. He bent to kiss Charlotte, then sat next to her. "How was everybody's day?"

They each spent a few minutes complaining about their

jobs. Nathan as a sales manager at a glue manufacturer; Charlotte was a receptionist at Hallasey Toyota; and Anya worked in the analytical lab at Datco paint, which sounded more glamorous than her job actually was. Testing paint viscosity minute after minute, day after day, week after week, month after month until she grew old and died.

Six o'clock came. "Did Marc call?" Charlotte asked.

"No," Anya said. "I'm sure he's caught up in work, or traffic. You guys should probably go ahead and we'll meet you there."

"No, no. We'll wait. We're in no hurry."

Quarter past, then 6:30 came and went. Anya played Huey Lewis on the boom box. They finished their wine cooler, then split another.

"Seriously," Anya said. "You guys go. We'll be there by seven."

"Why don't you come with us?" Charlotte asked.

"We could leave a note on the door," Nathan suggested.

But Anya knew Marc. He'd be pissed to find a note on the door and her not waiting for him.

"Go. Seriously," Anya insisted. "I'll drive myself if he isn't here by seven."

After Nathan and Charlotte left, Anya switched to Prince's *Purple Rain* cassette and helped herself to another wine cooler. She did the dirty dishes in the sink, swaying her hips and singing along with Prince. Even if everybody said he was gay, Anya found him sexy as hell. Some guys just look good with a little makeup, that's all. She hung up her work clothes and tried to put her shoes back into some semblance of order. She cleaned out her purse and was just about to sweep the kitchen floor when Marc barged through the apartment door.

"Hey, sexy. What's happenin'?"

Anya sent him a look telegraphing her annoyance. "It's

7:25 and you said you'd be here at 6:00." Marc pulled her into a kiss and tickled her sides. She hated when he did that. "Stop it!"

"Sorry, babe. A couple of the guys stopped by O'Connor's for a pop after work."

"That was two and a half hours ago," she protested.

"One beer, two. Who keeps count? Give me a sec to drain the main vein and I'll be ready to go. Sound good?"

Anya tried to ignore the sound of Marc's pee splashing into the toilet, bathroom door left wide open. She hoped he'd at least put the lid up. Fat chance! She put her coat on and wondered at how long he kept peeing. Either he hadn't gone since this morning or that was at least a four-beer pee. *Christ,* she thought. *I'm 26. Single and sexy and this is the highlight of my Friday night? Calculating how many beers he drank from the sound of his whiz?*

When the pissing stopped, Marc came back into the kitchen and grabbed a Budweiser from the fridge.

"Come on." Anya cringed at the whine in her voice. "Charlotte and Nathan are waiting on us."

"It's cool. One for the road, ya know?"

She waited for him to get into his car and lean over to unlock the passenger door. She got in and closed the door gently, just like he'd asked her to. A few months earlier, she slammed the door to his 1972 Camaro and he nearly popped a blood vessel. His car was his true love. His baby. Fully restored with a 350 big block engine, rear spoiler, Cragars, and a shiny jet-black paint job that he did himself. He might not be the classiest guy in town, and he might be late more often than she liked, but there was no denying he was good at body work, and painting was his specialty.

He asked her to hold his beer while he pushed the cassette into the player. AC/DC came blasting at her from the car's stereo, complete with a 100-watt amplifier. His expensive sound system was desirable based on the way Marc's guy friends salivated over it.

He reached over and held her hand. "You're looking great, babe. How was your day?"

Anya wanted to be mad, but what would that get her? She told him her day was good. He told her about a Mustang he worked on. He suspected it had been hit in the rear at some time, because the taillights were about a quarter inch off, as was the trunk lid.

Marc brightened up when he talked about cars, like he did when they first met at a mutual friend's pool party. When he turned and saw her in a turquoise bikini, he morphed into a cartoon. Eyes wide, mouth gaping, she almost wiped drool from his face. When he walked her to her rusty 1969 VW Bug, he spent 10 minutes convincing her to let him take care of the rust and body rot. She accepted his offer to fix her car and to go to dinner with him.

That was six and a half months ago. He still hadn't painted the car, but at least he did some of the Bondo work and the engine was running smoother.

They slowly grew into a routine. Pizza and beers after work. Hitting a club to hear a band or comic most weekends. Cuddling on the couch watching *Cheers* on Thursday nights. He even occasionally agreed to watch non-action movies now and then. She learned to accept him and his idiot roommates while they drank and smoked pot and acted like life was a never-ending *Saturday Night Live* skit.

The Porthole had a pretty good crowd based on the number of cars in the parking lot. They parked in their typical spot, about 12 miles away from any other car so no one could park next to and potentially dent Marc's baby.

"You hungry?" she took his hand. "I'm starving."

"Me and the guys had some wings." Marc pulled his hand away and lit a cigarette. "But if you order some of those nachos, I'll gladly have a few."

She felt a hum the instant the door opened. The warmth of the people, the laughing and talking and click of pool balls in the back room. On stage, Ron Grossler picked his banjo, singing about thanking God he's a country boy in an affected twang. He was one of a dozen or so regulars at the Porthole's open-mic, two-for-one-shots Fridays.

Glancing around, they made their way to a booth where Nathan and Charlotte leaned in close, talking as if alone on a tropical beach. Marc bent to give Charlotte a quick hug and Nathan an awkward high five, then was off to the bar to fetch drinks.

"Glad you made it!" Charlotte sent Anya a genuine smile. "We were just about to order. That cute Mexican guy was asking for you."

"Stop it." Anya tucked her purse in the corner of the booth and slid in. "Marc was working late. Did you decide on what you're getting?"

The question was a formality, as Charlotte and Nathan were as predictable as night and day. Nathan would get the All-American burger. Mateo, the cute waiter, jokingly called it the Gringo burger—with fries and a Miller Lite. Charlotte would get the turkey club, no mayo, please, and a white zinfandel.

Marc returned with a pitcher of beer, two glasses, and a couple shots of whiskey. "It's Friday night, y'all. Time to flush away our blues!"

Anya poured each of them a beer, while Marc pushed a shot in front of her. "A little Jack to get the weekend started?" He raised his eyebrows several times like he'd seen some actor do in one of the obnoxious movies he loved.

"I'm going to wait until I have some food."

"Suit yourself." Marc knocked back the shot and chased it with half his beer. "Like mother's milk," he said for the hundredth time. He put his glass down and lit a cigarette. "How's the wedding plans?"

Anya sipped her beer while Marc made idle conversation with Nathan and Charlotte. He'd never say anything negative directly to her, but she knew he found them oppressively boring. And he conveniently often had other plans when she wanted the four of them to get together.

"I know it's expensive, and of course you want it to look beautiful," Marc was saying. He had the second shot in his hand. "But really. Everybody's shitfaced by the time we eat the cake, and nobody really pays attention. Was it chocolate, or vanilla, or butterscotch crème?" He tossed the shot back and poured himself another beer. "You never hear somebody say, 'I loved Bruce and Roxanne's wedding. The cake was sooooo good!'"

They all laughed.

"I need to hit the head. Back in a flash." Marc got up, bringing his beer with him, working his way through the crowd, greeting his many friends on his way into the back room.

"Someone's coming." Charlotte leaned toward Anya and whispered with a sly grin. She nodded across the room. "Great timing."

When Anya looked over, she saw a dark-haired, caramel-skinned waiter delivering food to a nearby booth. Everybody called him Matt. He mentioned to her a few weeks back that his real name was Mateo. She told him she thought Mateo had more sparkle. As if he felt her eyes on him, he turned and smiled. "It's about time," he said. "Your poor friends are starving."

"My friends are big enough to order if they want to," she said. She meant to be funny, but it sounded stilted to her. "They're just hoping I'll pick up the check is all."

"Pay day, is it?"

"Something like that," she said, then turned to Charlotte. "You guys go first."

As expected, Charlotte went first and ordered the turkey club, no mayo. When Nathan ordered the All-American burger, Mateo glanced her way and winked.

"And you, Miss Rockefeller?"

"I'll have the *nachos grande,* spicy. And some mozzarella sticks."

"Any refills from the bar?"

"We're good, Matt. Thanks," Nathan said.

"No problem. I'll be back with your food in a few. Just flag me down if you need anything."

They chatted about the wedding for an eternity before Mateo returned with their orders. After placing the plates down, he also put down a small plate with four slightly shriveled jalapeno peppers on it.

"I know you like hot food," he said to Anya. "The cook and I have been playing around with some new ideas for appetizers, and I figured you could be our guinea pigs. These are jalapenos that have been cleaned and par boiled, so they won't be as hot as if you just ate a whole raw one. They're stuffed with cheddar and bacon bits. Let me know what you think."

"Thanks, Mateo. Are they physically hot? Should we let them cool?" Anya touched one with her finger.

"They just came out of the oven, so give it a minute."

Someone shouted "Matt" from across the room, and he moved to their table.

"I'm not touching those things," Charlotte said flatly.

"Ditto here," Nathan agreed. "Way too hot for me."

Anya considered using a fork, then just picked up one of the peppers with her fingers and took a small, tentative bite. Mateo was right—the pepper wasn't too hot, just a hint, and the cheese and bacon made for a delicious flavor. She popped the rest of the pepper in her mouth and watched Charlotte's eyes bug out.

"I hope you don't regret that."

"Me, too," she said between chews. She figured Mateo knew she liked hot food, because she always asked for nachos with the hot salsa. He also knew Charlotte and Nathan wouldn't because of their white-bread, gringo orders. So, maybe he did have the hots for her like Charlotte thought.

Anya figured Charlotte thought Marc was handsome, with an attractive bit of bad boy in him. But she knew Charlotte thought Anya could do better. Maybe, maybe not. But was Mateo better? A waiter and amateur guitarist at the Porthole Pub in Nashua, New Hampshire?

He was nice, though. Shy nice, and very different from Marc. While he wasn't exactly handsome, he wasn't bad looking either. He had soft brown eyes, and wicked nice teeth. With some new clothes and a proper haircut, he might...

"What the hell are these?" Marc slid in next to her and scarfed down one of the stuffed jalapenos. He chewed thoughtfully and poured the rest of the pitcher into his glass. "Did Pablo make these special for you?" His eyebrow curved up again. "Hot peppers to try to make you drink more?"

Marc pulled her over and kissed her, working his tongue into her mouth before she realized what he was doing. She pushed him away. "Easy does it," she said, the heat of the pepper lingering in her mouth. "No more spicy food if that's what it does to you."

"Or maybe you should get us another pitcher and shots and ask Juan to make us up another batch?" Marc sipped his beer and somehow managed to stuff a third of the nachos on her plate into his mouth. The sound of his chewing reverberated like a thousand soldiers marching over a field of twigs, despite the din of people talking and the blonde singing

Linda Ronstadt onstage.

"His name is Mateo," Charlotte said.

Marc looked at her for a long second. "I know."

Without another word, he snatched the empty pitcher and stalked to the bar for a refill.

o o o

Anthony the cook removed a hot plate of bacon-wrapped scallops from the oven with one hand and pulled a fry basket full of clams with the other. With the sleeves on his white tee shirt rolled up, the angry scars on his beefy arms were on full display. "As you know," he said, "I was sentenced to Saint Mary's on the south side of Chicago for elementary school."

Mateo dressed the two salads on his tray as Anthony regaled him with a story that started with his daughter's second-grade trip to the Boston Children's Science Museum.

"We took exactly two field trips. In fourth grade we got to tour Joliet Prison, sans the electric chair, no matter how much we begged." Anthony placed the hot plate of scallops on Matt's tray. "In sixth grade, we got to see the Armour slaughterhouse. Back in those days they killed the beef with a five-pound sledge, and hung the pigs by their hind legs before slicing their throats. Sister Mary Alice made sure we all got to witness that." He put a basket of clams onto the tray. "You're all set."

"That's fucked up," Matt said, holding the tray over his right shoulder and pushing the swinging kitchen door open with his left.

He made his way to table 17. The two middle-aged couples stood out at the Porthole. Mostly, the place appealed to the 20-something crowd. These folks must be rounding 40, which was fine with Mateo. The ladies had obviously spent time so they looked good, and one of the guys was wearing a button-down shirt. They looked like better tippers.

"Here we go," he said as he distributed the food. "Are we all set on drinks?"

"You know," the lady in a blue sweater said, eyeing her husband's plate, "I think I'll have an order of scallops, too. They just look so good."

"Excellent choice," Matt answered. The scallops were delicious, but a royal pain in the ass to make.

Onstage, Marion, a regular, played her Martin acoustic and sang a slow version of "Dear Prudence," while her girlfriend Noel sang background harmonies and thumped a beat on her own guitar. They sounded really good, he thought. It amazed him, the talent that lived around here. You'd think half of them would be trying to make it in Boston, but maybe, like Matt, they were content to just have regular jobs and play a little on the side to feed that occasional need for the spotlight.

He glanced around the tables in his section. He didn't see any needy customers, so he stepped over to where Anya was chatting with her friends. "Everything good here? Can I clear these plates?"

Anya's friend Charlotte stacked the plates, silverware on top, and handed them to Matt. "Thanks." He dumped the ashtray on the top plate, then returned it to the table. "How'd you guys like the jalapenos?"

"Charlotte and Nathan are wimps," Anya teased her friends. "But Marc and I loved them."

Matt tried not to wince at the asshole boyfriend's name. Which, of course, was absolutely ridiculous. So what if Anya was friendly and pretty and didn't dismiss him as the help like most customers did? She had a boyfriend, and although the guy seemed kind of like a dick, Matt didn't actually know him. But he gave off that vibe, and Matt knew to steer clear.

"Seriously. You should put them on the menu."

Matt smiled at Anya. "I'll let the cook know you approve."

"You going to play tonight?"

When Anya spoke, he paused. She knew it was Friday night and he was busy, and yet she was making conversation. Was she interested? Or just looking for attention, because her date was in the back room getting shitfaced and shooting pool with the losers?

"I hope to. Any requests?"

Charlotte, who seemed to be hanging on their every word, clapped. "Do you know any Cat Stevens? I love Cat Stevens."

"How about some Croce?" the tall guy, Nathan, chimed in. "'Bad, Bad, Leroy Brown' is a great song."

"Sure, I know it," Matt said. "But I've never played it. Sorry."

A drunk girl three tables over held up an empty glass and called to him.

"What was that Bad Company song you played a couple weeks ago?" Anya ran her fingers through her thick hair. "I really liked that one."

"'Seagull,' from the *Bad Company* album. I'll see what I can do."

When he looked into her eyes, he pretty much forgot about the boyfriend in the back room. Matt picked up a few more empty plates and took a bar order from a table of drunk girls who may or may not have been of legal drinking age.

"The stuffed jalapenos got two thumbs up," he told Anthony when he walked back into the kitchen.

He took the tray of food for table 5 and headed back out to the dining room.

Around 11:00, the kitchen was shutting down. He mostly attended to drink orders. Many of the tables were empty now. It was obvious by the mistakes and forgotten lyrics that those who were performing onstage were feeling the alcohol they'd consumed.

Matt grabbed an empty tray and took a lap around the back room. A dozen or so people sat on stools or stood around listening to the music and watching the two pool tables. Through the cigarette smoke haze, he saw Anya's boyfriend lining up a shot behind his back. A lit cigarette dangled from the corner of his mouth. He was obviously showing off for his opponent, a teenaged girl with bloodshot eyes and a black Molly Hatchet tee shirt. She leaned heavily on a pool cue for support. With a quick flip of his wrist, he knocked the cue ball into the seven ball, which landed with a soft click in the corner pocket.

"That's how it's done, baby!"

The girl shook her head while Marc's two goofball friends cheered him on. The one with the scraggly beard and a baseball cap sporting a fake dog turd on the brim, obviously a fan of Batman comic books, said, "Ka-blam!" and high-fived Marc. The other, a pimply misfit wearing a 'Show Me Your Beaver' tee shirt, added, "Nothing but net."

Perhaps he wasn't sure of the difference between billiards and basketball. Matt gathered up empty pitchers, beer glasses, and empty shot glasses. As he circled the second pool table, Marc was setting up for his next shot. He leaned back from the table, with his foot only a few inches from the wall. Matt paused, letting him shoot.

Marc drew the cue back, taking the shot, hitting the cue ball too hard, missing the three in the side pocket. He turned to Matt and glared. "You fucked up my shot."

"No. I waited here while you fucked up your shot all by yourself." Matt stepped past Marc.

A skinny guy with a copper-colored goatee, who was eyeing the Molly Hatchet girl like a cat next to a fishbowl, said, "Uh-oh."

Matt did his best to act cool, ignoring the idiot while grabbing two empty shot glasses. He brought the empties to the bar, wondering what Anya saw in that guy. He was handsome, Matt supposed, but he exuded an asshole quality. Anya and Charlotte and Nathan just seemed more... normal. The guys who hung out back, playing pool, were losers who got drunk, acting like idiots, only impressing each other. Anya was deeper than that. She was *better* than that.

Boz, a giant of a Bacardi-and-Coke drinker, with a Red Sox tattoo on one arm and a New England Patriots tattoo on the other, turned and nodded. "Whatsup, Matt?"

"It's Friday, and my shift's almost over," he replied. "You guys all right here? Sandy taking good care of you?"

"Sandy's the best," Sara, a regular who looked like she could probably fit into Boz's pocket, said.

"Damn straight." Sandy, the bartender, set a tray of drinks before Matt. "One pitcher of Miller, a Long Island Iced Tea, and two shots of Cuervo Gold. Table 11." She also put down a shot with a slice of lime in it. "And one for you." She winked. She knew he liked to loosen up at the end of his shift, especially if he was going to perform.

"She *is* the best." He forgot about Marc and knocked back the tequila, savoring the burn as it slid down his throat. "Muchas gracias." Picking up the tray, he turned and nearly ran straight into Anya.

"Oh shit," he said. "I'm sorry. You snuck up on me."

She and her boyfriend had slurped down quite a few drinks. At her body weight, she had to be pretty buzzed. "Just heading to the little girls' room," she said with a grin. "Tell me, Mateo..."

He enjoyed the way his name flowed slowly out of her mouth, seeming to swirl about in the air like some meaningless song before his brain registered that was his name. "I saw you doing that shot. Drinking on the job. But don't worry." She took one of the shots from his tray and gulped it down, then delivered a devilish smile. "I'll never tell."

She gave him a quick hip bump, then sashayed to the ladies' room. He stood still, admiring her backside. Sandy cleared her throat behind the bar and helped him remember he was still on the clock.

o o o

Marc lit up another smoke and watched the girl—Kathy, maybe? Or Katie?—get lucky and sink the ten ball without scratching. She really was a terrible pool player, even when not tipsy. She was cute, trying to convince him she was 21, attempting, and failing, to match him drink for drink. She probably didn't weigh more than 100 pounds, a buck ten, tops. He watched as she eyed an impossible shot on the two ball. He knew he should let her miss the shot, getting the inevitable over with. But what fun was that?

"Don't take that shot." He put his beer down. "Try this instead." He pointed to the eleven ball. "Hit the cue right here, and the eleven will hit the six and drop it right in the side pocket. But don't go all Mr. T on it. Just kiss it slightly."

She gave him a quizzical look, then nodded. She moved toward the wall where a skinny guy with a scraggly goatee sipped his bottle of Bud. Normal bar etiquette would be to move so the girl had a clear shot. But this guy—Marc didn't know him, but thought he was a friend of Kenny's—just stood there. Kathy, whether because she was too drunk or just didn't care if the guy was in her way, stepped in front of him, leaned over, and lined up the shot.

"Easy," Marc reminded her. He noticed goatee guy staring at her ass, like one of those starving children he saw on TV, eating a bowl of rice.

She slit one eye, pulled the cue back, and took the shot. Marc knew before she even touched the cue ball that the force was too hard and she was going to miss. What he didn't expect was for her to hit the eleven so hard it would fly off the table. She turned, anger and spit flying out of her mouth in equal measures. "Don't touch me, asshole."

Goatee guy raised up his hands innocently, a shit-eating grin on his face. The girl, red-faced and obviously upset, stalked to the table near Marc and drained what remained of her beer.

Marc's friend Derek, sporting that stupid dogshit hat he loved so much, handed him the escaped eleven ball. Marc set it back in the table's center, then picked up the cue ball and handed it to the girl. "You get a do-over," he said. "You can put the cue anywhere on this end of the table and take your shot."

Goatee guy now stood about two feet to the left. Marc looked at him and said, "Just let the lady finish our game."

"Yes, sir." The guy gave him a half salute.

Marc sipped his beer and took a drag off his cigarette. She made the shot easily, then missed getting the twelve in the corner. He butted his smoke, then proceeded to sink his next three shots.

Anya drifted into the back room, hovering as he called, "Eight ball, corner pocket." He hit the cue with a little backspin, perfectly executing the shot.

"Next," he said with a grin at Kathy/Katie as she slunk to lean her stick with the others on the rack.

Anya stepped closer. "Hey, Babe. You should come join us. Charlotte and Nathan are probably going to take off soon."

"I just won," he said. "I've got to play this next game. How about I join you right after?" He bent to give her a quick kiss, then reached into his pocket and handed her a crumbled five-spot. "Grab us another pitcher, will ya?"

Anya took the money and moved to the bar. Marc noticed both of his friends ogling her ass as she moved toward the music in the other room.

That Mexican-looking waiter was singing a Beatles song, and he actually sounded pretty good. He could tell by the way the guy smiled at Anya that he had it bad for her, but he wasn't worried. All the free food in the world wouldn't change who sweet Anya would be going home with tonight.

Kenny, a regular who sold bags of weed that were often a little light, had just finished racking the balls. Marc set the cue ball about four inches from the right bumper, just where he liked it, and hit the one ball with well-practiced force. He sank both a solid and a stripe, saw that the thirteen ball was his best shot, and called it. The game proceeded, with Marc sinking two balls to Kenny's three. Kenny chatted, telling him about a hiking trip in the White Mountains and how his '74 Maverick had turned 200,000 miles while on the Kancamagus Highway.

"Get your fuckin' hands off me!" When Kathy yelled, red-faced and spitting fire, all conversation in the back room stopped. Chatter quieted in the big bar area too. "Dirtbag." She looked like she might rip the eyes right out of goatee guy's skull.

"Lighten up, sweetheart. I'm just trying to be friendly." He reached out a hand, as if to brush her cheek. She slapped it away. He laughed, an attempt to put her in her place.

"Listen, man. Leave her be." Marc was drunk—he had to be drunk, because the words came out of his mouth before he even thought them.

Goatee guy, who kind of resembled a devil now that Marc got a good look at him, turned and scowled at him. "Ain't nobody askin' for your opinion, pretty boy."

"Ease up," Kenny told his friend.

But Marc moved the pool cue to his left hand, clutching it tightly while balling his right. He gave goatee guy his most menacing stare. "I'm telling you again, leave her alone."

Goatee guy gave a wolfish grin, revealing tobacco-stained, yellow teeth. "Or what? You gonna sic that sweet bit-o-snatch you got waiting in the other room on me? I could teach that bitch a thing or two."

Marc dropped the pool cue on the table. Who did this skinny, ugly fuck think he was talking to? Marc Thompson, the third of the four Thompson boys, was no stranger to fighting. He and his brothers had pounded the hell out of each other growing up, and then pounded the hell out of anyone who crossed their paths as they grew from angry teenagers to volatile men. Marc's brother Hank broke a guy's jaw once just for making a stupid mother joke. No, nobody who was thinking with a clear head crossed one of the Thompson brothers, especially one who had been drinking all night.

"What did you say, dick breath?"

After that, things streamed by in a blur. Marc took two quick steps toward goatee guy, kneeing him in the gut while grabbing him around the neck and banging the back of his head into the wall. Meanwhile, goatee guy swung a half-full Budweiser bottle toward Marc, smashing it into the left side of his skull, causing a large gash and a torrent of blood to spill down his cheek. Stars and a dark night sky suddenly overtook his vision. Even so, he punched and punched, on instinct, hitting flesh and bone, blood spattering his knuckles. Someone hit him in the back, and a pool cue broke over his opponent's shoulder. From the sounds of grunting and screaming and glass breaking, a full-scale brawl must have commenced in the bar. Once his vision cleared, he saw Big Boz tossing people left and right, and the girl scratching angry claw marks down some dude's face. People were screaming, pool cues were being used as batons.

Marc ducked to his left and looked around for Anya, hoping she was somewhere safe in the larger bar area. With all the chaos, he had little hope of finding her. He was searching for an escape route when goatee guy hit him with a hard right square in the jaw. The lights went out for a second. He was on the dirty floor, then he felt a steel-toed boot kicking him in the side. His ribs screamed in protest. Then the kicking stopped. A broad hand scooped him up.

"You okay, man?"

Still dazed, Marc shook his head, which only made it hurt more. Blood dribbled down his jawline. He tried to focus. It was Boz.

"Yeah. I'm good."

"You're bleeding. It don't look too bad," Boz said. "Better head to the men's so I can get a look at it."

Chatter buzzed in the bar, but the fight was over. Boz grabbed him by the shoulder and muscled his way through the crowd like an NFL linebacker.

"Where's Anya?" Marc asked.

"She's fine," Boz said, pushing a guy who was holding a bloody napkin to his cheek out of the way. "I think she left with those friends of hers."

Marc sighed in relief. Nathan and Charlotte would get Anya home safely. He'd pick up some flowers and apologize to her tomorrow. Right now, he probably needed a couple stitches.

o o o

Anya's attention snapped back. She peered in confusion around the bar. How long had she been daydreaming? She looked down at the nearly full pitcher of beer and cringed. She was definitely drunk.

She remembered Mateo singing. Something she didn't recognize. Maybe the Allman Brothers. Then he finished with that Beatles song, "The Two of Us," she thought. He even did the part in the beginning when John Lennon recites poetry. Something about digging a pigmy, and how Doris eats her oats. What the hell does that mean, anyway? Is Doris a pig? Who knows? Who cares?

"The Two of Us," now that was interesting. Why did he pick that song? Was he thinking of her? If he was, what should she infer—was that the right word?—from him picking that song? She was probably overthinking it.

That's what she was daydreaming about before a female in the back room yelled. Anya couldn't be sure what the woman said, being only 25 percent present in her body when she heard the scream, but it sounded like anger, not pain. Probably not pain. Pain usually was followed by longer wailing.

Now, angry men's voices. She focused, thinking one of them sounded like Marc. The bar still seemed full, but the music stopped. The angry shouts grew louder. Then she heard dog-shit-hat-Derek, in his annoying nasally voice, say, "Punch the fucker, Marco." No question that was Derek's voice.

Anya slipped out of her booth and took two steps toward the back room. Half the patrons in the big room turned to see what was going on. Her way was blocked. But over the shoulder of a girl she knew in high school, she watched Marc go after the creepy guy. Marc grabbed the guy by the neck, then kneed him in the crotch. Then creepy guy slammed Marc in the head with a beer bottle and he keeled over.

Marc's friends, Derek and Timmy, immediately came to his defense, but then Kenny hit Timmy with a pool stick, and all hell broke loose. The crowd pushed away, and she was carried with it for a second until a hand crooked around her waist and pulled to the right.

"Don't go near there," Mateo said.

She turned and looked at him—eyes brown, pupils wide and alert, concern etched into the corners of his mouth. There was a slight bit of sweat on his forehead, the sweat of a hard Friday night shift. His arm, still clasped around her waist, felt solid and secure.

She was 26 years old, single and good looking. Her boyfriend was in the middle of a barroom brawl, and she was in the arms of a handsome guy, who she'd been flirting with for the last month because her loser boyfriend, currently engaged in a bar fight, barely gave her the time of day except in the bedroom. What, she asked herself, was she waiting for? Might as well jump.

Anya Weber did the only sensible thing she could in that instant. She put her hand across the back of Mateo's warm neck, pulled him toward her, and kissed him. Eyes closed, she poured her hopes, her longing, her need to feel important to somebody into that kiss. And though Mateo seemed hesitant at first, he relaxed into her.

Anya broke the kiss, ignored the disappointment in Mateo's eyes, and asked, "Does the kitchen have a back door?"

Fighting was still going on around them. Glasses were breaking. People scrambled towards the door.

"Sure does," he said.

She took his hand from her waist, held it firmly, and pulled him through the swinging kitchen doors.

They nearly smashed into a red-headed waitress who peered through one of the door's small round windows. She stepped back quickly. They came to a serving counter. A hairy baboon of a man wearing a disgusting apron covered in God-knows-what, bent over a steel grill top, scraping off bits of fat and oil with a large metal spatula, hunkered nearby.

The baboon chef asked, "What the fuck's going on?" Anya slowed and let Mateo take the lead. She held his hand and tried not to reconsider.

They cut through a section where two guys washed dishes, reggae playing on a portable radio in the windowsill. Mateo ignored their stares, hustling Anya past a big sink full of dirty pots and pans, through a screen door, past a big walk-in freezer, and out into the employee parking lot.

In the cool night air, she felt like she'd stepped out of a space capsule onto the moon. The air was brisk and clean. No smoke, no spilled beer, no fryeolator or greasy onion ring odors. No music or yelling or punching or frenzy. Above them, the stars and moon sent down a shimmery, welcoming glow.

"Which car is yours?" she asked, then frowned. "You do have a car, don't you? Please tell me you have a car."

"Sure," he said, still walking quickly past a row of two or three pickups. There was a nice big car after that, a Cadillac, or maybe a Lincoln, and she thought how nice it would be to find someplace to go in a luxury ride. But Mateo went past the nice car, pulled out his keys, and opened the door to an ugly mustard-colored box that was half rust and looked like the tires were all different shapes and sizes.

He held the door open for her and gave a clownish smile. "Your chariot is ready for you, m'lady."

"Chariot, hunh," she said, sliding across the ripped vinyl seat. "Where's the horses?"

"Under the hood," he said, waiting for her to swing her legs in before closing the door. It might not be a chariot, she thought, but the service was a pleasant change from what she was used to.

Mateo went around and got in on the driver's side. He slipped behind the wheel, turned the key in the ignition. Thankfully, the old beater started. In fact, it ran pretty smoothly. *God*, she thought. *I've been spending too much time around car geeks.*

"Where to?" Mateo asked.

Anya scooched over until her thigh brushed his and kissed him again. It was a little awkward, but his lips were soft and warm and reassuring.

"Do you have roommates?" she asked.

"No. I live in a small flat above my landlord's garage. It's not nearly as impressive as my chariot, but if you keep your eyes mostly closed, and we only light one candle, the place has a lot of ambience."

"Ambience." She slid back over to her side, wanting to glance in the mirror to see how she looked, but refrained. "That's exactly what I want."

Mateo backed the car up, then steered over to Route 26 and headed north. Anya noted that he used his blinker, even in the parking lot, so that meant he was either very safe or just weird. She decided on the former.

"That was some crazy shit in the bar, hunh?" he asked. "Did you see what started it?"

"No," she said. She paused, wondering what to say next.

"I'm pretty sure your, umm, friend, was fighting with another guy. I saw those two going at it, then I just hustled to find you."

She stroked his arm, then took his hand. "Thank you."

"No problem. I'm just glad we got out of there before... well, before it got too crazy."

Anya didn't want to think about Marc, or the fight, or the bar, or anything but this moment. She scooted over again and put her head on his shoulder. "No more talk about that stuff. Tell me about you."

He thought for a minute, then said, "I have a cat. His name's Elmer."

She giggled. Elmer... like Elmer Fudd. What a funny

name for a cat. Another good sign?

"Let's try again." She thought for a minute, then said. "If money weren't an option, where would you go on vacation?"

Despite her buzz, she knew this was a loaded question. She'd asked Marc the same thing once. Without hesitation, he'd answered, "Boston. I'd go to the annual car show in the afternoon, and catch a Sox game at night, and crash in one of them fancy hotels with a Jacuzzi. That'd be sweet."

"Kathmandu," Mateo answered.

"Kathmandu? Why Kathmandu?"

"There's a Bob Seger song." He sang softly, "If I ever get out of here... I'm goin' to Kat-man-du."

"Sure," she said. "I love Bob Seger. But I don't even know where the hell Kathmandu is."

"It's a city in Nepal, in a valley in the Himalayas. Lots of temples and ancient artwork and stuff. I don't know much more about it than that. But it's far away, on the other side of the world, with people living very differently than us, and I'd like to check it out."

She stared out her window, gazing at the stars and the outline of trees in the moonlight. She'd been to Florida once with her parents when she was in high school, and they'd visited her Aunt Wendy in Connecticut a few times. But a foreign country? A foreign culture? Eating foods she'd never heard of? The idea intrigued her.

He turned on his blinker. They eased into a bumpy driveway, gravel crunching beneath the tires, past a wood-shingled two-family colonial toward a detached garage around back. He slid out of the car, then opened the door for her. He held out a hand and she took it, although it probably would have been easier to get out on her own. Hand in hand, he led her to the side of the garage, and up some rickety wood steps to a landing where he fished in his pocket for his keys. Once he retrieved them, he slid them in the lock, then paused.

"Shit," he said. "Shit. Shit. Shit."

"What's the matter? Just try another key."

He backed away, leaving the keys in the door lock, pressing his palms into his forehead. "My guitar," he cried. "I forgot my guitar."

She looped his arms around her waist. Fingertips touching his face, she made him look at her. "I'm sure your guitar is fine. The cops have already cleared the place out. Sandy or somebody'll make sure it's safe until tomorrow." She kissed him softly, a desperate, anxious feeling thumping in her chest. "Let's go inside."

He smiled at her, and her insides throbbed.

Mateo opened the door and they entered the darkness together.

CROOKED HALO

"Me and Jesus, got our own thing goin'
Me and Jesus, got it all worked out
Me and Jesus, got our own thing goin'
We don't need anybody to tell us what it's all about."
– "Me and Jesus" by Tom T. Hall

Father Dunn stepped out the rectory door, savored the early spring air, and slipped his car keys back into his jacket pocket. The long winter had finally gone dormant, so he decided to walk a bit and enjoy the outdoors. He strode through the suburban neighborhood. Most people were tucked inside their three-bedroom capes and colonials cleaning up dinner dishes, or watching mindless television.

Sharon was a primarily blue-collar town about 25 miles south of Boston. Paul Dunn considered living there a welcome change from the projects in Lynn where he'd grown up. As he passed a gray house with a double porch, a large German shepherd sprang from its hiding spot behind a couple of nearby trash cans. The dog growled, baring its teeth, instantly sending a tight thread of fear through him.

"Jesus—you scared the shit outta me." Father Dunn gave the dog's head a good rub as it tried to lick his hand. "Careful, big fella. You don't want to start something you can't finish."

After the dog loped back to his hiding spot, Paul Dunn continued to Hillside Ave. While still residential, Hillside led downtown. If you could say Sharon's few mismatched shops—one that sold subs, two video rental places, and a Dunkin' Donuts—constituted a downtown. At the corner where Hillside intersected with Summer Street, two teenaged girls in leggings and what could best be described as shirt dresses dragged on cigarettes while trying to look cool, probably waiting for boys their parents wouldn't approve of.

Without seeming too obvious, he checked to see if they were his parishioners. They weren't. "Evening, ladies," he said as he passed. They didn't answer but burst into giggles a moment later.

Father Dunn glanced into the Cumberland Farms convenience store as he went by. Next door, the H&R Block firm was closed, and a mother was screaming at a misbehaving child in one of the upper apartments. He thought about what he was in the mood for. Tonight was the Hagler versus Leonard fight, which could be considered a special occasion. Hagler lived in Brockton. A real local hero. Father Dunn considered him the best middleweight boxer to have ever entered the ring. His only question: How many rounds could Leonard last before Marvelous Marvin knocked him out?

A six-pack of Michelob was his usual go-to, but tonight he might splurge for wine instead.

He was 30 feet or so from Hillside Liquors when he heard glass breaking up ahead, followed by angry shouts. The door of the liquor store flew open, banging so hard into the adjacent wall it seemed a miracle it didn't shatter. A young man in a black leather jacket spilled out, followed by another wearing mirrored sunglasses and a Red Sox cap. Each carried two handles of booze.

Do I know...? Father Dunn's thoughts were interrupted when the red-faced store owner stormed through the door, swinging an aluminum baseball bat at the boys running down Hillside.

"I'll kill you sons a bitches!"

Without thinking, Father Dunn leaped after the boys. They were 20 years younger, their bodies torqued with adrenaline, and they had a generous head start. But he was wearing jeans and his Adidas, and he still liked a good chase. As a hoodlum in Lynn, he'd run from the cops and from rival gangs countless times. As a grunt in Vietnam, he'd run down, and run from, enemy soldiers like his life depended on it, because it did.

The kid with the baseball cap was panting and turned to see who was behind him. Big mistake. The large bottles of liquor slowed him down, so it didn't take long for the priest to catch up and shove the kid into a parked car. Bottles shattered. The boy thudded into the car and over the hood. He hit the pavement like a dropped sack of garbage.

The guy in the leather jacket never slowed, but turned to peek over his shoulder. He chucked one bottle into a front yard as he turned up a driveway. Thirty steps behind, Father Dunn figured George Street was where the boys parked their car. They probably thought they'd grab a few bottles, outrun the shop owner, turn at the end of the block, and quickly get into their car and drive away. Instead of following leather jacket, the priest continued to George Street, turned right, and slowed his pace.

George was a one-way, and a dusty-blue old Datsun B210 was parked ahead. Before he fully caught his breath, he heard a chain-link fence rattle and knew his suspicion was right. Bowing his head, he charged toward the car. His timing was perfect. The instant the guy in leather thought he was in the clear, Father Dunn tucked his shoulder like a fullback and knocked the boy to the ground. The bottle of Jack Daniel's flew from his hand, shattering after bouncing off the Datsun's roof.

The youth twisted under his weight and attempted a punch. The gesture was futile, as the priest turned into it with a muscular thigh then pinned the arm. A powerful fist hit the kid in the sternum, temporarily stopping his breathing.

"Stephen Degatto. I thought it was you. What would your poor mother think?"

"F-f-father Dunn?" the boy wheezed. "What the fuck..."

"Watch your language, son." The priest stood, yanking the unstable boy to his feet. "This your car? Let's get in and have a little chat."

He moved to the passenger door, which was unlocked, just as he suspected. He slid in and waited for Stephen to dust himself off. Once he had, Father Dunn told him to drive somewhere before the cops showed up.

"What about... my friend?"

"Your friend can take care of himself. Drive."

The boy's hand shook as he struggled to fit the keys in the ignition. The car turned over several times before catching, then exhaled a dark cloud of oily exhaust.

"Jesus Christ," Father Dunn said. "Can this shitbox make it to the church?"

The kid shifted into first, his nervousness transmitted through his ragged clutching. Without further words, they drove to Saint Michael's and parked underneath an old maple tree.

o o o

"I'm really worried about her, Father. Last night after dinner, she didn't ask to be excused from the table. She just got up and walked into the TV room. My husband told her to get her skinny butt back in and help clear the table, but she just gave him the fing... sorry, made an obscene gesture... and went outside to Lord only knows where. You know we try, Father. And we're scared to death she'll follow in her brother's footsteps, but..."

Father Dunn leaned forward in his side of the confession booth, rubbed his temples, asked Jesus to give him the right words. The Coreys were good people, one of only a handful of black families in his parish. They attended church regularly. Rosemary sang in the choir and taught CCD classes on Wednesday nights. Their daughter, Angela, was one of his first baptisms when he came to Saint Mike's. Their oldest, Kent, started running with the wrong crowd and never graduated high school. It was an all too familiar and horribly sad story. Now he was 19, hooked on dope and living on the streets. No doubt he was stealing for drug money, and walking the path straight to hell and damnation. Father Dunn had friends who had chosen that path, and he'd even taken a few steps on it himself. Thank God for Father Grant, who knocked some sense into him and helped him follow the path to salvation rather than prison.

Rosemary finished her tale. Father Dunn tried to send her off with some hope. "Your son is always on my heart, and in our prayers. Angela's a good girl. I'll have a talk with her. Maybe someone besides her parents will have more of an influence."

"Bless you, Father. Harold and I surely do appreciate it."

"Bless you, Rosemary. Go forth and walk in the love of Christ."

Father Dunn bowed his head and prayed for the Corey family. He tried to visualize Kent healthy and strong and studying for his GED. He pictured Angela smiling on her way to school, secure in the knowledge that God is always with her. He thanked Jesus for the opportunity to help bring about God's Kingdom.

Someone new entered the confessional. Father Dunn asked Jesus to guide him and slid the confessional screen over.

"Bless me, Father, for I have sinned," came the voice. It took a second, but the priest could almost always figure out who was unloading their sins. This was Howard Anderson, owner of a prominent office supply store in Newton. The guy was probably worth close to a million, but only slipped a twenty into the collection basket on the one or two Sundays he and his wife attended church each month. Father Dunn had asked the couple over to the rectory for lunch about six months ago, working the conversation around to the topic of giving to God what is God's, and the importance of pledging, but his words went unheard on the cheapskate.

"I have sinned, Father. I know I have, and I feel terrible. But, I don't know. I... I just can't seem to stop."

"Out with it, my son. God already knows your sins. Confess now and leave it here. Only then can you properly repent and return to the path of righteousness our Lord intends for you."

"Yes. Of course. Sorry." He sniffed back what sounded like real tears. "There's a woman, a girl, really—she's 23. It started innocently enough, you know. Sharing a soda at break time. Conversation when she worked late closing the store. Then one night, we went to Campano's Pizza after work..."

"I don't need to know what you had for dinner," the priest interrupted. "Get to the point."

"We slept together."

"How many times?"

"That night? Twice."

"In total. How many times."

"I'm not positive. Seven, eight I think."

"You're a married man with children of your own, committing adultery and breaking your vows. You are taking advantage of a young woman who probably has deep-seated issues of her own and sees you as the father that she desperately needs love from. Does that sound about right?"

A huge sigh came from the other side of the screen. "Yes."

Father Dunn let the silence hang there, weighing on Howard Anderson like a leaden yoke.

A full minute later, he said, "You know this needs to stop. God is very forgiving. But he also knows how easy it is to backslide into dishonorable behavior. You need to take steps to assure that doesn't happen." Again, he paused. "As penance, you need to let the girl go. Explain how it was a mistake and give her three months' severance and a glowing letter of recommendation."

"Three months?" Anderson muttered out loud. "That's unheard of."

"In addition," Father Dunn continued. "The school gym needs a new floor. You'll donate $10,000 to the church to cover it, and every time your sons play on that court, you'll think about how grateful you are that we have such a forgiving God. And you'll attend church more regularly, each week asking and praying to be a more righteous man."

"Ten grand? What is this, some kind of extortion?"

"This is a confession booth, where the price of sin is balanced. You have a lovely wife, two precious children, and a very successful business. All that could go away if you aren't diligent and careful. Now go in peace, and remember our Savior died for our sins. You're getting off easy with a tax deduction."

o o o

The priest knocked gently at first, then a little louder. Behind the door, he heard the thud of drumming and some crazy guitar work.

"Who is it?"

He didn't answer, just knocked again. The door swung open; an angry teenaged girl said, "What do you want?" followed by a look of shock and stupefaction.

"Hello, Angela. Mind if I come in for a minute?"

"Father Dunn? What... why... uh, sure. Come in."

When the girl moved to the stereo to shut the music off, Father Dunn asked her to leave it on. "But maybe you could turn it down a little?" His eyes moved around the room. Several stuffed animals sat at the top of the bed. On the floor were a math book and a spiral notebook. The open page was half covered with lines of writing. On the dresser stood several photographs, including one of her and her brother in bathing suits at the beach. In a corner, a chair sat with a laundry basket perched in it. He placed the basket on the floor, pulled the chair out, and took a seat.

"I hope I'm not interrupting anything important," he said.

Angela tidied the work on the floor and put it in a pile on her bed, where she sat. "Nothing important, Father."

"What were you working on? Homework?"

She glanced at him, then looked down at her bare feet. "Nu-unh. It's nothing. Just some words."

"What kind of words? A poem? A story?"

"More like words to a song," she said. "I know it's stupid. It's just something I do sometimes."

He considered asking to see her lyrics, but thought better of it. "Who are we listening to on your stereo?" he asked. "I don't recognize it."

"Sorry," she said. "You probably hate it. I can shut it off."

"No, don't. It's interesting. Who is it? And why do you think I'd hate it?"

"Because my parents do. Most old people hate new music." She glanced up suddenly. "Sorry. I mean, you aren't..."

He laughed. "Don't worry, Angela. I understand what you mean."

They listened for a few bars. "This song's called 'Don't

Disturb the Groove' by the System. It's one of my favorites."

"Catchy," the priest said, although in truth he hated the syntho-pop this generation thought of as music. "Do you play any instruments, Angela?"

She shook her head. "I tried flute back in fourth grade, but I didn't like it."

"Is there any other instrument you'd like to play?"

"Guitar, but they don't offer that at school. Only band instruments like trumpet and violin."

Father Dunn felt like a cartoon lightbulb turned on over his head.

○ ○ ○

The priest slowly rolled up and down the aisles of the Sharon High School parking lot until he found the dusty blue Datsun he was looking for. The spot next to it was vacant, which he took as a good sign. He parked, checked his watch, and waited. Ten minutes later, several clusters of students drifted out of the school, some making their way onto the waiting buses, others moving to their own vehicles in the parking lot. One group of boys slowly meandered to the back of the lot, smack-talking each other, not bothering to hide their cigarettes. Father Dunn got out of his car, wearing a black shirt and priest's collar. All the boys noticed, and one kid looked downright terrified. He figured that was Stephen's accomplice; the one who performed a tumbling routine on a parked car while attempting his getaway. The cluster quickly broke up, and a boy in a black leather jacket eyed him warily.

"Afternoon, Stephen. Mind if we have a word?"

The boy pinched out his cigarette and pocketed it so smoothly the priest couldn't help but smile.

"I know we still owe you 40 bucks," the boy said preemptively. "Kev... my friend had some other bills, but he's good for it. I promise."

The priest returned to Hillside Liquors the day after the simply unbelievable had occurred—Marvelous Marvin Hagler had been beaten, his first ever loss as a pro boxer. He spoke with the store owner about the theft. He said one of the boys was a parishioner, and he wasn't a bad kid, and Father Dunn would be sure he stayed out of trouble and repaid the owner for his losses. After some bitching and grumbling, they settled on $200. Which was criminal. Father Dunn paid the debt. So far, Stephen and his friend had paid back a hundred and sixty bucks.

"I wanted to thank you for the work you did around the church last week. The gardens look shipshape." The priest held the boy's gaze. "As for the money, I know you're good for it. But I was hoping you could help me with another matter."

The Degatto boy deflated.

"I'm looking for a guitar. Doesn't have to be fancy, just something for a beginner. If you could find me one among your cohorts, I'd be willing to forget the rest of the debt, including the work around the church—although it's good for your soul, and is a great way to grow closer to our Lord."

"Electric or acoustic?"

"Acoustic," the priest said, thinking of Rosemary and Harold Corey and the noise an electric guitar was capable of making. "And I better not read about one going missing from a local pawn shop in the paper, or I'll have to kick your ass."

A wicked smile grew on Stephen Degatto's face. "Local?" he said. "I wouldn't think of it."

o o o

The Andersons owned one of the finest homes in Sharon. A huge white colonial with a slate front porch and tall white marble pillars that made you think of the Greek Parthenon. At least, that's what Father Dunn thought the Parthenon looked like; he'd never actually been there.

He admired the perfect landscaping, the groomed flower beds, and the fountain that had only recently been turned on. He pushed the doorbell. From inside the house, a gong-like sound reverberated.

A moment later, a stern-faced woman with eyes the color of a gold-speckled robin's egg opened the heavy oak door. Her countenance softened the moment she saw who it was. Tight lips broke into a magnificent smile that surely made her orthodontist proud. "Why, Father Dunn—what a pleasant surprise! Forgive me, but I thought you might be one of those pesky window or vinyl-siding salesmen. Please, do come in."

"That's very kind of you, Camille. I'll only stay a minute."

He stepped into a tastefully decorated foyer. It had polished hardwood flooring, an oriental rug, and two matching vases large enough to hold a keg of beer each. Gabriel, the younger of the two Anderson boys, appeared from what was either the living or possibly game room, wandering over to hide within his mother's floral skirt.

"What a nice surprise," Camille said. "I hope everything is all right?"

"Absolutely," he said. "I just stopped by to have a word with Howard. Is he home?"

"No, I'm afraid not," Camille said. Her painted-on smile drooped. "With him it's always work, work, work. Late nights and now Saturdays, too. I've told him since he's the boss, he should be able to spend more time at home with us and let the store manager handle things, but that's not my Howard. Would you like some tea? Is there anything I can help with?"

"No thank you, Camille. I just stopped by to discuss a

little business with your husband."

As Father Dunn spoke, his mind rapidly analyzed the situation, calculating and recalculating to figure how best to proceed. "A few weeks ago, Howard told me he'd fund the new floor in the school gym, which we desperately need. It was very generous of him, and someday your Bobby and little Gabriel there, not to mention all the other kids in the parish, will benefit."

Camille's eyes grew wide, and Father Dunn caught a glimpse of the little girl that was still in her.

"Really now. I almost have to get a crowbar to get Howard to open up his wallet when I need something."

The priest laughed. "Perhaps the power of the Holy Spirit caught him that day. Anyway, I don't want to interfere with your day. Please just tell him I stopped by, and to give me a call when he has a few minutes."

"I surely will." Camille gave his arm an affectionate squeeze, then she scooped up little Gabriel, who was still playing shy. "See you in church tomorrow."

"God bless," he said, and left.

o o o

A heavy June rain poured down when he visited the Corey home for a second time. He exited the car, frowned at the downpour, opened the back seat of his car and retrieved the guitar, wrapped almost comically in a pair of Hefty garbage bags. It hadn't occurred to him when the Degatto boy delivered it that he might need a case. Oh well, live and learn, as his dear old mother was fond of saying.

He trotted with his package up the steps to the porch and knocked. Angela answered, her hair in two long braids, still dressed in her school uniform.

"Hi, Father Dunn," she said with a smile. "Come in."

"Is your mother here?"

"Yup. She's in the kitchen making supper."

He went to say hello to Rosemary Corey, then rejoined Angela in the family room. She was watching a rerun of that idiotic nighttime soap, *Dallas*. Better than running the streets, he supposed, but wasn't there something educational kids today could watch? National Geographic or maybe Jacques Cousteau?

He took a seat on the well-worn plaid couch, setting the guitar down beside him. "How have you been, Angela?"

"Good," she said. "I got a B+ on my math test today."

Father Dunn smiled. "That's wonderful. Congratulations." He ran a hand through his wet hair. "And how have things been with your folks? Last time we talked you promised to ease up on the back talk and help your mother more around the house."

"I been real good," she said a little too quickly.

He raised one eyebrow. "How about when your father asked you to take out the trash the other night?"

"That was an accident," she said nervously. "I didn't mean to drop it. And I apologized 'bout the mess."

"Don't worry, child. God doesn't expect us to be perfect, but he does expect us to try to be." He paused. "Everyone but the Lord Jesus is imperfect. But we need to strive to always be better. Now, enough preaching for today. I brought you something."

Her eyes grew as big as baseballs when he unveiled the guitar. "Here," he said. "See what you think."

"Me?" she said. She didn't touch the instrument.

"Yes. It's for you. I wouldn't know what to do with the damned thing."

She took it reverently, wiping away a few water droplets with her skirt. She traced the pick guard, which resembled the letter M, with her index finger, then balanced the guitar on her thigh and strummed the strings. Her smile at that moment could have lit up all of Fenway Park.

"Now, I know we don't offer guitar at Sacred Heart, but once you go to Sharon High, they offer guitar and piano and all sorts of music classes. In the meantime, you know Mark, the youth group leader? He's going to give you a few lessons to help get you started. I'll have him work out the details with your mother, and I'll see if he can get you a case and a strap and whatever else you might need."

He couldn't tell if the girl was listening. Her head was bowed as if in prayer, and she fingered the strings and strummed, making nothing but noise. But the joy on that kid's face? That was heartwarming.

"Thank you," Angela said with watery eyes. "I love it."

o o o

He put a twenty down on the bar, emptied his pint, and slid off the stool he'd occupied for the last three hours.

"Calling it a night, Paul?" a red-nosed guy to his right asked.

"'Fraid so, Pete. Gotta work tomorrow."

"Fuckin' Sox," his new friend said before downing his glass of Jameson. "God, I hate the fuckin' Skankees."

He smiled and headed out to the parking lot. Here at the Irish Mist, a dive in Quincy where he'd never run into a parishioner, he was just Paul, not Father Dunn. If anyone asked, which they sometimes did, he said he was a banker. That always put a glaze in their eyes. Not that he was ashamed of being a priest—just the opposite, in fact. But sometimes, he needed to take the collar off and just be one of the guys yelling at the television as the Red Sox lost yet another game.

He drove home with the window down and the radio

turned up. He only had four pints, but it wouldn't do to get pulled over and risk getting his name under the police blotter in the local paper. Half an hour later, he pulled into the rectory driveway. It was a little after midnight and the neighborhood was fast asleep.

He'd just locked the car door when the first guy stepped out from the neighbor's bushes.

"Kind of late, isn't it, Padre?"

The stranger was tall, maybe six-two, and skinny. White, but he couldn't make out much more since the lighting wasn't good. He heard steps to his left and turned to see a second guy. If the first one was Abbott, this was Costello. Maybe five foot six, with huge gym muscles shown off by his wife-beater tee shirt. He opened and squeezed his hands shut, itching for a fight.

"Watching the Sox," Father Dunn said. Privately, he appealed to the Lord for wisdom and strength.

Always take out the bigger threat first; he'd learned that lesson on the streets. That will put the fear into the others. A second later his fist connected solidly with Costello's nose. It came away splattered with blood. He turned quickly to throw a left at Abbott, who he knew would be closing in.

But before he connected, Abbott struck his leg hard with a tire iron. They both heard the bone break, and the priest went down hard. He rolled to his side and Abbott hit him again, cracking a rib, maybe two.

"I got a message for you," Abbott said. "Mr. Anderson don't like you asking for money or coming around bothering his wife. Understand?" Abbott poked him in the neck with the tire iron. "Understand?"

"Yeah."

As Abbott stood up, a blinding flash of pain shot through Paul Dunn's head. A bloodied Costello kicked him with a heavy boot.

"Ease up, Eddie," Abbot said. "He got the message."

"This motherfucker broke my nose," Eddie/Costello said. "I'm gonna fuck him up."

Father Dunn managed to roll toward his car, so the next kick broke his clavicle instead of his skull.

"Enough!" Abbott shouted. But Eddie Costello grabbed the tire iron from Abbott and shoved him aside. Father Dunn attempted to kick the goon, but the effort was too weak. When Costello/Eddie raised the iron bar above his fireplug head and swung it down, there was only a brief flash of pain, followed by a warm, omnipresent light.Then nothing but a gently fading memory of a part he played for a short while.

THE DAY FREDDIE MERCURY DIED

"Some say love, it is a river
That drowns the tender reed
Some say love, it is a razor
That leaves your soul to bleed
Some say love, it is a hunger
An endless aching need
I say love, it is a flower
And you, its only seed"
– "The Rose" by Bette Midler

Art listened to a long phone message from his sister, asking if he and Taylor would make it up north to the lake house this Christmas. It was four days before Thanksgiving, and he seriously doubted Taylor would ever see the lake house again. The coffee in the mug on Art's desk was on the cooler side of lukewarm. How long had it been sitting there before he'd taken a sip, and what had he done in the meantime? Answers: more than 45 minutes, and very little. He'd booted up his computer, checked for electronic memos, and deleted the two he'd received. How many times could he plead too much work, not feeling well, the car is in the shop?

"Art, Clyde is up my ass looking for the quote from McMaster."

He turned in his chair and poked his head around the corner of his cubicle. Three cubes down, Vic Hammond's head poked around his own cubicle. Vic had the sad eyes of an old hound dog and had finally embraced his approaching baldness. He shaved what little he had crowning his big wrinkled head. About a year ago, Vic grew a bushy, overly thick mustache to compensate for what he lost on top. The look was grossly outdated, and the mustache served mostly as a lint brush for loose crumbs and random dust particles.

"Can you nudge your friend, what's his name over there, and get them to shit or get off the pot?"

"No problem, Vic. I'll see what I can do."

"By the way, how's Taylor doing? Did those new vitamins do anything?"

Vic's wife worked for a vitamin manufacturer called VitaKing. While they sold vitamins in the usual way, the real push of the company was to try to get people to buy them on the World Wide Web. Vic claimed it was the way of the future, but Art couldn't imagine putting his credit card number out there where any shyster could get it.

"A little better, I think," Art said. "Probably going to take some time is all."

"Francine swears by that stuff, and she's never been sick a day since I've known her. You sure it isn't lupus, or one of them immune diseases?"

Art ignored both the twist in his gut and the question. "I'll give my contact at McMaster a call and see if they'll fax you those numbers this morning."

He took another sip of cold coffee and pictured Taylor alone at home, probably still in his pajamas. Art had already taken three weeks of vacation days, running to doctors, to hospitals, to immunologists, to acupuncturists, to herbalists and naturopaths. How much had they spent on guava juice and exotic herbal teas and beet root smoothies and hydrogen peroxide baths and ultraviolet light therapy? All without positive results.

He'd love to visit the lake house again. To go cross-country skiing on the lake with Taylor. To eat his sister's famous four-bean chili or Tom's homemade pizza. To play Rummy 500 with his niece and nephews. To lose himself in Stephen King's latest novel. To curl up by the woodstove with a glass of wine, laughing and joking and never hearing the dreaded word again.

He made the call to McMaster, worked on his monthly report, and dreamed about scallops. Not just any scallops, but big, silver-dollar-sized sea scallops, baked in a small casserole dish with butter, garlic, breadcrumbs, and a nice blend of Parmesan and Romano cheeses. Succulent and sweet as maple syrup on ice cream. The way they made them at a restaurant called The Heights in Brookline where he and Taylor had their first date.

Art met Taylor at a New Year's Eve party hosted by Elaine Powell, a mutual friend who made a bundle in Boston real estate. The party was held in an expensive Cambridge loft. There were too many hipsters, and Art hid his discomfort by drinking too much. He was out on the tiny balcony overlooking Massachusetts Avenue when Taylor stepped out and joined him.

"Mind if I smoke?"

"Medically speaking, it's a terrible habit, but I won't try to stop you." It was a stupid thing to say, but 28-year-old Art was little better than 17-year-old Art when it came to talking to handsome strangers. Even so, Taylor smiled, giving him his first glance at those flawless teeth and a playful glint in the eyes that charmed everyone Taylor encountered.

"You look too young to be a doctor," Taylor said, still holding the pack of cigarettes.

"I'm probably old enough, but not nearly smart enough," Art said. "I got a C minus in high school biology and decided English was more my thing."

"I think the world has more than enough doctors and lawyers controlling our lives." Taylor extruded a cigarette from his pack and lit it. "What we need is more thinkers. People who look at the big picture and can condense it down so the average person can understand it. No bullshit, no hyperbole."

"The *USA Today* of philosophy," Art said.

Taylor let out a hearty laugh. "I'm Taylor Cahill. Smoker, Red Sox fanatic, art connoisseur, and philosopher wannabe."

"Art Daniels," he said, taking the proffered hand. "Slightly overweight purchasing agent for a company you've never heard of, lover of pasta, Styron, and Broadway musicals."

As he released Art's hand, Taylor said, "Any thoughts on Miss Dolly Parton?"

The confusion on Art's face must have been obvious. He added, "Consider it a friendship litmus test."

"I'd love to be her chiropractor," he said.

Taylor gave Art another version of that smile that could melt chocolate when a tall guy with close-cropped platinum blonde hair, flawless bronzed skin in an Armani suit poked his muscular frame through the door. If he wasn't a professional model, Art thought, he sure missed his calling.

"Taylor, there you are." The accent was European, perhaps Spanish or Italian. "I told Trevor we'd stop by before the ball drops."

Taylor exhaled a great plume of smoke with a sigh, snuffed the cigarette out in an ashtray full of sand, petrified gum, and old butts. With a touch on the shoulder and a wink they were gone, and Art was left more alone and isolated than when he'd first stepped onto the balcony.

Three months later, Art shopped at Faneuil Hall with his sister and her family, mindlessly people-watching, rather than picking over the tacky tourist crap in the shops. He saw Taylor carrying a bag from Pier 1. He stepped away from the "I'd Rather Be at Fenway" tee shirts and cans of Boston Baked Beans to say hello.

Taylor recognized him instantly, greeting Art with a strong hug and a peck on the cheek. "You know, I was thinking about you, my pasta-loving friend, a few weeks ago when I was at Scarpetti's. Their crostone toscano with cipolline in agrodolce was amazing."

The first thought to cross Art's mind was that he did not have any idea what those words meant. But God, did they sound delicious when Taylor said them. That thought, however, was quickly shoved aside by the undeniable fact that Taylor had called him friend. Taylor Cahill, dater of gorgeous male models, had been thinking of him.

"Are you free some night this week? C'mon, don't tell me you're busy."

Art and Taylor exchanged phone numbers and made a tentative date for the following Saturday.

Scarpetti's booked a wedding party that evening, so they tried a new place called The Heights in Brookline. Art ordered the scallops, wanting to show Taylor his tastes were broader than simply pasta. Taylor surprised him by ordering veal, which prompted a lengthy discussion on the treatment of veal calves. Which inevitably led to conversations on the production of meat in America, the growing trend of vegetarianism, how they felt about people who were vehement vegetarians yet wore leather Birkenstocks, the pitfalls of Reaganism, the dream of universal health care. And the dreaded virus.

Taylor knew four people who had died. Art knew two, and four who had tested positive but weren't showing signs yet. They finished their evening with a shared dish of tiramisu and a snifter of Grand Marnier. The date ended with a kiss so hot it nearly melted Art's fingernails.

The workday dragged on. A teleconference with the Goodall Corporation in St. Louis. A phone call home, where Taylor didn't pick up. A brainstorming session facilitated by a co-worker, who Art thought was better suited for selling used cars than business restructuring strategies. A returned call to say thanks to his contact at McMaster, another unanswered phone call home, and an early departure to catch the bus down to Harvard Square. Art planned to hit the Coop on his way home to buy the new book by Amy Tan everyone was talking about, *The Kitchen God's Wife*. He'd heard a good review on NPR, and it sounded like something Taylor would enjoy.

Two middle-aged women stood in line in front of him as he waited to make his purchase. They were obviously friends and were exact opposites. One was tall, with perfectly coiffed auburn-tinted hair, carefully applied makeup and an expensive skirt and blouse set, probably bought at Lord & Taylor. The other woman was short, dressed in faded jeans and a rumpled consignment shop blouse. She wore no make-up and looked like she cut her own hair with dull scissors.

The taller one asked her friend if she'd heard that Freddie Mercury died that morning.

"Oh my God, no. Please tell me you're kidding."

"It was all over the news this afternoon. All the radio stations are playing old Queen songs. 'Bohemian Rhapsody,' 'We are the Champions,' 'Bicycle...'"

"What happened?" the shorter woman asked. "Another drug overdose?"

"AIDS. You really need to watch the news now and then. I understand throwing out your television, but you have got to be more aware about what's happening in the world."

"My therapist agrees that avoiding the news is better for"—she glanced at Art, who was pretending to read the blurb on the back of his book—"my mood. And what am I really missing? War. Murder. Raping of children? I'll stick with yoga, herbal tea and ignorance, thank you. Anyway, was Freddie gay, or a druggie?"

The women took a step forward as the next customer was served. "Maggie, pull your head out of the sand," the tall one said. "The band's name is Queen. They're all rump-wrangling queers."

Art fought the urge to weep at the news of Freddie Mercury's passing. It was an immense loss. But this, this callous, middle-school name-calling by a woman who appeared to be educated and worldly? This shocked him. He stepped out of line, put the Amy Tan book down on the sales rack, and left the store.

He walked aimlessly up Mass Ave, fighting the urge to cry, to scream, to kick something. How could people be so callous? Yes, it was arrogant, and yes, it was pretentious, but Art liked to think Cambridge people were smarter. More refined. More enlightened.

Art's attention returned when he nearly walked into a couple of kids who looked to be twins, maybe three or four years old. They chased pigeons picking at pieces of pretzel on the sidewalk. The kids charged the birds, who flew away, causing the children to erupt in giggles. Art stopped to watch the kids return to their mother, who sat reading the *Globe* with a cup of coffee at an outdoor café. Snickering conspiratorially until the birds returned, they charged again, laughing with all their might as the birds abandoned their food and once again took to the sky. Art watched the scene repeat for several minutes. For a moment, a smile creased his sad face as he wondered at the children playing.

He walked past the nail salon, the gyro shop, the used sporting goods store, the hundreds of people making their way home from work focused on dinner or catching the T or going out clubbing that night. As he stared, the people turned into holocaust victims, to skeletons, to piles of dust blowing in the wind down Boylston Street.

Over half a million people in the United States were infected with the AIDS virus. In the last decade, nobody even knew how many had died of the virus, since it was still a taboo topic. Slow, agonizingly cruel deaths. The only compassion America could muster went to a teenage boy in Indiana who contracted the virus through a blood transfusion. What a shame, people said. Look how brave he is.

Three teenage boys sat on sticker-covered skateboards passing a crudely rolled joint outside the T station at Central Square. All of them sported multiple earrings. One of them wore a poorly drawn homemade Celtic cross tattoo on his forearm. Another rocked a green-tinted Mohawk. The boy with the tattoo glared at him, eyes bloodshot, pupils the size of dimes. "What you lookin' at, faggot?"

Several snappy responses danced on the tip of Art's tongue. *The turd I shat this morning looked better than that stupid tattoo. Your future cellmate is going to love your pretty mouth. Your mother should have gone ahead with the abortion.* Once again, Art failed to engage. He descended the stairs, dropped his token in the turnstile, and moved down the platform. An African-American woman with short dreads, dirty jeans, and a Jamaican flag tee shirt played an old acoustic guitar. There was a long scratch toward the back of the guitar's face, and the pick guard was in the shape of a capital M. Most of the commuters walked by without so much as a glance, although a few did toss some loose change into her tattered guitar case.

Art stopped to listen. The singer's voice was raspy and contained a masculine quality. She moved fluidly up and down the neck of the guitar, closing her eyes when singing, focusing her concentration on pulling the song from her soul.

"A friend of mine, he used to smile, but we ain't talked in a long, long while. We used to jam, dance and play. Now he's in bed, wastin' away."

On Valentine's Day, Art came home from work to find a red-eyed Taylor naked on the toilet. There was a bloody towel wrapped around his arm. Art gingerly unwrapped the makeshift bandage to find a two-inch gash near the elbow.

"Jesus, Taylor. What happened?" The skin was so thin and pale it wouldn't have taken much.

"I fell in the shower," Taylor said, a quiver escaping his words. "It's nothing. I'm fine."

"It's not fine, and you're a terrible liar," Art said. After wrapping the wound with gauze and medical tape, he took Taylor to the emergency room. The woman at the admissions desk probably thought she was discreet, but Art saw her eyes move from him to Taylor to the blood, followed by a grimace and a command to please take a seat. A male orderly wouldn't let him go into the room, but Taylor told him later about the nurse's horrified look when he told her he was HIV positive. And how they dressed in what appeared to be hazmat suits, then double gloved to put in six rudimentary stitches.

The scar it left was worthy of a lawsuit, but instead of seeing an attorney, Taylor insisted they go to a stylist to chop off his thick locks. "This way I won't need to wash my hair so often," he'd insisted.

As far as Art could tell, Taylor still shampooed and conditioned every day.

Art took out his wallet, removed a twenty, folded it into a triangle, and dropped it into the singer's case. She glanced up at him. Without missing a beat, she nodded in appreciation and started singing the next verse. The tune changed while Art daydreamed, and now she was picking a slow song.

"When this is blown over, and everything's all by the way, when I grow older, I will be at your side to remind you how I still love you."

Art exited at Alewife station and moved with the herd up the metal stairs to the parking garage. It took nearly 25 minutes to drive the three miles to Arlington Center. Then he walked to a Szechuan place called Beijing Palace and ordered a hot and sour soup for Taylor, and garlic chicken with asparagus for himself.

When they decided to move in together, Art's place in Dorchester was too small and too blue collar for someone in the art world, as Taylor was. Taylor's loft was too full of memories of Pierre, his last lover, so they settled on a two-bedroom, 900-square-foot fourth-floor apartment in Arlington. Art donated most of his furniture to the Salvation Army and they'd furnished the new place with Taylor's belongings, and of course, the paintings and prints on the walls were all part of his collection.

The highlight of the apartment was the balcony off the living room. It was small, but large enough for a little table and three chairs. It faced east, and since their building was at the top of a hill, the view of downtown Boston was spectacular. They enjoyed drinking coffee, watching the sun rise over the city in the mornings, and easily as many glasses of wine while the sun set in the west, illuminating the tall buildings in a golden aura before the onset of dusk.

Taylor wasn't watching television or reading in the living room. The apartment was unnervingly still.

Art found him in the bedroom. Taylor lay motionless. He panicked until he saw a small rise in Taylor's chest, heard the slight snore escape. *Alive,* he thought. *It's okay, he's alive.*

Before they moved in together, before either of them could make that kind of commitment, they both were tested. The results were negative. They moved in. Their love blossomed despite so many differences. Taylor liked the glasses all turned downward in the cabinet, arranged tallest on the left, shortest on the right. Art didn't like the television on when they were eating and despite Taylor's love of jazz, Art preferred late '60s folk music—Judy Collins; Peter, Paul and Mary; Simon and Garfunkel. Taylor had a nearly photographic memory for people, faces, lyrics, and even baseball statistics, while Art was better at remembering ideas and concepts.

In time, they learned to give space when space was needed; a hug when physical contact was best. They talked endlessly about trips they would take someday. And they dreamed about the combination coffee shop/ bookstore/ art gallery they hoped to open up someday.

Someday.

Someday, they would travel to Florence. Someday, they'd watch the Boston Pops perform on the Fourth of July from their yacht in the harbor. Someday, they'd move to Greenwich Village, have a clambake on Martha's Vineyard, get front row tickets to see Robert Morris in "The Piano Lesson," catch a home run ball at Fenway Park. Someday, they'll find a cure.

Art set the table for dinner. He put on the kettle for tea, when Taylor came from the bedroom, dressed in his robe and the LL Bean slippers Art bought him their first Christmas in the apartment.

"Hi, honey," Taylor said with a smile. "How was your day?"

"I called you twice this afternoon. You didn't answer."

The smile on Taylor's face evaporated. It returned a second later, but it was forced. "I went out today for a bit. Felt like a walk after hearing the news this morning. It's all over the TV and radio. I had to get out of the house."

Art moved towards Taylor and pulled him into a hug. He was careful not to squeeze too hard. All the muscle, the strength that had flowed from Taylor in their first hug, had melted away over the last year and a half. His skin, once so warm and rich, now resembled an old almond shell. Art tried to say, wanted to say, "How are you feeling?" But the only thing to escape his lips was an exhale before a sob ricocheted through his body. He had to be the strong one. He had to support Taylor. But in that moment, he felt about as strong as overcooked linguine.

The darkness engulfed Art. Was life nothing more than a string of endless good-byes?

Taylor held him, somehow conveying the strength that used to come so easily to him. He put his chin on Art's shoulder and softly sang, "Working nine to five, what a way to make a living."

Art couldn't help but laugh. "Are you singing Miss Dolly at a time like this?" He pulled back enough to see a mischievous sparkle in Taylor's eyes.

"It's enough to drive you crazy if you let it..."

Taylor's husky baritone always touched his heart. "You really are a sick bastard."

"I'm your sick bastard, though."

Taylor rubbed Art's back, quietly whispering over and over that it would be okay. Everything would be okay. He never was a good liar.

Freddie Mercury died November 24, 1991

We still feel the silence.

THE LETTER

"It's hard to rely on my good intentions
When my head's full of things I can't mention
Seems I usually get things right
But I can't understand
What I did last night"
– "Good Intentions" by Toad the Wet Sprocket

I woke to the sound of the nurse's squeaky shoes and optimistic voice saying, "Hello, Sweetheart. Are you hungry? Can I get you some juice?" The sugary voice wasn't directed at me.

I slouched in an uncomfortable pleather chair by the window in a hospital room. My eyes popped open, and I took in the source of the voice. A big-shouldered woman with chestnut hair wound tightly into a large bun on the top of her head checked pulse and blood oxygen and IV lines while simultaneously straightening out a crooked blanket. She addressed my 13-year-old niece Cassie, my kid brother Sam's daughter.

At 79 pounds, ugly purple and green bruises marked her arms and shoulders. Her bald head peeked out from the Jamaican flag bandana I brought her a few weeks ago. It was pulled to the side. She more closely resembled a wartime refugee than the pizza-loving, field-hockey-playing, honor-roll-making seventh grader that she really was. She shook her head and the nurse said she'd be back in a little while in case she changed her mind.

The sun put a warm hand on the side of my face as I sat up. After a short groan and crackle in my bones as I stretched them into their intended shape, I said, "Sorry, Cass. I must have dozed off." I ran a hand over the tiny hairs on my own scalp, an unconscious habit I'd developed since shaving it. "What'd I miss?"

"Oh," she said in a voice that made her sound like she'd been smoking two packs a day for a decade or more, "Laura Bush came to say hello. So did Oprah. Then the Notre Dame Marching band paraded up and down the hallway playing the 'Star-Spangled Banner.'"

What a smart-ass. No wonder I love this kid so much. "That explains why I was dreaming about the American Revolution. Paul Revere was wearing a red, white, and blue tutu, riding around frantically on a horse hollering something about the nurses are coming, the nurses are coming."

A hint of a smile grew on her face as she rolled her eyes.

"How you feeling?" I asked. Then I remembered our conversation from the previous day. Cassie told me she was sick and tired of everyone asking her that. I put my hands together like a little kid praying and bowed. "A thousand apologies, Cassie-san. What I meant to ask was how is your belly feeling?"

She made a ble-e-e-ch sound, which was 13-year-old speak for 'my stomach feels like it's full of sharp rocks and used motor oil, thank you.'

I moved to the bed and sat beside her. I'm not the intellectual one, not the charismatic one, not the guy who always knows what to do in a pinch. I'm just Uncle Bill, or UB as Cassie sometimes likes to call me. I'm the uncle who brings her to Fenway to see a Sox game and buys her too much junk food, so we need to pull over so she can puke on the drive home. I'm the guy who buys 40 boxes of Girl Scout cookies just so she sells the most in her pack, or troop, or whatever they call it. The uncle who takes her to the track and gives her two dollars a race to bet, who showed her the ins and outs of five card stud when she was eight, and let her drive my old Honda around the Walmart parking lot early on a Sunday morning last summer. I wished with all my might that words of comfort would come, but they never do. I took her soft hand in mine and bent to kiss her forehead. She smelled of kid sweat and industrial laundry soap and the generic medicinal odor that permeated every hospital I've ever been in.

This was Cassie's sixth round of chemo. Each time they pumped the poison inside her, she grew thinner and weaker. Her bright eyes dimmed more and more each time. While her friends were on summer vacation at the Cape, or swimming at a lake in Maine, or planning their dinner with Cinderella on their way to Disney, Cassie was pumped with enough toxins to bring her to the edge of death before yanking her back into life. It just wasn't right. I held Cassie's hand. Her eyes opened and she smiled as my brother Sam and his wife, Tasha, came into the room.

"Hey, baby doll," Sam said. He walked over and shook my hand as his wife examined her daughter like a gemologist studies a rare blue diamond.

"How are you feeling, sweetie?"

Cassie glanced at me with a 'see what I mean' look then told her mother she was doing okay. Generally, the chemo went all right while they pumped it into her. Over the years, the doctors had mastered the art of combining prednisone and anti-nausea medications prior to the chemo cocktail, so patients didn't feel too bad during the infusion. It was generally a few days later that the sickness came, the pain in the joints and bones, the feelings like her finger- and toe-nails were going to fall off.

"I brought you some mail," Tasha said as she draped her coat across the chair. "There's cards from the Muldrews, your cousins in Florida, a *Seventeen* magazine thanks to your Uncle Bill." She shot me a look, reminding me how displeased she was that I purchased her 13-year-old a subscription to what my sister-in-law considered a trashy magazine. "And a letter with a Las Vegas postmark," she continued.

"Listen, kid," I said. "I'm going to stretch my legs for a bit and let you visit with your parents. Need anything while I'm out? A rack of ribs? Some jalapeno poppers maybe?"

Cassie snorted, both in disgust and to show me she loved me, I'm pretty sure. I grabbed my faded denim jacket and headed for the exit.

A woman struggled to bustle through the entrance to the oncology center. Quick-stepping over, I opened the door, holding it while she juggled her purse and the bag she carried. I guessed her to be in her thirties, but it was difficult to tell. A white do-rag covered her bald head, contrasting with her dark skin. Her eyes were puffy, and she was as thin as a clothesline, as my grandma would say. But when she turned towards me and smiled, it brightened her features, revealing her true beauty.

"Thanks," she said as she walked by.

"Sure," I said, but she was already 10 feet away and probably didn't even hear me.

Walking down the street, my mind drifted back to Cassie, and I tried not to think about the letter with the Las Vegas postmark. Her symptoms began to show in February. A teacher at the middle school called, concerned that Cassie kept falling asleep in class. She had noticed a significant weight loss and bruises spotting her arms. She wanted to ensure everything was okay at home.

I found out about her cancer in a text message. Cassie wrote, "Cancer☹." Being old-fashioned, I called her, but she didn't answer. When I arrived at the house, Sam had just gotten home and I don't think my presence was exactly appreciated. I took Tommy, my nephew, out, and we picked up sandwiches, even though no one was hungry.

Tommy kept asking questions, like "Did Cassie have tumors?" And "Where are they?" And "What's going to happen?"

Tasha snapped at him. I took him into the living room to play video games. I tried to explain how some cancers are in your blood and bones, and Cassie was going to be okay, but he'd have to really be on his best behavior until she was all better, because his mom and dad were going to be pretty stressed out until then.

I'm no doctor, and I didn't much know what non-Hodgkin's lymphoma was at the time, but I think I did okay explaining it in a way that a third grader could understand. At least, I hope I did. I mean, this is why I never wanted kids of my own. You never know the right thing to do, and if you mess up, which always happens, you end up screwing them up for life. It's just too much pressure, that moldable little thing, looking to you for guidance and advice. Much better to just visit, take them out and give their folks a break and have fun with them. Make them laugh, make them smile, then drop them back home so their parents can do the heavy lifting.

It was after Cassie's third chemo treatment that I got the idea for the letter. She was in her room, refusing to go out. After her first treatment, she still had a full head of hair. Then a few days after the second dose, it started coming out in clumps in the shower, in her brush, and to Cassie's absolute mortification, in her English class. Sam and Tasha wanted to keep her in school as long as possible. Keep life normal and all that. It was devastating for a young girl to face all those stares and deal with comments though.

Cassie holed herself up, refusing to come out of her room. I went over, hoping to persuade her out. When I knocked on her door, she barked, "Go away." I let myself in and sat on the edge of her bed.

"I brought you a box of 20 Buffalo wings," I said. "Medium spicy."

"I'm not hungry," she said. Then after a pause, "Thanks, anyway."

I placed them on her bedside table and gently rubbed her back. She faced the wall, and I could see the few lonely patches of hair on her scalp. My eyes burned. It took everything I had not to lift her up, hold her, and bawl. Instead, I focused on the music she was listening to. A guy who sounded like he might not shave yet was crooning about love being more precious than gold, or some such crap.

"Is this the Black Ties?" I asked, trying to engage her. The Black Ties were her favorite group. The pop radio waves across the country, and probably most of the civilized world, played their latest song at least twice an hour until everyone over the age of 15 was so sick of it they'd choose to get an un-anesthetized colonoscopy rather than hear it again.

She nodded but didn't say anything.

"What's the lead singer's name again? Derek Brown, David Blue..."

"Damon Black," she said.

"That's right," I said, smacking my forehead with my palm. We'd talked at length about what a great singer she thought he was, and of course, how every girl in the universe thought he was sooo cute and hot. We'd even looked online for the band's tour schedule, but they were in Europe for the rest of the year.

Cassie turned suddenly to look at me, eyes red and swollen from crying, one eyebrow gone while half the other still hung in there. "Look at me," she said. "I'm hideous."

"Sweetheart, you have never been hideous a day in your life," I said. "Well, maybe when you were first born. You kind of looked like Winston Churchill there for the first day or two. But once they cleaned you up and got some food in you, the sunshine came into your eyes and you've been brilliant ever since."

It didn't work. She felt like shit, she looked like shit, and she knew it. I tried to remember what I was like in seventh grade, slicking my hair back, struggling into too-tight jeans, trying to imitate the older boys who I thought looked cool, stuttering any time a girl tried to speak to me. Believing everyone thought I was a dork, every girl found me too short, too ugly, too eccentric, and just not worth bothering with. And then I tried to imagine how much worse it could have been if I were bald and had the big C.

An hour later, I was in the barber's chair getting my head shaved when the idea hit me. Cassie was way down in the dumps, and nothing I or anyone else could say would lift her up much. But what if someone else tried? Somebody she really adored and admired? What if I could get that guy from the Black Ties to give her a call, or even just send her a short note? That would put that spark back into her eyes.

At home that night, I spent some time on the internet looking up potential ways to contact Damon Black. I found a fan site and emailed him there. I located an agent in Los Angeles who claimed to represent him, so I sent a query asking for Mr. Black to send a dying girl a note. It was hard to write that last part, and I don't believe Cassie is dying—I can't believe Cassie is dying—but I wanted to whom it may concern to take my note seriously. I found the Black Ties' myspace page and sent a message, and also found Damon Black's myspace page and sent him a personal message. Although, with probably a quarter million friends, I doubted he'd ever get to it.

A week went by, and I didn't hear anything from the band. Cassie's eyes nearly bugged out of her face when she saw my shaved head. Then she laughed, which made the whole stunt worthwhile. I read aloud from her history book, some boring stuff about the Civil War, so she could keep up. And I tried to help her with pre-algebra, but math was never my thing.

After her fourth round of chemo, I tried messaging the other guys in the band, who also had huge followings. I bought one of their CDs so I could see who the record label was, and I sent them a letter as well. Another week went by, and then another.

I returned to the hospital with a cup of coffee for Sam and a box of donut holes in case Cassie might want one.

"Uncle Bill, you'll never guess who wrote me a letter!" My eyebrows shot up, and I tried to formulate a response. She shouted, "Damon Black! Damon Black wrote me a letter!"

"You can't be serious!"

"I am," she said. "Can you believe it? Here, listen."

I handed Sam his coffee and put the donut holes on the bedside tray as my niece began to read.

Dear Cassie,

Me and the other guys in Black Ties are sorry you're so sick. It always bums us out to hear that one of our dedicated fans isn't doing well, especially a girl as smart and funny and beautiful as you. I know you're doing what you need to get better, and even if you feel kind of crappy now, in a few months you'll be done with your treatments and you'll feel like your old self. Better than your old self. The sun's gonna shine down on you, and you'll be stronger than ever. I believe in you, Cassie, so hang in there, and don't give up. Don't ever give up. I want to see you in the front row of a concert when we're back in the states.

Keep on,
Damon Black

Cassie looked up from the letter, her smile as bright as the floodlights at Fenway during a night game.

"That's awesome," I said. "Totally awesome."

"I know, right? I can't wait to see the look on Katie and Meghan's faces when I tell them." She looked down at the letter again. "How do you think he knew about me? I mean, how did he know my address? And about my treatments?"

"Well, uh, um, I don't really know. Somebody told him, I guess." I glanced around the room and saw Tasha staring at me like a hunter stares down the barrel at a 12-point buck. My brother, on the other hand, was shoving a fourth or fifth donut hole down his gullet.

"Somebody who knows you must have told somebody in the band. The important thing to remember is that Damon Black believes in you and wants you to get healthy again."

"Do you think he'll write again? Maybe he'll send me an autographed picture next time."

"I wouldn't count on that," Tasha butted in. "He's busy touring and all."

A different nurse came in to poke and prod and take Cassie's vitals. I took advantage of the moment to say my good-byes and head out. As I stepped into the elevator, I felt someone close behind and turned to see my sister-in-law.

"You wrote that letter, didn't you?"

I used the defensive technique I'd developed at age 12 to get around answering difficult questions. I put on my best poker face and stayed mum. Did I mention that I'm not much good at playing poker?

"Don't lie," she said. "I know you did. I can see it in your face. But what I don't know is, what the hell were you thinking?"

I next went for diversion. "What gave it away?"

"Do us both a favor and never try your hand at forgery," she spat out at me. "No celebrity has the time or inclination to write letters to sick little girls, and even if they did, they'd have some flunky do it on band letterhead paper, and it would be a form letter. And it wouldn't use the words 'bummed out,' which nobody under 40 ever uses anymore. And they'd know that the band's name, the black ties, isn't capitalized."

Judge Judy rested her case as the elevator doors opened on the ground floor. Even so, she wasn't done with me yet, following right behind as I stepped into the lobby. I turned to face my domineering sister-in-law and saw how disheveled her hair was. Little streaks of gray tinted the usual light brown color. Dark bags clung beneath her glassy eyes, only one of which had badly applied mascara on it. Her skin was pale, rather than the lively just-back-from-the-beach look I normally associated with her.

"I know you love her and want to be the knight in shining armor who rides in and makes everything all better, but you have no clue how much this is going to hurt her when she figures out what you did. It's going to knock her down twice as hard as it might have lifted her up. Did you even think about that? Did that thought ever cross your mind?" She waved her arms around like she wanted to hit something, but was too upset to locate a target.

"Tasha, there's no reason she needs to find out I sent it. She's a kid—"

"She's a smart kid with smart friends. It's not like I work for the fucking FBI, and I knew you did it before she'd read the first paragraph. You have that friend, Mitchell, who lives out in Vegas. You had him send it, didn't you?"

I stared down at the oddly shaped floor tiles. Damn. She had me. And if Tasha figured it out so easily, so would Cassie.

"Listen, Tash. I'm sorry. I just, I just wanted to lift her spirits."

"I know that," she said, running clawed fingers through

her hair. "But how am I going to pick up the pieces when she figures it out?"

I didn't have an answer. I never seemed to have an answer. Why did I pull the fire alarm back in middle school? Why did I abandon my friend Tucker at a bar in Somerville when he was so drunk I knew he'd never make it home alone? Why would I ever bet a thousand dollars on the Patriots in the 1986 Super Bowl? Why did I sneak out with Darlene when Lisa was really everything I wanted in a woman?

Outside, dark clouds covered the sky, and rain started pouring. Another divine message from the universe? By the time I made it to my car, water dripped from my ears and my denim jacket was fairly well soaked. I longed for a cigarette and cursed myself for giving them up five years ago. Tommy was a baby then, and Cassie told me she didn't like the smoke. The news was full of stories about how secondhand smoke was bad for kids, so I finally bought the damn patches and quit. Right now, I'd kick a dog for a nice smoke.

I fingered the keys, started the car, turned on the wipers, and pulled forward to the visitors' parking exit. As I waited, I saw a drenched woman shuffling down the sidewalk with heavy bags ducking under the meager shelter of the bus stop. As I eased out and got closer, I saw the white leather do-rag contrasting with her mocha skin and pulled to the curb.

The electric window on the passenger side didn't work, so I opened my door and stepped out. "You need a ride?"

She stared at me, the rain coming down harder now, and I imagined I must look like I was standing under a waterfall. She shook her head.

"Come on," I said. "You're getting drenched, and you know you don't need to get sick. Let me give you a lift."

She continued to stare, probably thinking how best to handle this nut job. As I put one foot back in the car, she stood taller and made her way to the car. I slipped in and opened the door for her. She slid in gingerly, putting her bags between her legs on the floor. She held her keys in her right hand between her fingers, ready to strike and do damage if needed. I smelled the dampness on both of us, and a slight vanilla scent that must be perfume or lotion or something. I waited for her to buckle up, then eased the car away from the curb.

"I'm Bill," I said. "Bill Donnelly."

"Hey, Bill," she said. "I'm Angela."

"Where can I take you, Angela?"

She glanced around at our dreary surroundings. "LA might be nice."

"LA?" I laughed. "All that smog, the plastic people, the earthquakes, the rent? They can keep it. Where you gonna get a good calzone in LA? And who are you gonna root for—the Clippers? The Dodgers? C'mon—get real."

Now it was her turn to laugh. "I take it you're a local?"

"Yeah, more or less. I was born up in Stoneham, then made my way to Revere and eventually to Boston. I've been bouncing around here for the last 25 years or so. You?"

"Similar, 'cept I'm from the South shore. Born in Sharon. Been in Dorchester since '95."

As I contemplated whether or not to ask about what kind of cancer she had, she took control of the conversation.

"You know River Street?"

I nodded, slowing to allow a dumbass on a rice rocket to get well ahead of me.

She said, "Your head's shaved, but you don't look like you just got chemo or radiation."

"I was visiting my niece. She's 13. About a month ago I shaved my head, you know, in solidarity."

"Was she happy you did it?"

"Not sure," I said. "I think so. Now she just makes fun of

me, but that's okay."

"What's she got?"

"Non-Hodgkin's lymphoma," I answered, a bad taste in my mouth as I said it.

"How's she handlin' it?"

I shrugged. "She's tough. It's more than any kid should have to deal with, but my gut tells me she'll end up even stronger."

"Is your gut always right?"

I turned to look at her briefly. She was watching me, still on guard, but perhaps a touch softer around the eyes. "Almost never," I said.

I made the turn on to River and passed a couple of Thai and Vietnamese restaurants that weren't there the last time I was in this area. Angela directed me to a large brick apartment building and told me to park in the back. "You want to come in for some tea? It'll help take the chill off."

I said sure and tried to carry her bags, but she wouldn't let me help. Inside, the building smelled of mildew, cat piss, and wet concrete. Her apartment was on the seventh floor. We rode up in the elevator with a woman dressed in one of those Islamic headscarves. It must take a lot of courage wearing a covering like that given the current climate in this country.

Angela's place was tight, but tidy. The main room nestled a small kitchen area, a table for four shoved against one wall, a couch, and a TV. Beside the TV was a stereo, and a green guitar case sat in a metal rack that looked like it was made for it. The window revealed an excellent view of the building next door.

Angela put on a kettle and excused herself while she changed into dry clothes. I hung my wet jacket on one of the kitchen chairs and studied a collage of photographs over the couch. Each picture contained a shot of a woman playing guitar.

In some she was playing solo, in others she was a part of a group. The woman in the picture had long braids, but I could tell it was Angela, although it was hard to say how old the photos were. In the center picture, she was onstage outdoors somewhere. Eyes closed, she was singing; the sunlight gleamed on the copper-red finish of her acoustic guitar, and she seemed totally lost in the music.

"You like regular, or something herbal?" she asked.

I turned, not having heard her come back from the other room. She now wore faded jeans that hung a little too loosely and a purple hoodie. "What are you having?"

"I don't like it much, but I'm having plain green. The docs say it's good for me."

"I'll have the same then." Stealing another glance at the photo montage, I said, "Do you still play?"

She didn't say anything for a few beats. "Music adds texture to life, and will always be a part of me. But I gave up the dream a while ago. I still play around town sometimes. The Social, O'Leary's, Jasper Hill. But lately, I get so tired. My voice just don't hold out."

"Was that Tracy Chapman I saw you with?"

She smiled for a second, making me want to do something silly just so she'd laugh.

"Yeah. I opened up for her back in '95. She's a wonderful lady, and she was good to me."

"You play with anyone else I might know?"

"I played with lots of folks. Don't know if you'd know 'em or not." She took the kettle off the stove and filled our cups. "I opened for Modest Mouse back in '93, before they got so big. Susan Tedeschi, Paul Speidel, Vinnie Sarino, Luther Johnson. Ancient history now." She put the cups and a plate with several stale cookies on the table and beckoned for me to take a seat.

A flash of inspiration hit. "You wouldn't know Damon Black, would you?"

Her brow furrowed. "Who?"

"Damon Black? The Black Ties? Forget it." Oh well, it was worth a try. I sipped the tea and she must have seen something in my expression.

"Tastes like grass, right?"

"Grass with a bit of fertilizer, I'd say."

She tried to hide a grin and sipped her own tea.

"So, what keeps you busy these days?" I asked.

"Radiation treatments," she said. "Five days a week for eight weeks. I'm a little over half done."

"Breast cancer?" I used to work with a woman named Marge. She had cancer in her left breast, so I was somewhat familiar with the treatment.

Angela nodded, then told me about finding the lump only two months after getting a clean mammogram. They did a lumpectomy, then another, then the rounds of chemo. The doctors said her prognosis was good, but what else are they supposed to say?

She told me about her time as a street musician, then the few years she felt sure she'd make it, only to fade into obscurity. Now she worked at her aunt's office supply company, which was good because nobody gave her grief when she needed to take off for treatments or just to go home and sleep. We talked that way until our tea was done, then she offered me a beer, which I took her up on. Before I knew it, I was opening up to her about Cassie and the whole letter debacle that afternoon.

Angela sat quietly and listened as I spilled my guts. Once I was done, she said, "The Damon Black question makes sense now." She took a long sip of beer and wiped her mouth with a napkin. "My grandma used to say, 'The road to hell is paved with good intentions.'"

"That was one of my mom's many expressions back in the day. Socks come in pairs. Stop crossing your eyes or your face will freeze that way. Unfortunately, I've always been immune to the wisdom of my elders."

"Amen," she said, lifting her can and clinking it with mine. "So, what you gonna do?"

I closed my eyes, seeing Cassie there in her hospital bed, feeling as though someone was pressing their thumbs into my skull and it was made of dough. "I honestly don't know. My gut tells me to leave it alone and see what happens. If Cassie doesn't figure it out, it's all good. If she does figure it out, well, I'll be on the top of her shit list."

Angela pulled the bandana she'd covered her scalp with off, revealing tiny hairs on a perfectly symmetrical head. "I thought we already established that your gut feelings ain't worth shit."

I had to laugh. "True. I can't argue with that."

She scratched her head and studied me for a minute. "Do you believe in prayer?"

My mind raced back to CCD classes, Saturday confessions, incense logs, Sunday Mass with Father Anthony at Saint Peter's when I was a kid.

"I want to," I said. "I really want there to be something or someone out there who cares for us, who looks out for us, who wants to help us. But it's hard not to have doubts."

"Everybody has doubts," she said. "Mother Teresa had doubts. Martin Luther King Junior had doubts. But love is a powerful force. Love is the strongest thing of all. You love your niece, and she loves you. When you pray, you feed your love energy into your niece—I'm sure of it."

She rolled her head around, stretching her neck. I could tell she was tired and I should probably go.

"My head's a little fuzzy and I'm not expressing myself well. What I mean to say is, when you put your love out there, be it in a prayer or whatever, the person benefits simply from the knowledge that you love them. That opens up the channels for energy transfer."

Next door a television set turned on, demonstrating how thin the apartment walls were. That didn't seem to faze Angela. "What you did, you did with love, even if it wasn't the smartest thing you ever did. If your niece figures it out, you need to let her know that. Let her know you aren't perfect and maybe made a mistake, but it was love that drove you to it, and that same love will allow her to forgive you."

"I hope so." I put down my empty can and stood to go. "I sure hope so."

ELVIS'S TOILET

"If you're lost, you can look and you will find me
Time after time
If you fall, I will catch you, I will be waiting
Time after time"
– "Time after Time" by Cyndi Lauper

Frank Giardini turned onto the dirt road just past the 'Elephant's Trunk Flea Market' sign. The old pickup clanged and banged along the uneven path, every bump and jolt reverberating through the springs in the worn vinyl bench seat. Frank steered clear of an old lady in some sort of antique Easter bonnet as she pulled a wagon with a dog statue behind her. The first row in the parking area was full, but he found a spot in the next one. He glanced at his daughter, Emily, but she was fixated on her phone, presumably texting one of her friends.

"Ready to find some bargains?" He smiled big, hoping she'd catch a little of his enthusiasm.

"You sure about this?" Emily looked around doubtfully.

"I told you, me and your mom"—Frank paused like he'd just hit an unexpected speed bump at the innocent mention of his ex—"we got virtually everything in our first apartment at flea markets. I promise, you'll be amazed at the treasures."

"Looks a little more like crap," Emily said as she opened her door and stepped from the borrowed truck.

Frank quickly joined her, considered for a second taking her hand, then remembered Emily was almost twenty now, not seven. She was about to start her third year at George Mason University in Virginia, majoring in biology with her eye on medical school. Frank knew she could do it. Emily was smart, much smarter than he or his ex were. She even got an $8,000 a year academic scholarship to George Mason, a school he still had his doubts about. He'd heard it was a training camp for ultra-right-wingers and anarchists, but Emily just rolled her eyes whenever he brought the matter up, so he kept his mouth shut. Mostly.

"Okay, review with me one more time. You're looking for a dresser, a desk, maybe a bookshelf, and a lamp or two. Sharon has a TV, right?"

"You got it," she said as they approached the entrance. "I'm taking my bed and my stereo. I might need a throw rug for the living room."

"I thought you said Sharon's mom got you guys a rug at a tag sale?"

"She did," Emily said. "And it's hideous. Like cat vomit on moldy burlap."

Frank paid the two-dollar entrance fee for each of them and waited as a crusty guy who looked older than Moses's grandfather stamped their hands. The flea market was set up with an aisle straight ahead of them, and lanes shooting to the left and right. Even though it was just past ten o'clock, early in Frank's mind, the place was busy and full of bargain-hunting customers and overeager sellers.

"How do you want to tackle this?" Emily asked. "Do we split up and search, or go together?"

"Let's stick together. I might need to give you a lesson in Haggling 101."

Emily shook her head and they walked past a young couple selling old coins, some porcelain canisters, and, believe it or not, a pair of African American salt and pepper shakers. The ceramic couple were fat and happy, and their skin was actually painted black, not brown. These must have been from the '40s or '50s, and were about as racially insensitive as you could be in the twenty-first century.

"Dad!" Emily pointed at the figures. "Can you believe that?"

A sour look crossed the faces of the young sellers when they heard Emily's comment. "These are valuable historic pieces," the man said.

"How much are they?" Emily asked. "I'd like to buy them just so I can grind them into dust."

"Eighteen dollars for the pair," the female seller said. "You can do whatever you want with them."

Frank took Emily's elbow and urged her along. It quickly became apparent that there were three types of sellers presenting their wares. The polished sellers offering new, probably stolen, goods: sunglasses, spices, plants, hair products, even underwear. These people had established set-ups with large boxes of goods and just waited for customers to come to them.

Then there were the real flea market enthusiasts. They usually had rickety tables, sitting in lawn chairs in front of their cars with out-of-state plates. They were selling what they considered collectibles, much like the first couple with the salt shakers. This crowd sold old dolls, musical instruments, vintage signs, Depression glass, antique furniture and the like. Much to Frank and Emily's surprise, they saw three more sets of salt and pepper shakers shaped like Black people, plus a Black lantern boy that, offensive as it was to imagine, someone must have displayed once in their front yard.

The third type of sellers, according to Frank's classification system, were the blanket-dwellers. These folks were mostly younger, hippie-types who probably lived in their cars and traveled around, displaying their various wares on old tattered southwestern-style blankets, the type he and his ex bought in Mexico for ten bucks on a vacation pre-Emily. Some sat in weathered lawn chairs, some parked themselves on the ground or in their cars, doors open in case they needed to get out to make a sale.

"Dad, look at this." Emily headed around someone displaying vinyl records, Barbie dolls, VHS movies, and other crap on a queen-sized bedsheet. Emily walked to the car where an old school desk sat with a wine-bottle lamp on top.

Frank's mind wandered back to Christmas 1980, two months after he started dating the woman he later married, had a child with, and then divorced. Their relationship was new, not too serious yet, and he gave her two tickets to a Cars concert, assuming she'd take him. She gave him a homemade gift, a wine bottle crammed full of Christmas lights. He had no idea how she ever squeezed so many red and green and blue and yellow lights into the bottle, or how she got the cord through a small hole at the bottom. But it was unique, and he appreciated it, and her.

"Is this desk for sale?" Emily asked the seller, a well-muscled, bleached blonde woman.

"Everything is for sale," the woman said, her voice deep and gravelly. "I'd sell you these pants I'm wearing if you made me a good offer." The woman smiled to show she was joking, a good-natured soul, a friend. Someone you could trust. "That's twenty-eight dollars. Thirty-five if you want the lamp, too."

Frank lifted the lamp, pushing aside all thoughts of his ex. He ran his hands over the desktop, imagining the kids who must have sat at and sweated and slept on this very desk over the years. He lifted the lid and peered into the storage cubby underneath.

"What do you think?" Emily whispered.

Frank pushed and pulled a little, determining that the desk was solid. It was smallish, but Emily and Sharon's apartment was only 480 square feet, so smaller might be better.

"Will you take twenty-five?" he asked.

The seller was lighting up a cigarette and Frank could see the wheels turning as she exhaled out a large plume of smoke. "Gimme thirty and I'll throw in the lamp."

Emily looked at him, her eyes as bright and hopeful as his ex's had once been. As he took out his wallet, the seller said she'd keep the desk and lamp until they were ready to go back to their vehicle. "There's wagons up front you can rent for a dollar. But don't waste your money." She flexed her large biceps. "You two look strong. You can handle it."

Frank paid the thirty bucks and they moved on. At the end of the aisle, there was a food truck selling corn dogs. The odor of the hot grease tweaked Frank's appetite. He considered asking Emily if she'd like to get one with him, but pushed away the thought. Emily was in a vegetarian phase and the temporary pleasure of a hot corn dog wasn't worth her lecturing about the evils of animal fats and nitrates.

In the next row, an older couple sold furniture. The man, whose white hair put him somewhere in his seventies in Frank's mind, was wearing denim overalls. The woman, presumably his wife, wore a faded housedress, a scowl, and gray hair pulled back tight. Give him an old timer's farmer's hat, Frank thought, and they'd be Ma and Pa Kettle.

Most of the end tables, high-backed chairs, and armoires were antique, or so the tags claimed. Each was about a hundred bucks more than Frank would ever spend. Emily did find a dilapidated dresser in the back, though. "Come take a look," she said as she methodically pulled out each drawer. "I could sand it and paint it and it'd be good as new."

Frank inspected the piece. It was solid wood, with a reddish lacquer finish that was destroyed on top, probably from someone keeping a houseplant on it. Water and wood just don't get along. He ran a fingernail along the side and watched as the old lacquer came up. "How much is it?"

"The tag says $90, but I bet we can get it cheaper."

Frank smiled to himself, glad Emily had grasped the subtler aspects of flea market shopping. But he knew his daughter. As good and creative as Emily's intentions were, she'd never refinish this dresser. He could. And, if he painted it, the sanding wouldn't have to be perfect anyway.

Years ago, his ex came home from work one day with a beat-up bookcase. She found it in somebody's trash, but thought it would give them a place to store the baby's rapidly growing collection of Dr. Seuss books. Frank took the bookcase into the basement and spent a few evenings sanding it down to bare wood. He liked working with his hands, and also the peace and quiet in the basement. Sure enough, a reasonably nice piece of furniture appeared from underneath the blemished varnish. He didn't know what kind of wood it was, but thought he'd stop by Grossman's Hardware and pick up a light-colored stain. Then, the day after he told his ex he was done sanding, he went down to his fortress of solitude and saw the bookcase, freshly painted neon yellow, on top of some newspapers on the basement floor.

"Don't be ridiculous," she said. "The yellow matches the crib. And no kid wants to look at wood. They want bright colors. And, by the way, you're welcome."

Frank brought his attention back to the matter at hand. "We'll take 75, but that's as low as we'll go," Pa Kettle said. Even Frank's story about sending his only daughter off to her own apartment didn't soften them. He bought it anyway.

The next two rows had nothing but blanket-dwellers selling crap they must have picked out of whatever town dump they lived near. He thought about going back and making an offer to a guy who was selling a nice oriental-style rug, but the man was nuts if he thought it was worth $150. Perhaps if he offered $75.

"Cool! Dad, come look at this."

Emily had turned the corner. At the first seller's table in the next row, she held up a nice-looking acoustic guitar.

"I don't remember a guitar being on your list." Frank glanced at the seller, a red-haired block of a man with a ruddy complexion that probably didn't get along well with the sun.

Emily strummed the guitar. It was horribly out of tune, but it did have a nice sound, with great resonance. "Didn't you play guitar when you and Mom first met?"

Again he felt a quick, sharp pain in his chest. "I made a lot of noise and wouldn't necessarily call it 'playing.'"

Emily handed him the guitar. Frank admired the reddish sheen, much like the old dresser, but in better shape. The surface of the body of the guitar was faded and a little worn in places. A long scratch behind the unusual pick guard seemed to be the only flaw. This guitar had been played a lot. It needed some polish and to get out of the sun.

"Tracy Chapman played that guitar. You know who she is?"

The seller's voice was squeakier than Frank would have expected, based on the seller's size. "Sure," Emily beamed. "'Talkin' 'bout a Revolution'—I love that song."

Tracy Chapman's guitar my ass. Frank figured this guy must think they were country bumpkins. "How do you know this is Tracy Chapman's? Was, I mean." He figured the guitar had a better chance of being the beater he'd used to try to woo his ex than it had of being Tracy Chapman's.

"Look at the CD in the guitar case," the seller motioned to a battered green guitar case beside Emily.

She lifted the lid and took out a CD.

"On the back there, see? That's her with this guitar. I got it off her niece."

Emily squinted, then handed the CD to her father. Frank

also squinted. The photo was small, a tiny African American woman standing by a microphone, guitar in hand. But was it this guitar? Who could tell?

"It ain't easy to see, but if you look close you can see the pick guard's shaped like an M, just like this guitar. It's it, I swear." The guy held up his hand, as if he had just sworn to testify in a courtroom.

Frank pulled the CD closer, then held it further. It was impossible to tell whether the guy was bullshitting them. He handed the CD back to Emily to analyze. "How much you asking for it?"

"Two-fifty," the guy answered. "But, seeing as you two look like really nice folks? I tell you what. Give me two hundred and I'll let you steal it."

"I'll give you a hundred," Frank said. "Cash."

"A hundred fifty," the seller countered. "Cash."

They settled on one-thirty. Emily was giddy with her new treasure. Rather than leaving it with the guy while they finished their shopping, she insisted on putting it in its case and strapping it on her back like a Sherpa. They were about to move along when something caught Frank's eye. Next to a black trunk that looked like it might have come from a pirate ship was a toilet, plain white, complete with lid and tank. On top of the tank was an Elvis figurine, standing maybe six inches tall. It was the '70s Elvis, in a white jumpsuit and oversized, gaudy sunglasses.

The figurine was like a magnet, compelling Frank to look closer. As he picked it up and discovered it was plastic, not ceramic, he noticed the price tag on the toilet. $500! *Give me a break!* He blinked twice and looked again. And there it was, $500, plain as day. Frank turned and saw the red-haired seller putting Frank's money into his wallet while eyeing him with a smile.

Frank couldn't help himself. "Whose royal ass sat on this

crapper that makes you think you can ask 500 bucks for it?"

The seller grinned as he tucked his wallet into his back pocket. "That, my friend, is no ordinary crapper. And, I am impressed with your instinct. The King himself not only sat on that crapper. He shat in that crapper, and he died on that crapper."

What a bullshitter. Frank knew he should probably go pull the truck up and get Emily to help him haul their stuff to it. And yet, he stood.

"Are you trying to tell me that this is Elvis's toilet? Elvis Presley, King of Rock and Roll?"

"The one and only." The seller scratched his belly and moved closer to talk to Frank. "Everything I got here has a story to it. That's why I put the little Elvis doll on the top there. Just like Tracy Chapman's CD, it's verification of sorts."

"Verification?" Frank didn't try to hide his astonishment, not only because the guy knew such a long, five-syllable word, but because of his outlandish claim. "So, a plastic Elvis doll from a sweat shop in China is your validation that this was once Elvis's toilet?"

"Course not. That's more of a conversation starter. Plus, I really like the way Elvis looks in his Phoenix jump suit. Back in his Vegas days, when he was at his best. I love that song, 'Suspicious Minds,' don't you?"

Emily wandered back to rescue her father. "Come on, Dad. You're really interested in that toilet? That's just weird."

"Just give me a sec, Em. You go on, I'll find you in a minute."

He turned back to the seller who needlessly reorganized some fake roses in a vase sitting on what he would probably claim was Jackie O's bedside table.

"You really expect someone'll believe this is the toilet that Elvis died on?"

"I can't make nobody believe nothing. But I do have a letter of authentication."

Frank shook his head. Another five-syllable word.

"It's signed and dated by the contractor who took this toilet out of the Graceland mansion a few years back when the place was refurbished."

When the seller took a step forward, Frank could smell the stale scent of cigarettes and old coffee on his breath. The man picked up the Elvis figurine and touched it reverently with an index finger. "After Elvis died, money-hungry Priscilla turned Graceland into a clown show. She took anybody's money and let them in, then sold them all sorts of fake Elvis memorabilia on their way out. I hate to say it, but that's probably where this guy"—he made the Elvis figurine dance in the air—"came from."

Frank knew that what the seller was saying was true. He and his ex had stopped by Memphis on their honeymoon, a week of sun and fun and, most likely, Emily's conception, on Pedro Island. His ex begged him to stop by Graceland on their way home. He was young and stupid and in love, or so he thought, so they stopped. They did the tour, ate peanut butter and banana sandwiches, and bought Love Me Tender shampoo in the gift shop.

"Lisa Marie, Elvis's daughter, inherited Graceland when she turned twenty-one." *This guy's quite the talker*, Frank thought when the seller rattled on.

"She obviously inherited her father's smarts as well, 'cause the first thing she did was shut it down for a bit while the mansion was rehabbed for the tours that go on there today. She did it up right, very classy. Nowadays more'n a half-million people a year visit the place. Probably more popular than the White House."

Frank glanced away from the seller, saw Emily looking over someone's dozen or so leather purses, which undoubtedly fell off a truck somewhere, and returned his attention to the seller's story.

"I think she shut it down for two, three years, which must have pissed her mother off. This was before *Dallas* was a hit and all of a sudden everybody remembered who Priscilla was. Anyhow, I got connected to one of the contractors. The one who gutted the bathroom where Elvis OD'd. Being a smart man, he hung on to the toilet for a while. And now it's mine, and could be yours."

Frank glanced over at Emily, chatting away with the purse seller. She ran a hand through her hair, a gesture that reminded him of her mother. Hair lighter, a bit rounder after the birth of Emily, but still a nice figure. Nice enough to catch the attention of Tim Warren, a co-worker who Frank had shared beers and watched football with, back when he was too stupid to see what was going on.

He thought they were happy. They'd made it through the difficult years when Emily was a colicky baby, then the terrible twos. They'd managed through the miscarriages, and her shitty boss at the bookstore. They went to the Cape in the summer, to the movies once every month or two. Hell, even everything in the bedroom seemed better than good—exceptional—back then. To him, anyway.

He came home to an empty house almost five years ago. Emily was at play practice, and he noticed right away the picture of the old sea gull was gone, the one they'd bought in Falmouth that had been on the wall for over 10 years. So were her clothes, several antique clocks she'd picked up over the years, and the crock pot. What kind of woman takes the fucking crock pot?

The final blow came in the bathroom, of all places. Frank went in to check for her makeup case. It was more of a deluxe tackle box, he used to kid her. She had blush and foundation and lip gloss and eyeliners and God only knew what else in that thing. All of which cost them a small fortune, he sure knew that. But at the time, he thought it made her happy. What a fool.

The case was gone.

The note was in a little blue stationery envelope, tucked in the corner of the bathroom mirror. He opened it with shaking fingers, a stew of sadness and anger boiling in his belly, and read her last scrawled words. Predictable crap about how they had been too young, how the magic was gone. "I can't take it anymore. I need to find out who I really am." Just like one of those sappy country songs she used to make him listen to.

Frank tore the note lengthwise, then lengthwise again. Then he ripped the strips, one by one, until he had a small mountain of paper pieces, some still damp from his tears, in the sink. He dumped them right where they belonged, in the crapper, to be flushed away. Just like his marriage.

"You okay, buddy?"

The seller's squeaky voice rescued Frank from his maudlin memories. He looked at the guy, who seemed curious about where his customer's thoughts had taken him.

"You was gone there for a minute, pal. Thought maybe you was going to have a seizure or something."

"I'm fine." Frank reached over and depressed the flusher on the Elvis toilet tank. No surprise, nothing happened.

"Thanks," he said. "I appreciate your time." Frank Giardini shook the seller's hand, then moved to find his daughter.

As he approached, her new guitar on the ground carefully leaning against her leg, Emily turned her million-dollar smile on him. "Which do you like better? This one..." she showed him a black leather purse on her right shoulder. "Or this one?" She turned to show him a maroonish colored bag on her other shoulder.

He looked at his daughter, love flooding his heart.
"Whichever one you want. That's the one I like best."

MY BEST CLIENT

"A friend of mine, she cries at night, and calls me on the phone
She's waited long enough she says, and still he can't decide
Pretty soon she'll have to choose, and it tears her up inside"
– "Nick of Time" by Bonnie Raitt

Melinda put one hand on her client's chin and turned her head to the right. She closed her eyes, then opened them fast and wide, like an old-fashioned window shade flying up, hoping to figure out what the problem was. It worked. The eye shadow wasn't dark enough, and the blush wasn't right on her client's cheeks. It needed to be tapered more from the bridge of her nose to better accentuate her high cheek bones.

Taking a step back, Melinda squinted behind her large, plastic-framed glasses. She knew smaller frames were in style now. Her daughters, Deborah and Sharon, had poked fun of her glasses often enough, but these worked perfectly fine. And her husband Douglas would crap a Twinkie if she spent $150 on a newer, more stylish pair.

"Don't you worry one bit, Miss Polly. I'll have you fixed up in a jiff."

She chose a violet-blue from the Maybelline section of her extensive makeup kit. She knew from experience that ladies of Miss Polly's generation preferred Maybelline over the newer, flashier brands.

"Don't worry," she said, brushing in quick, light strokes above Miss Polly's eyes. Like an artist, she thought. "Now, where was I?"

Melinda turned her head right and left, closely observing her creation. She smiled, happy with the results of her work.

The violet-blue was the right choice.

"I was filling you in on last night's re-run episode of *Seinfeld*. That George, he just kills me. Last night, he and Jerry were somewhere, and when he thought nobody was looking, George picked a big chocolate dessert out of the trash and began eating it. Can you believe it? I think it was an eclair, but I'm not exactly sure what that is. It was hilarious. Least I thought so. Douglas looked at me like I was heading for the looney bin, but that's only 'cause he don't like Seinfeld." Melinda bent closer and lowered her voice. "Some of the characters are Jewish, you know."

Next, Melinda took a clean cloth and wiped Miss Polly's face outward from her nose. She blended in a little foundation and just a touch of the melon blush. "The funniest thing George ever said, at least in my opinion—Lord knows he says lots of funny things—but in one episode, I forget exactly which one, he said to Jerry, 'Never eat anything bigger than your head'. I think he was gnawing on this big piece of cheese. Yup, that was it. I don't know why, it just cracked me up. Douglas looked at me like I had a screw loose, again, and told me he'd like to eat my head. Like a praying mantis, that's what he said. Does that make any sense to you? Most times I think he's the crazy one, that's what I think. But he's always telling me I'm the stupid one. Dumb Melinda only went to cosmetology school while Mister Big Shot went to college."

Melinda lowered her voice again, tilting Miss Polly's face to the left to make sure the blush on her cheeks was exactly even. "Between you and me, he only went to Knoxville Community College, and though he says he graduated with honors, I've never once seen a diploma. Not once. And I've cleaned every square inch of that house a million and one times."

Melinda selected a tan eyeliner pencil and added just a teeny-tiny bit to the edge of her client's right eyebrow. "Well,

Miss Polly, I do declare you look stunning. Never better."
Melinda ran her fingers through Miss Polly's hair one more
time to puff it out just a little more. "You are not only my
best client, you absolutely are the belle of the ball."

Melinda took Miss Polly's hands in hers, closed her eyes,
and bowed her head.

"Dear Jesus, thank you for allowing me the chance to get
to know Miss Polly before she passed. Please welcome her
with open arms and a big smile. I ask this in your name,
Amen."

She packed her things, washed up in the bathroom, and
hit the lights on her way out, leaving Miss Polly to rest in
peace until her wake that evening.

Mr. Phillips worked on some important-looking papers at
the funeral home's front-office desk. The place was dead
silent, though Melinda didn't feel completely comfortable
with that description. But it was the first description she
thought of.

"Everything go okay?" Mr. Phillips, always dressed in the
same dark gray suit, took a yellow envelope from his desk
and held it out toward her.

"Just fine. I hope her family will be pleased."

"You do great work, and I get all the credit," he said with
what might loosely be considered a smirk.

Do undertakers ever smile, she wondered, *or were they
trained to hide any bit of happiness, especially in front of
grieving customers? Botox probably would do the trick. A
little injection in the corner of each side of the mouth.*

"Thank you." She accepted the envelope and tucked it
into her purse. Forty-five bucks. Cash.

Mr. Phillips rose and opened the door for her. "You'll be
here for Mr. Worthington on Thursday morning?"

"Yes, sir," she said, already thinking about the things she
needed to pick up at the grocery store on the way home.

o o o

Melinda made sloppy joes, one of Douglas's favorites. While Melinda gathered the dishes and stored the leftovers in the fridge, he finished his beer, going on and on about how the Democrats are crazy socialists out to ruin our society. Deborah, her youngest, sat quietly, her food only half eaten, in her black jeans and black tee shirt, printed with a logo for a band called 'Jane's Addiction' on the front.

What kind of a band would call themselves a horrible name like Jane's Addiction? Can you imagine anything pleasant sounding coming out of a bunch of, what do they call them, 'Goth' musicians, all in their black clothes and black hair and black lipstick? No wonder they're all so depressed all the time.

Everything was going just fine until Deborah, as usual, decided to open her smart mouth.

The landline wall phone rang. Douglas glanced at Deborah. "Get it, will you?"

"Why should I answer it?" Deborah said, her voice full of teenage defiance. "It's not gonna be for me."

Melinda never thought of herself as psychic, but she felt the energy in the room change. She knew her husband, so she knew she better intervene.

"Please do as your father asks and get the phone, Deborah."

"Why do you always take his side?" Deborah asked, not moving a muscle toward the phone. "It's two feet away from him, and I'm all the way on the other side of the table."

"I said answer the goddamned phone," Douglas growled.

Without uttering a word, Deborah flashed her father the middle finger. Douglas jumped to his feet, his five-foot-six body knocking into the table. The vase full of mums Melinda had picked that afternoon fell over and broke. Water and glass shards spread across the table, onto the floor.

Douglas's temper was like a hornet with a hangnail. He reached to grab Deborah. But, quick as a flash, she was up. Both of them were running around the kitchen table like Wile E. Coyote and the Road Runner.

Melinda grabbed Douglas by the shoulder, but he shoved her aside. The distraction at least gave Deborah an extra second. On her 16-year-old legs, she sprinted down the hall and out the front door.

Douglas, a lifelong smoker, never stood a chance. He slammed the front door, threw the deadbolt, and marched back into the kitchen. Melinda braced herself. Douglas wasn't a violent man—she'd never put up with that. But he did have a mean streak and an Old Testament way of thinking.

"Do not let that little bitch back in the house. That was the last time I'm putting up with her shit. Let her sleep out in the woods for a few days. It'll do her good."

"Douglas." Melinda's stomach grabbed when she saw his cold, dark eyes. "Doug, please. You don't mean that. She's just going through a phase."

"Yeah, a phase. Just like Charles Manson and the Son of Sam went through a *phase*. Phase my ass."

When he stepped on broken glass with his work boots, Melinda summoned up enough willpower to keep from asking him to please not do that. He grabbed his beer from the table and emptied it in three quick gulps.

"You spoil her," he snapped, crumpling the can between his hands and dropping it to the table. "You still baby her and take her side. She's not a toddler anymore, and it's well past time that she learned some goddamned respect." He moved to the fridge, broken glass in his wake. "Look what she did." He waved toward the wreckage in his path. "Just look at this fucking mess." He opened the refrigerator and extracted a fresh can. "You raised her. You can clean this shit up."

Without looking at her, he stormed into the living room and turned on the TV.

Melinda sighed, releasing tension she didn't realize she was holding. *All in all, that went better than it might have,* she thought. She surveyed the damage and decided to tackle the broken glass and water on the floor first.

Two hours later, the kitchen was all cleaned up and the table was set for the morning. Douglas snored in his recliner while Fox News droned in the background. Melinda unlocked the window in Deborah's bedroom so she could get in when she came home. Then she dialed her daughter Sharon's number.

"Hey, Mom."

Melinda sighed, a biological reaction to the sound of her firstborn's voice. How she missed her. Sure, birds have to leave the nest and all that. But oh, how she missed her. Sharon was away at college, studying science. She and Douglas were so proud of her, even if her hubby had a hard time showing it. He grew up in a household that was about as warm as an icebox. He just didn't know how to show what he really felt deep down.

"I called earlier, but nobody answered."

"Oh," Melinda said, deciding she shouldn't tell her daughter about the incident at dinner. "We were having a discussion at supper and couldn't pick up."

"What did Deb do?"

"She didn't." Melinda pulled her hair into a ponytail, then released it. "Well, she disrespected your father, and he got a little hot under the collar. You know how he gets."

"Yeah, I know. Is Deb okay?"

"She's fine, just fine. Everything is good here. Tell me about you. You had a quiz this week in math, right? How'd it go?"

"It was a midterm. I feel pretty good about it. Calculus is

tough, but Emily has a good head for it and is helping me figure it out."

Melinda heard a fridge door opening in the background, then the click of a can top. "Is that beer, or soda?"

"It's Diet Coke, Mom. Geez. Do you think I'm a lush?"

"Of course not. But mothers worry. That's our job. Where's Emily tonight?"

Sharon and her friend Emily moved out of the dorms into an apartment at the end of the summer. Douglas wasn't happy about it. He knew all about college kids and said he wouldn't pay for his daughter to party her life away. But Sharon was a good student, with a scholarship and a part-time job washing dishes at the dining hall, and she convinced Douglas that renting with Emily would be cheaper than staying in a dorm with a full dining plan. Melinda sighed, sad, knowing Sharon thought her father's first love was his wallet.

Emily was a sweet girl from Connecticut. When Douglas drove Melinda, Sharon, and a bunch of her belongings up to Fairfax in August, they met up with Emily and her dad, who, according to Douglas, had a goddamned *Gore Lieberman* sticker on his car—a Toyota, instead of an American car. Fortunately, Douglas didn't make a stink. At least not until later on the drive home.

They all worked together to move the stuff into the apartment. The place wasn't big, but there weren't rats or crackheads hanging about, either. The men carried the beds and mattresses and dressers inside, while Melinda chatted with the girls and put what little they had away in the kitchen and Sharon's bedroom. When Melinda saw Emily's guitar, she asked her to play something, but Emily said she was just learning. With a little cajoling, though, she showed off her guitar, which had a beautiful amber polish and an unusual M-shaped pick guard under the sound hole. Emily strummed a little of the John Lennon song "Imagine" before Douglas not-so-subtly said it was time they hit the road.

A few weeks later, Sharon reported to her mother that the roommates got along great, and no, Emily didn't invite boys over, never mind strange ones. And yes, they'd received the big batch of chocolate chip cookies she'd sent, and yes, they were delicious.

Melinda missed her terribly.

"I know it's early," she said. "But have you given any thought to Thanksgiving? Emily is more than welcome to come. You could stay as long as y'all like. Does she bake? We could make pies—pumpkin, pecan, and apple—you know how your father lives for apple pie."

"Come on, Mom," Sharon interrupted. "First, that's like a month away. And second, you know that's not a good idea." Sharon exhaled loudly. "Look, Emily's my friend. Do you think I want to expose her to Dad's lectures on how Al Gore is a fascist, or how God hates gay people, or how the Bible tells us that women are subservient to men and don't belong in positions of power?"

"Now, stop. He's not that bad," Melinda said. "Just a little old-fashioned and opinionated, that's all. Once he's got a belly full of turkey and pie and the football game's on, you won't hear a word out of him."

"You and I both know better than that," Sharon said. "For now, let's just say I'll think about it and get back to you."

Then Melinda filled her daughter in on the happenings around town. How the Jones's oldest boy had joined the Army, and a new Krispy Kreme was going in down on South Street, and why in the world would one little town need more than one Krispy Kreme? "Love you, sweetie," she said before hanging up, then stood silent and alone in the kitchen for a long minute.

Melinda was thrilled that Sharon was so smart and was out making her way in the world. *She's got more guts in one finger than I've got in my whole body*, Melinda thought. But Lord, how she missed her.

o o o

Melinda turned on the overhead light switch. "There," she said. "Much better." She plopped her makeup case on the prep table and smiled at her client. "Good morning, Mr. Worthington. Do you mind if I call you Mr. Bob? Worthington is a big, ritzy kind of name. But since we're going to work together, I'm Melinda and I'll just call you Mr. Bob."

Mr. Bob was mostly bald, with what her teacher, Miss Lilian back in cosmetology school, used to refer to as a toilet seat, meaning he still had hair in the back and sides, fortunately kept short. She had no idea how to work with those men who decided to keep what little hair they had long.

She pulled on a few wispy strands. "I'm thinking you're a number five, Mr. Bob. I'll start with a five clipper and if need be, we'll move to a four."

Melinda trimmed her client's hair, then used a dust vac to clean up the loose hairs. She informed Mr. Bob that there was a frost warning for the following day, and that she still had some tomatoes left in her garden to pick. The beets would probably be okay for another few weeks. Halloween was coming, and she bought a big bag of Butterfingers from Walmart, but she kept them from her husband and her daughter or else they'd be long gone before a single trick-or-treater showed up at their door.

Melinda used her electric razor to give Mr. Bob a nice shave. She found it a little creepy how men's beards continued to grow after they died. She matched the correct foundation to his skin and began the process of bringing Mr. Bob back to life, as best she could. Only Jesus could really bring him back to life, of course. She hoped he'd wait until she was done if that was the plan, thank you very much.

"I took my youngest, Deborah, out for driving time last night. I needed to run over to the Dollar General for some shampoo and cotton swabs and figured she could use the practice. She's got her permit, and she isn't a bad driver, but I worry about her." Melinda considered her color choices before picking a concealer to help Mr. Bob with those dark bags under his eyes.

"Do you have kids back home? I imagine yours are all grown and gone by now. Hopefully not too far. I think families need to stick together, don't you? My youngest, Deborah—the one I went driving with last night—she's a handful. My Douglas..."

Melinda paused while working around Mr. Bob's eyes. "He don't like it when I call him Douglas, insists I call him Doug. Apparently Douglas was the name of some famous slave, and he doesn't want anybody associating him with the other guy, which I think is silly. I like the name Douglas. It's got a grown-up, professional sound to it, don't you think? Doug sounds like the guy you call to pump out your septic tank."

Melinda studied her client's face. She should trim those ear hairs. Why do old men have to grow ugly hairs in and on their ears? What were you thinking with that one, God?

"First, let's work on your complexion a little bit. Just a touch, I promise."

The families of men didn't like to see them all covered in makeup. What they didn't realize is how gray the skin can turn after one's soul has gone to heaven, or the other place. How cheeks can sag, and little wrinkles can turn deep and hard to cover up. Her job, as she saw it, was to bring them back as best she could. Sleeping like angels, she liked to think.

"My Douglas forgets what it's like to be young. He thinks Deborah is full of the devil, but I know she's not. She's just trying to figure out who she is. It's sorta like trying on makeup. First you try bright colors, and figure out they aren't right for you. Then you try dark colors, and so on until you work out what fits you best."

She reached over and selected a different brush from her kit. "Lord knows, that girl can be trying. Every day I pray for patience. Jesus help me."

As Melinda worked, she remembered some of the crazy things she and Douglas had done in their younger days. Toilet-papering the principal's house on Halloween night. Drag racing in the middle of the night out on Route 45 with his buddies. Convincing her to go skinny-dipping after a night of dancing and too many beers at the Wagon Wheel. Where did that Douglas go? Why had he grown so hard?

"It's about change, really, if you think about it. Douglas wants things just so, and the truth is, things never stay just so. Kids grow up and need to find their own place in the world. They don't stay six or seven, always doing your bidding and trying to please you. I know, though. Maybe it's a mother thing. I mean no offense to you, Mr. Bob. I'm sure you were a good daddy and your kids all loved you. I sure hope so, at least."

Melinda brushed a little foundation under Mr. Bob's chin and neck. Once Mr. Phillips dressed him in his suit, the rest wouldn't show.

"Well, Mr. Bob, you do look better'n a shiny new penny. You've been my best client. Now, let me get my scissors and touch up those brows."

Melinda finished her work, made sure the area was clean and all her makeup supplies were stowed back where they belonged. She took Mr. Worthington's hand in hers, closed her eyes, and bowed her head.

"Dear Jesus. Thank you for allowing me to assist Mr. Bob here on his journey home to you. Please comfort his family, and welcome Mr. Bob so he feels right at home. I ask these things in your name. Amen."

Melinda shut off the lights and closed the door to the back room. She thought the correct word was mortuary, that's what Sharon said, but Mr. Phillips always referred to it just as the "back room." As she entered the office, she saw Mr. Phillips busily typing on his computer. "Just a second," he said.

She studied a vase of fresh yellow roses on the table near his desk. Did yellow really make people grieve easier? Or is it more a color of convenience? Obviously red is out for a funeral, and white is nice, but maybe too bland. *When my time comes,* she thought, *I want colors. Red, blue, purple, and orange. I want 'em all.*

"Everything go okay, Melinda?"

"Why yes. Mr. Bob seemed to have a little more discoloration on one side of his face, but I think I covered it nicely. His family won't even notice."

"You do fine work." Mr. Phillips stood, reaching into his jacket and producing her pay envelope. "Say, is that a new hairstyle?"

"No." Melinda unconsciously patted her hair. "I just put it up in a barrette. Something different is all."

"Well, it takes 10 years off you."

"Oh, listen to you, all butter and cream. I'll pretend you're being honest and say thank you." She accepted the envelope and tucked it in her purse. "Good luck with the service today."

"Everything should go fine. The Worthingtons are fine people, and I expect we'll be very busy."

She stepped outside and breathed in the fresh air. Her hand combed through her hair, wondering if maybe it was time for a change, maybe go a little lighter on the color.

o o o

Melinda and Douglas watched football in the living room. She glanced at him and decided to bring up the text. She made macaroni and cheese for dinner, the kitchen and dishes were done, and Deborah was holed away in her room doing homework. Or more likely, doing whatever she constantly did with her phone. Melinda knew to wait until a commercial came on, although she didn't even understand why there was a game on. She thought football was on Sundays after church, then Monday night. But this was Thursday night. Who could keep it straight?

Eventually, a car commercial came on and she turned to Douglas. "I got an interesting text from Sharon today."

"Yeah?" Douglas's eyes remained glued to the set.

"She said her classes were all going well, and she asked if we'd be interested in going to her and Emily's for Thanksgiving this year."

He turned towards her. "What'd you say?"

"I told her that I'd talk it over with you. But Doug, I think it's a good idea. Something different. She and Emily can show..."

"In that tiny apartment?" He glanced back at the TV, where a beer commercial was on. "We have a big, comfy house. And you always cook a great bird. Tell her to come here."

The game came back on, but she didn't want to give up. "Sharon's proud of her new apartment, and she wants to show us how grown up she is. I think we should go. It's not that far. I can make pies and help her with the turkey."

"And what the hell am I supposed to do in the meantime?"

"Doug, it's our daughter. She's reaching out to us. You can walk around Fairfax, or go find a store for beer, or go to the movies. Or, you could sit and chat with our daughter and her roommate and her family. That would be nice."

"What?" he barked. "Lieberman's lapdog's gonna be there. Now I'm definitely out."

Douglas snatched the clicker from the arm of his recliner and turned the TV volume up. The conversation was over. Melinda jumped to her feet and stepped in front of him, blocking his view.

"I miss my daughter and I want to see her. I don't ask for much, Douglas, but I'm asking for this."

She saw his face twitch when she called him Douglas, but he didn't say anything.

"Please, can't you be a little flexible on this? It will make Sharon happy. It will make me happy."

"We'll see," he grunted. "Now move your fat ass? You make a better door than a window."

Melinda went to the kitchen. She opened the refrigerator and got a beer for her husband. She knew how to play the game.

o o o

Children were always the hardest clients. She knew in her heart that the good Lord had a master plan she couldn't even pretend to understand. Somehow, somewhere, this was all His will. But a 15-year-old girl taking her own life? That just didn't make sense.

The paper reported it was an undiagnosed heart condition, and maybe there was some truth to that. But everybody in town knew the girl swallowed a bottle of pills and washed them down with her daddy's Wild Turkey. The high school was abuzz with the gruesome details. And the principal went on TV to say they brought in some sort of grief therapist to meet with the kids who needed to talk.

And here was Gabrielle Toltsman, peaceful and quiet, almost as if she were taking a nap.

"Oh Miss Gabby, I'm so sorry for all your suffering." Melinda took out a soft brush and began gently running it through her client's thick blonde hair. "You're up in heaven now, so I know your problems are over. But I can't imagine the pain your family's in."

A tear formed in Melinda's eye as she pulled the girl's hair back to trim the split ends. She wiped it quickly with her sleeve, then checked to see that the girl's hair was even.

She worked in silence, uncertain what to say to this tortured girl. Did Sharon or Deborah ever feel that way, so bad they had no other choice? She hoped and prayed not. So tragic. So damn tragic.

"I've got two girls of my own. Both a little older than you. Deborah said she heard who you were, but didn't really know you. She said you were good at singing and had a part in last year's musical."

The girl's face was so young, with only a little acne. Melinda knew just how to take care of that.

"My Sharon is in college up in Fairfax. She and her friend Emily just got their own apartment."

Melinda caught herself. Was it unkind to talk about things this poor girl would never have? A driver's license. Making out after senior prom. College, an apartment, a house and... life?

The family provided earrings for their daughter, who had four piercings. The top pair were pearl studs, which she doubted Gabby ever actually wore. Way too fancy and old-fashioned for a 15-year-old. The other pair were definitely hers, little silver cats dangling on pewter wires.

Melinda carefully applied an inexpensive strawberry lip gloss, also supplied by the Toltsmans, and remembered buying the same brand at CVS for Sharon when she was about Miss Gabby's age. This got her to thinking about Sharon and Thanksgiving.

Douglas hadn't even hinted he'd be willing to travel to Sharon's. In fact, he even brought home a 16-pound Butterball. He acted like it was a gift for her, but she knew damn well everyone at the plant got one for Thanksgiving. She knew the plant did it so they could cheap out of giving employees actual raises.

She thought about waking Deborah at the crack of dawn on Thanksgiving Day and sneaking out. They could drive up to Sharon's, have a wonderful day, and Douglas could just sit home and stew in his own juices.

But, in her heart, she knew that just wasn't right.

"Miss Gabby, you are precious, and most definitely my best client."

Melinda put her makeup away and vacuumed Gabby's hair from the floor and around her bedding. When she was finished, she took the young girl's hand in hers, closed her eyes, and bowed her head.

"Dear Lord, please greet Miss Gabby with extra love when she gets there. She's had a hard time down here on earth, and she desperately needs your love. Please also shine some extra love on her family. I'm sure they're having a terrible time of it. Lastly, please soften up my Douglas's heart and help him see how precious his own daughter is. Help him open his eyes before it's too late. I ask you this through the grace of your son, Jesus Christ. Amen."

o o o

Not surprisingly, Douglas didn't notice she hadn't taken the turkey out of the freezer to thaw and brine. Melinda hadn't bought five rolls of stuffing bread, or cranberry sauce, or green beans and a can of fried onions to make the casserole Douglas's mother used to make, the one he loved so much. Melinda made pies the day before Thanksgiving, just like she always did. That probably squelched any suspicions Douglas might have had about Turkey Day, as he liked to call it.

She set her alarm for six o'clock, but didn't need it. She woke up a little after five and slipped into Deborah's room. Deborah would want time to get ready. Melinda went downstairs and put the pies and a gallon of apple cider into the cooler, which she placed next to the door.

Returning to their bedroom, she went over to Doug's side of the bed. She took a deep breath and mentally asked Jesus to give her the right words. Douglas was turned away from her, balled up in a fetal position on his side and snoring through his open mouth.

"Doug," she put a hand on his shoulder and gave him a little shake. "Doug, hon, it's time to get up."

"What?" he croaked. "Hunh? What's the matter?"

"Nothing's the matter, sweetie. It's time to get up if we want to get to Sharon's on time." Melinda stepped away, moving toward the bathroom.

"What the hell you talking about?" Douglas, fully awake now, glared at her. "We're not going anywhere."

She glared right back. "*We* might not be going, but *I* am. You can stay home if you like. I'll leave you an apple pie, and that 16-pound turkey's in the freezer if you want to cook it."

"What the hell has gotten into you?" Douglas threw the comforter off and got out of bed. "I told you, we're not driving to goddamned Fairfax. We're having Thanksgiving here."

Melinda plowed forward. "Get yourself dressed. I'll make

you an egg sandwich for the road." She went into the bathroom to brush her teeth and do her makeup for the day.

When Melinda went downstairs, Deborah sat slumped at the kitchen table, still half asleep.

"Where's your father?"

"Dunno." Deborah hadn't bothered to brush her hair from the look of her.

Melinda, who Douglas once said could have been a short-order cook, whipped up three egg sandwiches on English muffins, wrapped them in tinfoil, and cleaned up the mess. There was still no sign of Douglas.

"Deborah, get your coat on. Bring a hat in case it's colder than we think."

As Melinda donned her navy-blue wool coat, Douglas stomped down the stairs. He stopped on the last step, making him appear six inches taller, looking hard at her. She returned his look and began to button her coat.

"Melinda, are you really driving all the way to Fairfax, and back home, by yourself? Are you really planning on leaving me here? Are you really dead set on ruining Thanksgiving?"

"Are you?" She turned back into the kitchen. "C'mon, Deborah. Time to go."

With the egg sandwiches in her purse and the cooler with pies and cider stowed in the trunk, she started her car and let it idle for a second. Deborah flopped into the passenger seat and struggled to get the seat belt fastened.

"Honey, why don't you get in the back. Your father is going to want to sit up front."

Deborah did as asked, and they both sat in silence for a minute.

"He's not coming, Mom."

"Give it another minute, hun."

One minute passed. Then two. Melinda closed her eyes,

uncertain what to do. After five minutes, she told Deborah to come on up to the front seat.

"We really gonna do this?" her daughter asked.

"Yes."

Deborah grinned. She looked happier than Melinda had seen in years. "Let's go, girlfriend."

Melinda backed out of the driveway onto the street, then turned north toward downtown and the highway. She paused, half-hoping Douglas would join them, half-hoping he wouldn't. *Even if he did come, he'd be cranky all day. He'd make her pay, that's for sure. Everyone else, too.* All she wanted was to spend time with her daughters. Not to fight or argue or talk politics or religion or anything unpleasant. Just one day of peace.

She took her foot off the brake and took a deep breath. Then she hit the gas.

THE BLUES ARE FALLING

"I'm still alive, but I'm barely breathing
Just prayin' to a God that I don't believe in
'Cause I got time while she's got freedom
'Cause when a heart breaks, no it don't break even"
– "Breakeven" by The Script

Tony Carter stood, guts all knotted up, trying to gather his courage. His armpits were raw and chafed from the crutches and his stump was starting to complain. He stood in front of the door to Dr. Elaine Schneider's office for 10 minutes or so. A dark gray door in a light gray hallway with medium gray linoleum. If you're looking for color and style, avoid the US Military. Several people in civilian dress passed by, glancing quickly at him, avoiding eye contact. Don't provoke the crazy guy visiting the shrink.

Quit stalling. Time to shit or get off the pot, as his father used to say. Tony stepped forward and knocked before he could change his mind.

"Come in."

At a glance, he took in the big houseplant in the corner of the office; the heavy maroon curtains; the picture of Dr. Schneider with George W. Bush on the wall; the artificial lavender scent; and the perfect placement of various items on the doctor's desk. Without getting up, she smiled and said, "Afternoon, PFC Carter. Please come in and take a seat."

Fortunately, the two chairs in front of the desk had arms. He dropped into the chair to the left and placed his crutches on the ground next to him.

"How's the leg healing up?"

Tony's first inclination was to answer something snappy. *I'm not sure—most of it is still in Afghanistan.* "Good," he said instead. Be brief and don't be a smartass. The sooner this was over, the better.

"How long were you outside before knocking?" she asked.

"Not long."

"That's good. I once had a navy officer stand out there for over two hours before he decided to bail. Seeking help isn't easy, Tony. Do you mind if I call you Tony? Outside these doors we have to be official, but in here I like to be respectful, but informal. One less barrier."

Tony stared at the fiftyish woman, with her short-cropped silver hair, her big shoulders and farmer's arms, which contrasted so dramatically with her little, baby-sized teeth and Lisa Simpson voice.

"Tony's fine."

"Great." She leaned forward and clasped her hands on the yellow legal pad on her desk. "Mind if I ask why you are here today, Tony? I'm curious because the previous times I've tried to talk to you, I got the sense you weren't interested."

That's because he wasn't. He'd pretty much rather tie his dick in a knot than talk to a shrink. There wasn't nothing wrong with his head. It's the missing leg that's the problem here. But in a moment of weakness, he'd told Nurse Sharon he'd talk to Schneider. Although he wasn't good for much else, he was a man of his word.

"One of the nurses talked me into it. She thinks I'm depressed."

"Do you think you're depressed?"

No, he wanted to say. *Who would be depressed about having their leg blown off, still pissing blood after two months from the shrapnel swimming around in his innards and soon to be ejected from the US Military without a job or a family or anywhere to go? What kind of whack-a-doodle would be depressed about that?*

Why had he listened to Nurse Sharon? Because she was a sliver of sunshine in his otherwise bleak days. She worked the morning shift and had a captivating smile and a bit of southern twang that reminded Tony of the girls back home. She had thick blonde hair, eyes soft and blue as a comfortable old pair of jeans, and a curvy figure that left him thinking about her long after she'd moved on to her other patients. When she said, "Mornin', Tony," her voice sweet as honey, he wanted nothing more than to ask her to take them both far away from there. A cozy little cabin high in the mountains by a lake, the smell of dusty pine paneling and newly split wood and fresh-caught trout frying in a cast-iron skillet. Then he remembered. How the hell is a one-legged cripple gonna get to a cabin deep in the woods?

Last Monday, Nurse Sharon caught him at a bad moment. His stump hurt something fierce, and he was ruminating about his screwed-up life. She caught him feeling sorry for himself. When she held his hands and talked softly to him, those eyes drilling holes right through him, it was a moment of weakness, not a chronic condition.

"No more'n anybody who just got their leg chopped off."

The doctor let the silence hang thick in the air for a beat before saying, "I assure you that there have been many people much worse off than you who have successfully rebuilt their lives, and I'd like you to hold on to that thought. But, I don't want to get too far ahead of ourselves. Why don't you tell me a little about why you joined the service?"

Although it seemed like an eternity, it was only about a year and a half ago that Tony made the decision to join up. He was in his second year at Eastern Kentucky University, a physics major. Science had always been his favorite subject in school, and Mr. Marshall, his high school chemistry teacher, encouraged him to pursue it.

Tony had no parents to help guide him. So, while he made it to college, he felt adrift while there. Balancing acid-base reactions in chemistry class or calculating how far a ball of a certain mass hit with a certain force at a certain angle would travel in his physics lab just didn't seem to matter much. Even though Eastern was a state university and a bargain compared to a lot of schools, he took out huge loans to attend. Food and books and nights out drinking with his new friends were expensive. And it seemed that when he got into a carrel in the library to study with his astronomically priced calculus textbook, he couldn't help but wonder if it was worth it.

During his second year, he went to a kegger with a friend. He met a psych major named Cheyenne. She gave him a little white capsule she said was X. After taking it with a few more beers, he felt certain Cheyenne was the most beautiful and smartest person he'd ever met. The song "Torn" by Natalie Imbruglia was playing on the stereo, they were dancing and making out and he had no doubt he'd finally met his soul mate. That was until she left the party on the arm of a basketball player named Cedric. Sometime after that, Tony went into an empty bedroom, borrowed a blanket from off the bed, and crawled out the window and down the fire escape. He wandered back to campus and curled up under his favorite tree, a big old beech outside the library, and fell asleep.

"Left... Left... Left, right, left..." A lone voice called into the morning stillness, answered by a methodical, *thump, thump, thump* of boots on the ground. Tony sat up, rubbing the sleep from his eyes, and watched as about a dozen ROTC grunts marched across the quad toward the athletic fields. Each one in step with the other, feet firmly planted, no questions about where they were going or when they would get there.

The service never appealed to Tony. But, in that moment, on that crisp spring morning, as the first rays of daylight illuminated and wakened the sleeping campus, signing up called to him. Organization. Discipline. Dedication. Purpose. Drive. Preparedness. Action.

Four weeks later, Tony parked his rusty Corolla, its trunk full with all he owned, behind the garage of his friend Marty's parents' house. He hopped a Greyhound bus to Parris Island, in South Carolina's flatlands. For the next three months, new recruit Carter learned to march in his sleep, yell "Yes Sir" and "Aye Sir" at the top of his lungs even when he didn't have any breath, and to consume as many as 3,000 calories of food in under five minutes. He ran, he lifted, he swam, he breathed tear gas, and he learned martial arts. He kept to himself and others seemed okay with that. He walked out of Parris Island 12 pounds lighter, cured of his occasional insomnia, a United States Marine.

"No particular reason. College was expensive, and I wasn't enjoying it all that much, so I decided to give the service a try."

The doctor stared at him, probably trying to read him. Tony did his best to make his face expressionless.

"And how about moving forward? Do you have any plans for where you would like to go from here? Once you are recovered, of course."

"No. I have no idea," he said.

"Do you have family? I checked your records, and you don't seem to have had any visitors."

In his mind, Tony saw the photo of his parents standing by Cumberland Lake in the late 1980s. They were both tan and fit and so damn young—younger even than he was now. They held hands, his mom smoking a cigarette and rockin' a yellow bikini, his dad with a can of Bud in his other hand. The photo was framed and hung on the wall of pictures his mom carefully arranged. But about six months after Gloria, his stepmother, moved in, the photos all disappeared. First the ones of Mom, followed by Tony's aunts, his grandparents, then the rest. She started changing out the furniture, buying new drapes, installed new carpet in the bedrooms. She even tossed all of his mom's old albums—Cat Stevens, Jackson Browne, the Boss—Bruce Springsteen. Erasing all evidence of the family they used to be.

One afternoon, he and his dad headed to the hardware store. Tony worked up the courage to complain to his father about it. He remembered his dad looking at him and saying, "We'll always miss your mom, Tony. But, you know, she'll always live in our hearts." Returning his gaze to the road, he added, "As for Gloria, every bird wants to make the nest their own." And that was the end of that.

"No. No family." He paused, knowing she was looking for more from him.

He closed his eyes, another memory flashing across the screen in his mind. Gloria was hogging the TV, making them watch an old movie called *Ghost*, which made Tony long for his mother. He went to bed, thinking his dad and he should have a code word, in case one of them died and came back, so they could say it and recognize each other. They'd have proof positive that people came back again.

But he never decided on a good word. Cody, the name of his dad's first dog? Or Cynthia, his mother's first name? Saturn, his favorite planet? But anyone might say those words in the future, so it had to be something obscure, personal to them. Octaplatopus? Einsteinium? Nebulonica? Eventually, he fell asleep, and never brought it up with his father. Now, he wished he had.

"My folks died when I was young. I got a stepmom, but I

ain't talked to her in years."

"You've had a lot of loss for such a young man. Do you mind if I ask what happened to your parents?"

Here we go, Tony thought. Dissecting his past so she can write some psychobabble in her report on him that makes her feel like she's important. Got to justify this plush office and her generous government salary. Not today, lady.

"Ma died in a car wreck when I was six. Dad had a heart attack when I was 17. Been on my own since then."

"That had to have been very hard, Tony. I know talking about these things can be difficult, and I appreciate your openness. Loss and trauma can leave lifelong scars, but at the same time..."

Tony stopped listening. This wasn't going to help. He needed to heal up and get better at walking with his new prosthetic leg. He needed a pain pill or two to stop his stump from hurting so much. Then he'd figure out the next step. The Marines should help foot the bill for training or maybe college, but he couldn't really think about that stuff now. Getting through each day, each hour, was already too much to handle. The rest would just have to work itself out.

The doctor finished yakking and was looking at him for a response.

"Sorry," he said. "I was thinking about something else there for a second."

"What were you thinking about?"

"Nothing." He moved his hands to the arms of his chair, eager to get out of there.

"You just told me you were thinking about something else. Please, indulge me." She picked up her silver pen and drew a small circle on her yellow pad.

Tony decided to give her what she wanted. Maybe then he could leave and get back to his room. He'd get a Percocet, put in his earbuds and listen to some music. Drown out the negative thoughts forever ricocheting around in his skull.

"I was thinking about this guy, Becker, his name was. I met him in basic. He was a really good guy. From Texas, with a wife and twin babies back home. One day when we was over there, in a little village outside Diyala. We was playin' soccer with some village kids. Just kickin' a ball around, giving them candy and clean water and all, building trust and letting the locals know we were there to help. At least, in theory." Tony paused. "A village woman came up to him. Becker probably thought she was going to say thanks, or maybe ask for some extra candy bars, but instead she must have been wired. She hugged him, and as soon as she did I knew something weren't right. Women over there barely even leave their house, never mind approaching a Marine. I thought of pulling my gun, of shouting to Becker. But, before either me or Kramer could even twitch, the bitch blew them both to smithereens. Right there in the street in front of all those kids."

Tony closed his eyes, sorry he'd conjured the memory. "Me and Kramer hit the deck, then stupidly tried to see if we could save Becker. But he'd been vaporized. Specks of him were on the brick and the windows and probably on the kids. We hunted for his dog tags, but all we found was one of his boots and a clump of melted change he must have had in his pocket."

"And why do you think your mind went there while I was talking to you?"

Tony leaned over, grabbing his crutches with his left hand, pushing himself up with his right. "Because there's no point," he said. "None of it matters. There is no fucking point."

o o o

Tony considered putting on his prosthesis, but instead opted to just one-leg it to the bathroom with his crutch. He brushed his teeth and ran wet fingers through his hair, which needed a cut soon. He'd shaved just two or three days ago, so he probably wasn't looking too grubby. At least that's what he told himself.

Back in bed, he picked up the tattered copy of *The Shining* he'd found in the cupboard full of abandoned books by the nurse's station. The story was good, this freakish little kid who could see spirits and evil shit, stuck in a haunted old hotel in Colorado. But Tony found it difficult to focus. He'd get through a paragraph, or maybe even a page, then his mind would wander. He'd be back in boot camp, or playing foosball with his buddy Gerry at the dorm. Watching Becker getting atomized. Back sitting on edge next to McNemer in the supply truck, a Hummer in front of them scouting for hadjis, then hearing the whistle right before the RPG blew their truck in half. Feeling a twitch of pain in a foot that didn't exist anymore.

He heard a shuffle at the door, put the book down, and looked up. Nurse Sharon came in, smiling. Her hair was pulled back with a sparkly blue clamp kind of thing.

"Mornin', Tony. How y'all feeling today?"

"I'm hanging in there." He tried to sound upbeat. "Are those new earrings? Don't think I've seen them before."

Sharon's hand went up to touch her ear. "You like them? My sister gave them to me for Christmas year before last, and I always thought they were a little too flashy."

"Naw, they're nice. The blue stone in the middle matches your eyes."

"Well, you're too kind." Nurse Sharon put the blood pressure cuff around his left arm, then took his wrist in her hand to check his pulse. Her touch had an immediate effect on Tony's mood. Like stirring sugar into a bitter glass of iced lemonade.

"How's the pain today?"

"Maybe a six, or six point five outta ten."

"Mind if I take a look?"

Nurse Sharon pulled away his bedcovers to expose him in his boxers, the left leg bandaged about four inches below his knee, an angry gash still healing on his thigh. She unwrapped and examined his wound.

"You're healing up nicely, Tony. Good job. How's the PT work comin' along?"

It's miserable, he wanted to say. I hate every minute of it. "Slow but sure, I suppose."

He barely felt her touch as she re-bandaged his stump. Quite honestly, he didn't know how she could do it. He certainly wasn't used to the sight of the wound and the negative space of his missing appendage.

"You up to walking down to the cafeteria for breakfast?"

"You gonna join me? If you hold your nose, the eggs are almost edible."

"I'd love to." She gave him a flirtatious smile. "I really would. But I had my breakfast an hour and a half ago, and I've got a dozen other patients to tend to."

"You're breaking my heart, Nurse Sharon."

She made some notes on his chart, then leaned over close enough that he saw flecks of violet in her irises and smelled the vanilla in her perfume. "You be good, and I just might have a surprise for you after my shift's done."

She touched his cheek, light as a feather, the tenderness in her fingertips almost too much to bear. Then she left, and Tony felt the dull blade of false hope pressing at his innards. All the nurses were nice, but he felt something more around Sharon. At least, he thought he felt something. But it had to be his imagination, or maybe the Percocet. How could Sharon, or anyone, be attracted to someone so disfigured? So broken?

○ ○ ○

"What's the first lesson I told you to memorize, Carter?" The voice, more a growl than a command, was firm and manly and government-grade USA military. "Get up, Carter. Dig down inside you and find the strength to get up. That's the most important thing you'll learn here."

Tony lay sprawled on the hard blue mat in the physical therapy room. Elbow hurting, shirt drenched in sweat, his stump felt like someone was holding a welding torch to it. He tasted copper in his mouth from fresh blood, no doubt a result of his recent tumble. Or perhaps the previous few.

"You've done good today, Carter. Real good. Now, dig a little deeper, get your ass up so you can head back to your room for a shower." Deon's voice went up a decibel. "C'mon, Carter. No thinking, just do it."

Tony wanted to curl up and cry. In part, because he'd just fallen down again, like a goddamned toddler, but also because it was all just too much to take. Tony knew it was hopeless. Every time he tried to walk without crutches, his body betrayed him and gravity stomped him. The fake leg was like a frayed extension cord—you just couldn't trust it. The constant falling and the endless aches and pains and the fact he was a crippled 22-year-old with no future weighed like a sack of bricks on his back. And no pep talks or positive affirmations from Deon the PT would help.

Two strong hands grabbed him on either side of his rib cage and lifted him up about a foot. "Hands front, Carter. Push-up formation. Now."

He did as he was instructed. He seriously doubted his weary arms could manage his body weight. And yet, they did.

"Push to your knees, now up. C'mon, soldier, you can do this."

Tony wobbled as he tried to use his somewhat good right

239

leg to push his body back into a standing position. The prosthetic foot was too far back. He wanted to move it forward, he tried to move it forward, but instead he felt his equilibrium giving way like a badly stacked house of cards. He pitched frontward, throwing out his arms to cushion the fall.

An arm with muscles strong as a steel girder held his chest up, stabilizing him until he could get both feet back under him.

"Steady now." Deon spoke like a dad teaching his child to ride a bike. "Can you make it to your crutches, or you need me to fetch them for you?"

Tony turned to look at Deon, the physical therapist tasked with motivating him to walk again. Deon's skin was dark, almost the shade of black coffee. He was maybe five foot four, and had to be about 200 pounds, all of it muscle. With his shaved head and falcon-like eyes, he was an intimidating individual. He didn't talk much about himself, preferring to teach lessons like "the most important thing is to get up," and his other favorite, "Pain is just a state of mind. You control it. It doesn't control you."

After taking a deep breath, Tony pivoted on his prosthesis and turned to the wall where his crutches leaned. He bit down on the pain, squared himself, and then stepped forward with his fake foot. He thought of a straight line as he placed it down and put weight on it. A fire blazed at the end of his stump. But he kept going, stutter stepping with his good leg, then the bad one. Finally, he had the crutches and could take the weight off the prosthetic to give his stump a break.

"Nice job, Carter." Deon put a firm hand on his shoulder. "You're learning. You've got grit. You're gonna be fine. See you tomorrow at 14:00."

o o o

Exhausted from physical therapy and the Percocet he had talked another nurse into giving him, Tony half-napped on his bed. Some news show was on TV, but the sound was off.

In a murky haze, Tony was nine years old again, sitting on a high branch in an old maple at the back corner of their property. His stepmom was in the kitchen whipping up this week's version of shitty turkey casserole. Tony waited for his dad to come home from work. Up there, he could sit and think and clear his head without being hollered at or told to clean his room or watch his baby brother while Gloria went over to her friend's house for coffee, which Tony quickly realized meant wine.

Evening crept in. While the sky wasn't fully dark yet, more and more stars were visible. Tony used to sit in that tree, wondering if heaven was really up there among the infinite stars. Was his mother up there? And what about asteroids and space dust and even rockets and satellites? Those things were real, but was heaven?

Tony's father told him about Laika, a dog the Russians had launched into orbit back in the late 1950s. If a dog could go to space, why not a boy? Maybe he could figure out a way to see heaven.

The summer after high school, he read about Laika on the internet, and learned the dog died less than seven hours after takeoff. The Russians were reluctant to reveal the truth. Eventually, it came out that Laika died from distress. Stuffed into some doggie space suit and launched at three G's up-wards about 130 miles, that poor dog was so freaked his heart finally gave out. But up to that point, how that poor animal must have suffered. It had no clue, no control, noth-ing but suffocating fear, loneliness, and anxiety, followed blessedly by death. How much distress, he wondered, could a human being take?

Tony's eyes snapped open at the sound of someone at his door. Sharon was there, dressed in black jeans and a tight blue shirt, showing off her fine figure. She held a guitar case in her left hand.

"Sorry, Tony. Did I wake you?"

"Naw, I was just resting my eyelids. Come on in." Tony pushed himself up more into a seated position. "Actually, isn't it way past your shift?"

"I volunteered to cover for Helen. She had to leave early because her boy is sick."

"I'm sorry to hear that," Tony said. "But glad to have the chance to see you in your civilian clothes. What you got there? Are you planning on serenading me?"

Sharon rolled her eyes and smiled. "Lord, no. I don't have a musical bone in my body. Back home at church, Miss Joanne, the children's choir director, used to tell me to just hum the hymns, my singing was so awful."

"I have a hard time believing that," he said. "Maybe she just needed her hearing aids adjusted."

Sharon laughed. "Earlier today, I told you I had a surprise for you, and this here's it." Sharon put the guitar case on his lap. "This used to belong to my roommate, Emily. She took a job in New York and now she lives in a tiny little studio apartment without an extra lick of space. She left this guitar behind, and now I'm offering it to you if you'd like it."

Although the zipper resisted, Tony gave it a good tug and unzipped the weathered green case. Inside was an acoustic guitar, obviously used, with an unusual M-shaped pick guard. The strings were steel, a brassy color, and the body was a reddish hue, with a bad scratch that Tony thought he might be able to polish out.

Tony lifted the guitar, which was heavier than he expected, and held it in his lap like someone who knew what he was doing.

Sharon pushed the guitar case to the end of the bed and sat next to him. "Do you know how to play?"

"No idea," he said, randomly putting the fingers of his left hand under the neck of the guitar and on different strings. He strummed the strings with his right. The sound was far from pleasant. Yet, he randomly changed his finger positions, and this time it sort of kind of sounded like a real chord. "I've seen people play, and even thought of trying many times, but I've never actually tried it." He moved his fingers again, then plucked the strings one by one, which made him think of an orchestra tuning up. "How about you?"

"After Miss Joanne about threw me out of the children's choir, I decided music wasn't my thing. But Emily did insist on teaching me the G chord one night when we'd drank a whole bottle of chardonnay. Here, you put your finger on the top string, then your pointer on the one below that over here, then you got to stretch your pinky down here on the bottom string." Sharon took his left hand and helped him place his fingers as she spoke. "Try that."

He did, strumming with one finger. What resulted was definitely a good sound. Not perfect—one or two of the strings seemed off just a tad—but the sounds blended to-gether to make an overall pleasing tone. He strummed down again, then up. He smiled, and Sharon leaned forward and gave him a hug.

Tony's hands still held the guitar, so he couldn't return the hug. As Sharon pulled back, she paused, not six inches from him. Their eyes locked, and without thinking, Tony bent forward and kissed her softly on the lips.

He leaned back, surprised by what he'd just done. He was curious what Sharon's reaction would be. She bent forward, mimicking his motion. This time she did the kissing, the touch of her lips soft and sure. Then she smiled at him and shifted back to look inside a compartment in the velvety interior of the guitar case. She fished out two magazine-sized books.

"These should help you get started." She handed him *The Beginner's Guide to Acoustic Guitar* and *40 Campfire Songs* using something called the "tab method."

"You'll have to download an app on your phone to help you tune it. I think there might be some picks in the case, but if not, let me know and I'll get you some."

Tony put the books down on the bed and took Sharon's hand. "Thank you so much, Sharon. I really appreciate your kindness. But why are you doing this for me? I'm useless."

Sharon squeezed his hand and spoke firmly. "Tony Carter, you are not useless. I don't ever want to hear you say that again." She relaxed her grip. "I'm giving you this guitar because I believe in you. I know you can learn to play it, just like I know you can do anything you put your mind to. Just like I know you're going to keep working hard and heal up. Before long you'll walk right out of this place." Giving his hand another quick squeeze, she added, "And when you do walk out of here, you should give me a call."

She released his hand, and he immediately missed her touch. She stood, put a hand on his shoulder.

"I'm tuckered out and need a shower something fierce. You practice for a bit, get some rest, and I'll see you in the morning."

"I like the sound of that," he said.

"Of what?"

"Of all of it."

She turned and left. Tony felt pretty sure she was smiling as she did.

o o o

"Shit." Tony spit the word out as he threw the pick against the wall. The sound of the butchered B7 chord faded a lot faster than his sour mood. What the hell was wrong with his fingers? Why couldn't he get that damn chord? It wasn't that hard, but it was essential to "Folsom Prison Blues." With only three chords, it was one of the simplest songs you could learn on an acoustic. And now, like the dumbass he was, he'd have to get up and go retrieve his pick. Fuck it, he thought. Just fuck it.

As he started to put the guitar back into its case, an orderly with a patient in a wheelchair pulled partway into his room, then knocked.

Tony looked up, but didn't say anything. The orderly was tall and thin, with the posture of a dishrag and a small cross tattooed on the side of his neck. Tony had seen him around, but didn't know his name. He tried not to look at what was in the chair.

"'Scuse me," the orderly said. "This here's Brian. He was wondering if you'd mind if he listened to you play for a spell."

Tony could only assume the figure before him was a man. A thick oval bandage was taped over each eye. His head was shaved and all taped up, as were his hands and arms. He wore a loose johnny and medical socks covered his feet. The only exposed skin was on his lower ears, about half of his face and neck, and even that skin on the right side looked blistery and scorched. The lips were cracked and covered with some kind of salve. Tony hadn't seen that much gauze and medical tape since seeing *The Mummy Returns* at a dorm social his first semester back at EKU.

Tony wanted nothing to do with this guy, or with anyone else in this godforsaken place. He was having a hard enough time dealing with his own shit, never mind this unfortunate bastard. Why couldn't people just leave him alone?

Feeling obligated to say something, he blurted out, "Can he talk?"

"Don't ask me—ask him."

Although he felt kind of stupid, Tony asked, "Can you talk?"

"Some." The voice was so coarse and gritty it sounded like the poor guy's throat was packed with rock salt.

The orderly bent down, retrieved Tony's guitar pick from the floor, and handed it to him. "Looks like you dropped this. I'll be back in a few minutes. You keep playing."

"Actually, I was just going to..." The orderly pivoted and was gone before Tony could finish his sentence.

Tony sat, not having a clue what to do or say. He looked at Brian. The poor bastard sure had been in some awful shit. Burns, Tony guessed. An old song lyric popped into his head. Fire is the Devil's only friend. Should he ask? Did he even want to know?

"You coming along well," Brian croaked. "I been listening." He held up his hands, both taped up like he was wearing mittens. "Too fast, though. Slow down, then fast."

"You play?" Tony asked, then felt even stupider than he did a second ago when he'd asked the guy if he could talk.

"Not lately," Brian said, holding up his hands again, a hint of a smirk on his cracked lips. "Try to play slowly," he said, his y's sounding roundish, almost like w's. "First E chord, down then up. One... Two... Three... Four."

Not knowing what else to do, Tony put the guitar back in his lap, fingered an open E major, and strummed four times, down then up, slowly.

"Good," Brian said. "Now A. Remember, slow."

Tony repeated the same slow stroking pattern, down up, with the A major chord.

"Good," Brian said. He then had Tony move back and forth between the two chords, painfully slow in Tony's mind.

When would that orderly come back and get this guy out of here?

"Now, you know how to finger B7?"

Tony knew from the diagrams in his guitar book, and he could do it if he concentrated, but he flubbed it every time when he tried to play it as part of the song. He fingered the chord and strummed. Obviously he was off.

"Sound like your pointer finger is deadening." Brian hacked for a second, catching his breath. "Touchin' the B string."

Tony focused on moving his pointer finger and strummed again. Better, but not quite right.

Brian told Tony to move his left hand an inch more clockwise, placing his fingers higher above the fretboard. The position was less comfortable, but it allowed his fingertips to move straighter down on the strings, which resulted in a cleaner sound. For the next 10 minutes, Brian had Tony finger B7, strum up down, skipping the top string, then releasing the chord. He had Tony shut his eyes and repeat the exercise, drilling the muscle memory into his left hand. Finally, the steel strings pushed Tony's fingers as far as they could go.

"My fingertips have 'bout had it." He spoke. "Thanks, uh, Brian."

Soundlessly, Brian waved his thanks away, like it was nothing. Which, Tony thought, probably was true. Who knew how long this poor bastard would be here? And what the hell would he do once, if, he healed up? What was going on inside the guy's skull? Was he jealous that Tony could play, or at least attempt to play, a guitar? Was he happy just to have killed a half hour in another endless day?

Tony kicked his left leg out, the end of his scrub pants flapping where his foot should be. Then he looked at Brian and wondered how the guy could scratch himself if he had an itch? How could he wipe his ass?

"Can I ask you something?" Brian nodded, but in a full-body way, tipping his torso, probably because his neck hurt.

"How... I mean, obviously you're pretty tore up." Tony paused, trying to collect his thoughts, to say what he felt without coming across as a total douche nozzle. "How do you keep it together? How do you not just break apart into a thousand tiny pieces? I feel like a damn baby and I just got my foot chopped off. Compared to you, that's nothin'."

Brian turned his head slightly, as if he was trying to look at Tony. The tip of his tongue came out and he licked his cracked lips. "I play the blues," he said in that scratchy voice. "But, I don't sing the blues."

Just then, the tall orderly came back and asked Brian if he was ready to head back to his room. Brian sat there, as if holding Tony's gaze, only that wasn't possible because of the tape covering his eyes. Eventually, Brian nodded yes, then croaked to Tony, "Rock on, bro." He raised his right arm, all bandaged like, and sort of saluted Tony.

Without thinking, Tony returned the gesture, saying, "Later," then watched as Brian was wheeled back to his room. He put his guitar away, zipped the case shut, got off his bed, and leaned it in a corner where it would be safely out of the way.

He got back into bed, rolled on his side away from the doorway, and closed his eyes. Even so, he still saw Brian in his chair, the image seared in his memory. How much could a body take? Was it the human spirit keeping him alive, or just the miracle of modern medicine? What kind of life would he have after surviving such a trauma? Would it be better if he died?

Slowly, the tears came. Tony didn't bother wiping them away. What was wrong with him? Why was he so damn sad all the time? He forced himself to sit up, grabbing a tissue to wipe his eyes and blow his nose. Enough already. The past was past. What's done is done. He had to look forward. He had to keep working hard, get out of here, then give Sharon a call. Who knew? Maybe there would be something there to build on. Lord knows what she could possibly see in his sorry ass, but who knew?

You can do this, he thought. *You can do whatever she asks of you. You can put all the horrible shit behind and start again. You can. You will. You must.*

INDESTRUCTIBLE

"Don't get too close
It's dark inside
It's where my demons hide
It's where my demons hide"
– "Demons" by Imagine Dragons

Isaac Stone turned his head slightly right, waiting for his eyes to focus. Red blotches in front of him coalesced into 3:27 on his clock radio. Thirty years back, he'd just be coming in at this time. Now he reached over and turned off the alarm, which was set for 3:30. Three minutes early. He shut his eyes again, folded his hands together across his belly like a corpse in a coffin, and silently thanked God for granting him another day.

His morning routine, including making the bed, usually took him 25 minutes. He'd grab a fresh bagel later, so he skipped breakfast, put on his big flannel jacket, and pocketed his thermos of coffee and wool cap. Before leaving, he touched his index finger to an old picture of Paulette and Daisy, taken when she was about six. He also tapped the wooden sign that said 'Time To Make The Fucking Donuts' with his knuckles. An old Marine buddy had made it for him years ago, and he still couldn't pass it without smiling.

Outside, the still night bit him. Isaac slipped on the cap, put his hands in his jacket pockets, and started walking. It was three blocks to the bus stop, which used to take him ten minutes to walk, eight if he hustled. Now it took twenty, and hustling wasn't much of an option. His age and the pain in his hip slowed him these days. As the day went on the hip would loosen up a little, but the limp had become a constant companion long ago.

He caught the 4:18 in-town bus, sat in his usual seat, two behind the driver, and took his first sip of coffee that day. Strong and black, he savored the warmth and the bitter, nutty taste. Through the window, he watched as the projects turned to low-rent housing then to parking lots and store fronts. At Atlantic and Wayne, he nodded to the bus driver and got out. His hip was cramped up more than usual this morning. It reminded him how, 43 years ago, a piece of VC grenade got lodged in there, too close to the femoral artery to operate, the docs said. Better to leave it be.

When he unlocked the bakery door, it was 10 minutes before 5:00. Isaac turned on the lights, reached into his pocket for his thermos, and took a sip. "Time to make the fucking donuts," he said to the empty shop.

By the time the Dominican guys, Carlos and Manny, sauntered in around quarter of six, the yeasty smell of fresh baked bagels, the heat of five ovens and hot oil filled the kitchen. Thanks to yesterday's prep work, Isaac already finished four batches of donuts, along with six batches of bagels that were just about done. It was enough to take care of the early morning crowd.

At 6:30, Gloria arrived with Estelle, who Isaac suspected had a thing going with Martin, the shop's owner. As usual, they turned on the 'Open' sign and gabbed constantly between customers about female stuff. Boots and purses and JZ this and Beyoncé that. Isaac smiled and weighed out starter and rye flour for the two-dozen sourdough loaves next on his to-do list.

Manny and Carlos were good workers. They didn't talk much, preferring to sing along to the Spanish station they listened to on the radio. Carlos took over bagels and donuts. Manny worked the grill Martin had stupidly put in a year ago so they could make breakfast sandwiches and coffee. Theoretically, it was supposed to help expand the business. While Martin had that fancy business degree framed on his office wall, he didn't have half his father's business sense.

Back in '87, George McHale founded McHale's Bakery with a simple plan—bake great breads, cakes, pies, donuts, and so on. Success followed. The business doubled in size and attracted not just local customers, but orders from some of the finest restaurants and gourmet food stores in Bethesda.

Isaac floured his palms. With practiced hands, he worked the dough into a large block, then cut it into sections that would weigh 900 grams, plus or minus. He set them into proofing trays, then slid them into an empty rack. He checked the time, making a quick calculation and mental note for when the proof would be finished. Martin had purchased expensive whiteboards with multi-color markers, asking Isaac to record each batch, the times it proofed, baked, the weight of each loaf before and after baking. "This way I can study our process and optimize it," Martin said with that stupid grin, like he was talking to a child.

"You mean use my time to weigh and write shit down instead of baking, like I been doing since you was barely out of diapers?"

Martin didn't much like it when Isaac talked back like that. He thought it set a bad example for the other employees. Isaac admitted it probably did. He didn't much care. Martin didn't know jack-shit about baking bread or cakes or how to make a bagel that had just the right crispness on the outside, yet was airy and tasty on the inside. One summer, the kid worked at the bakery, and half of what he made couldn't even be donated to the shelter. Hell, the poor saps out by the dumpster even turned their noses up at them.

Martin's first mistake was changing the bakery's name to "Confectioner's Corner," which he thought would draw a more upscale clientele. The dumbass couldn't understand that his old man spent more than 20 years building the McHale Bakery name. Everyone associated that name with quality. Confectioner's Corner? *Who the hell wants to eat in a place with a name like that?* When sales dropped, Martin started weighing and recording and gathering data. Like whether a loaf of pumpernickel weighs 450 or 455 grams was the reason the shop lost money.

Then last year, it was the breakfast sandwich debacle. He took out a perfectly good, often-used oven to put in a damn grill. Sure, they probably sold a hundred sandwiches a day. But the profit margin wasn't nearly what a loaf of artisan bread cost, and they can't make as much bread without that oven. So, the shop's still not as profitable as when George was in charge five years ago.

Isaac glanced up at the clock when he heard Martin talking to the counter girls. It was just before 2:00, which was early for Scrooge to come count the till.

Estelle faked a laugh, which Martin responded to with one of his own. "You know me better than that!" he said, probably responding to some private joke between them. Isaac pulled a tray of cupcakes from the oven, put them down to cool, and then started bagging 120 brioche buns for Shuman's Deli, one of the few downtown businesses that stuck with the bakery after George died.

"Hey crew," Martin announced when he came into the kitchen. "How's it going?"

Isaac ignored him, while Carlos and Manny answered in Spanish. Isaac only knew a few words of Spanish, but he sure hoped the guys were either insulting Martin's *madre,* or suggesting that he lick their privates. A tiny smile creased Isaac's lips at the thought.

Martin turned and watched Isaac bagging buns. "Those Shuman's brioche?"

"Yup."

"You counting carefully? Last Thursday I double-checked, and you gave them 122. That's two over, and that's money out of our pockets."

Isaac continued bagging buns, a dozen per bag, 10 bags, plus a few because that's how you keep a longtime customer satisfied. He kept counting, all the while, staring at the bread knife sitting 12 inches away. He imagined reaching over, grabbing it, turning toward Martin, and stabbing the obnoxious asshole in the throat.

"When you finish, Isaac, come see me. We need to talk." Turning to head to the closet he called his office, Martin said, "*Bueno* job," to Carlos. Carlos waited until Martin's back was turned to laugh and shake his head.

"What's up?" Isaac stood in Martin's doorway. His desk and chair were so big, there was little room for anything else, and Isaac refused to sit in the metal folding chair intended for guests.

"Come in, come in," Martin said. "Please close the door and take a seat."

Isaac eyed his boss. Slowly, he turned, closed the door, and stood in front of the desk, with its oversized computer screen and sleek new phone. In addition to his diploma from the University of Maryland, Martin had pictures from his ski trips to Colorado and the Alps on the wall.

"Please, Isaac, take a seat. You've been on your feet all day."

"I'm good," he replied. "Thanks."

"Did you see the Ravens game last Sunday? That Jackson is a helluva quarterback. Threw for 386 yards. I tell you, I think we're headed for the playoffs this season."

Isaac just stood, absorbing this—what was it? Some lesson he learned in college, gotta pretend you're one of the workers and can talk at their level? When Martin paused, waiting for a response, Isaac simply said, "No."

"Well, you missed a great game. Great game." He shuffled a few pieces of paper on his desk. "I'm not going to bore you with the details, Isaac. I'm sure you've noticed that in this recession, business has been down."

Recession? What recession? Isaac scratched his neck with a floury hand. That shit was over three years ago. Now we got a brother in the White House, and the economy is doing fine.

"I've been juggling the numbers, and, ummm, unfortunately, I know you've been here almost twenty years..."

"Twenty-four, as of September sixth," Isaac said.

"Twenty-four, is that right? Wow. Long time. But that's a great segue to what we need to discuss. Isaac, I've always been a straight shooter, so I'm sorry to say that with our reduced margins and the downturn in business, I'm going to have to let you go."

Isaac stood perfectly still; not even his chest moved, though his heart wasn't sure it was happy with the lack of action. "Let me go?"

"Not today. You'll have two weeks, which will bring us to Thanksgiving. You can make sure Carlos and Emmanuel have all the holiday bread recipes, and then you can retire and enjoy your family. Have a nice Thanksgiving. I've noticed your, ummm, limp, and won't it be nice to get off your feet?"

Isaac flexed his hands. Strong hands. Hands that had made hundreds of thousands of loaves of bread, cakes, pies, cannolis, bagels, muffins, chocolate-filled cinnamon buns. Hands that hit walls, hit people, broke glass. Hands that once snapped the neck of a Vietnamese farmer who wouldn't quit his wailing when they were under attack.

"I was the first person your father hired to work here. After he and your mom, rest their souls, busted their backs to get this place rolling. Your daddy taught me everything he knew about baking, and I've been keeping this place goin' ever since. Carlos and Manny are good kids, don't get me wrong. But the both of them produce about half what I do. What about seniority?"

"Well, that's it, Isaac." Martin looked serious, yet hangdog. "Those guys work for about half what you do. It just makes the most financial sense. And I know you've been a valuable employee. Dad thought of you as a brother almost. That's why"—Martin opened the top drawer of his desk and removed an envelope—"I'm giving you a $500 bonus check, as a way of saying thanks for your years of dedication to Confectioner's Corner."

"Five hundred bucks? I get five hundred bucks for 24 years of 10, sometimes 12-hour days, working in that hot kitchen in July when it was 95 degrees outside, and 130 degrees by the ovens?"

Martin sat frozen, envelope outstretched toward Isaac, not speaking.

Isaac snatched the envelope and left. In the back room he washed up, tossed his apron in the corner, and put on his cap and jacket. He considered saying so long to the guys, but what was the point? He'd never see them again. He did stop behind the counter up front to fill a bag with old-fashioned, glazed, and chocolate-covered donuts.

"Thank you, ladies," he said to Estelle and Gloria, who'd never seen Isaac help himself to the store's offerings before. "Have a nice night."

Although it was early, Isaac didn't really have anywhere else to go, so he caught the bus to the transfer station, then took the eastbound to the naval hospital. He rode the elevator to the basement and turned on the lights in the meeting room. As he put on a pot of coffee, he tried to stop, or at least slow down, the anger that was swelling in his head. It won't do no good, as he knew better than anyone.

His rage, along with his drinking and what they now call PTSD, cost him his wife and daughter. It cost him friendships. And he knew, inside, as long as he kept it at bay, everything would be alright. So, he prayed a simple prayer. *God is good, all the time. All the time, God is good.* Isaac repeated it over and over and over again in his head until the anger stepped back and threw in the towel.

After putting out the donuts, he took an old-fashioned and was just pouring a cup of coffee when someone appeared at the door.

"Excuse me?"

Isaac turned and saw a white lady, probably mid-forties, too much makeup and gel in her hair.

"Is this the right room for the 4:00 PTSD support group?"

"We call it the survivor's club, but yeah, it's here."

"Good," she said, then looked in the hall behind her. "Come on, Philip."

A young guy peered carefully into the room like it might contain a trap. He entered tentatively, head bobbing up and down like a chicken's. Isaac had seen a lot of people come and go in this room over the past 10 years, and this guy looked about as shattered as any of them. Wire-thin and taut, his eyes were mere pinpricks. He scratched at his scalp like he had lice, even though he probably didn't.

"This is my nephew, Philip," the lady said. "Philip served in Iraq. We're hoping you all might help him."

"Isaac." he said, but didn't put out a hand. "Good to meet you, Phil. Care for coffee, or a fresh donut?"

o o o

Tony flipped the smoldering cigarette butt out the Acura's window onto the asphalt parking lot. Sharon's Acura. He spit out the window.

Sharon's apartment. Sharon's furniture. Her music. Her food in the fridge. He took a long pull off the forty, wrapped in a brown paper bag like some old bum on a park bench. Like him. The clock on the dash read 3:44, although he knew from the DJ on the radio that it was four minutes slow. He could change it, but he didn't. Instead, he took another swallow of beer. His day had been going fine. His big mistake, he knew, was not keeping track of the time so Sharon wouldn't catch him playing Assassin's Creed III on the PlayStation. Sharon's PlayStation.

"What a dumbass," he said to the dusty car interior. He knew better, and yet... and yet... what? He'd come up with a reason if he could, but even now, an hour since Sharon first screamed the question at him. "What the fuck is wrong with you?" He had no answer.

No butterscotch-syrup sweetness in her voice today. And he got it, he really did. She gets up at the ass-crack of dawn and works hard, on her feet for all but maybe 20 minutes in a nine, often 10-hour day. She's tired, and a little cranky sometimes when she gets home. Who wouldn't be?

So why, he asked himself for the ten-thousandth time—*can't you get your shit together?*

Tony had yelled back that he wasn't her lapdog and he didn't take orders from her, or anybody. He made a big show of turning off the PlayStation and slamming the controllers back under the entertainment center—not neatly on the first shelf, how Sharon liked. He made a scene about putting on his sneakers, grabbing his guitar, and yanking the Acura keys off the rack—Sharon's key rack. Even as he did, he knew he was being an asshole. *Why, though, he couldn't exactly say.* She had asked nicely, and he had agreed, willingly, to wash the dishes and clean the kitchen. To take out the trash and recycling, and to straighten up the living room. All that would have taken him, what, an hour?

It wasn't like he didn't do anything all day. He took the trash and recycling out and did most, well, some of the dishes. It wasn't his fault that he was tired and needed a quick nap. Then, after lunch, he practiced guitar, working on the intro to "Dead or Alive," one of Sharon's favorite Bon Jovi songs. Then he ran through a few more songs. Somehow, time just melted away when he had his guitar in his hands. Playing was good, though. Playing was Sharon's idea, after all. And it did help him relax. It helped him focus and forget about all the other shit weighing him down. When his fingers found the exact right spots on the fretboard, and the strings sounded crisp and clear, there was no past or present weighing down his thoughts. There was only the here and now, and here and now everything was under control.

After that, he just wanted to play a little video before tackling the rest of Sharon's chore list and getting ready for work. Work, he thought, taking another swallow of beer. Tony had been delivering pizza for Lorenzo's for a couple months now. It didn't pay a lot, but it was a job. Not to Sharon, though. She expected more. Sure, she said it was fine, for now. But he knew she wanted more. She always did. Ever since that day, his birthday, when he was still in the hospital. She first asked, then demanded, then rode him. "Tony, you need to... Tony, why don't you try to... Tony, registration for classes at the community college is this week... Tony, I heard Pulman's is hiring..."

She was a great girl, really, she was. They had fun together. And she felt so damn good curled up against him on the couch when they watched a movie or some stupid TV show. But she just didn't get that Tony needed more time. More space. A part of him wanted a better job, or to start up at college again. But a bigger part, the part that was driving this bus, said—maybe later. For now, I just want to chill for a bit. He polished off the forty and put it on the passenger floor with the others. He'd better remember to put those in the recycling before Sharon saw them in here and blew her lid. Reaching in the glove box, he popped a breath mint, checked his eyes in the rearview mirror, and retrieved the guitar from the back seat.

He entered room B314, which always smelled of damp concrete. He nodded to Isaac, who was talking to a scrawny, twitchy-looking redheaded guy who was scratching his arm like it was covered with ants. Tony put his guitar by a chair and got himself a coffee. Somebody brought donuts. He took a chocolate-covered one, broke it in half so people wouldn't think he was a total pig, then stuffed the entire half into his mouth. While he chewed, he looked at who was there.

Isaac urged Twitchy to take a seat. Malik and G-dog were talking about sports, like they always did. Austin and Nate sat quietly, hands on their thighs, eyes on the floor, either struggling to figure out the meaning of life or just trying to keep their shit together. With this group, you could never tell. Tony picked up his guitar and took the seat closest to the door. It was only one seat from Twitchy, which he wasn't completely comfortable with. But he liked to be close to the door. It just felt more comfortable. Safer.

Five minutes later, Graham came in carrying a super-market cake box, apologizing, like he did every week, for being late. Graham was the group leader. He was either a scatterbrain, or this harried, constantly flummoxed look was a part of his act to make them all believe he was a super busy guy, but not too important to help their crazy asses out. Every week, Graham wore some odd combination of clothing and accessories. Today was fairly mild, with thick silver-framed glasses, an eggplant-colored shirt, and a neon yellow tie.

"Okay," Graham said after pouring a cup of coffee. "Glad

you guys could make it. Seems we have someone new, so welcome." Graham paused, taking a sip of coffee. Twitchy was picking a fingernail and didn't seem like he was interested in engaging.

After a pause, Isaac said, "This here's Phil."

A robotic chorus of "Hi, Phil" came from the group.

"I'm Graham. I'm the facilitator of the Homefront Support Group."

He went on to detail his pedigree, his experience, and how much he cares and supports them all, and how much he enjoys helping to turn a screwed-up life around, blah, blah.

"Everyone is free to participate, or not—although I think you'll find us all more helpful and supportive if you join in. In your own time, but since you're here, why not?" Graham paused; nobody said anything. "So, how did you all do this week? Anybody?"

"I almost won the lottery," G-dog said.

"Really?" Graham asked.

"Got two numbers," G-dog answered with a flashy smile.

They had a group chuckle. Then, just a beat too late, like the electrons were having a hard time working their way through his brain, Twitchy let out a howling belly laugh. Tony thought he noticed Isaac moving his chair away a few inches.

"I got something," Nate said. He was from Boston or Maine or somewhere up North, and had sort of a nasally voice that grated on Tony's nerves. "Me and Carla went to the Terrapins game on Saturday. That's our third date, and I think it went good. Hell, I know it went good."

"Who won?" Austin asked.

"Maryland 70, Vanderbilt 83," Malik said, then added, "Sorry. Not my place."

Nate blabbered on for a few minutes about how hot this girl was and how she thinks he's awesome. Tony found himself hoping she was a good boxer and kept a hammer in her purse, since Nate had a history of solving most of his lady problems with a fist.

"Anybody else?" Graham looked at the group, hope in his eyes. "Since we have a newcomer—Phil, maybe you want to introduce yourself?" Everybody turned to look at Twitchy. He stared into the distance, slack-jawed like he was on a four-day bender. Or jonesing for a hit off his crack pipe.

The silence was getting to Tony, so he jumped in. "I had words with my girlfriend before coming here today."

Graham pulled his eyes away from the new guy. "What happened?"

"I was playing video games when she came home from work, and she got pissed that I hadn't finished all the chores she asked me to do."

"Why didn't you do what she asked?" Graham asked. "Were they reasonable requests?"

"Yeah, they was reasonable. And to be honest, I don't really know why I didn't do them. I meant to. But—and maybe some of you guys feel this way sometimes— but I just couldn't, you know, work up the energy."

"It's called depression," Isaac said. "The world's greatest motivation killer."

"Good point, Isaac. Tony, we've talked about this a little before. Have you scheduled an appointment with a psychia..."

"I'm sick of fuckin' shrinks," he interrupted Graham before he got started on his wonders of the science of the mind bullshit.

Ever the psychologist, Graham tried to divert his aggression. "Does anyone have suggestions that Tony might find helpful?"

"Sure," G-dog said. "Do the damn chores."

Tony glared, but could tell G-dog was just ribbing him.

"I'm no fan of the docs, either," Malik said. "They always wanting to put you on pills. Xanax, Lexapro, Prozac. Screw that. I say hit the gym. Pump some iron." Malik flexed his muscles, proof that he practiced what he preached. "It'll release those endorphins. That's the best therapy."

Tony listened, but dismissed the idea. He didn't have the energy to wash the dishes—how the hell was he going to work out at a gym? And where would he get the money? He couldn't even pay his half of the rent, never mind goddamn car insurance and gas and his overdue phone bill. Besides, Sharon's birthday was coming up in a few weeks.

"Get up at the same time every day, man, do an hour of chores, then go for a walk." Nate said.

When Austin suggested trying a new meditation phone app, Tony stopped listening.

"Can I say something?" Everybody turned to look at Twitchy, who spoke for the first time. He smiled, but there was no warmth to it.

"Sure, Phil." Graham encouraged him. "That's what we do here. We talk, we listen, and we help each other."

"What... I mean, do y'all believe in ghosts?"

Malik laughed. "Say what?"

Austin pulled out his phone and texted somebody. Isaac moved his chair a few more inches to the left.

Graham, always the professional, said, "Why do you ask, Phil?"

The guy started scratching at his arm again. "When I was over there, uh, we kilt a lot of people. First Sergeant said I 'exsanguinated' something. I don't even know what that means."

"Do you want to tell us about it?" Graham asked.

"Not really," he said. "I shot this dog, see. Couple of 'em, actually. Then the CO got pissed and they doped me up and sent me home."

"You shot a dog?" Malik looked like he hoped he'd heard the guy wrong. "A couple of them?"

But Twitchy didn't answer. Instead, he closed his eyes, hugged himself like he might fall apart, and began rocking, back and forth, back and forth. Isaac stood and put a hand on his shoulder, while the rest of them just sort of sat there stupefied. This dude was a mess, and he needed way more help than he was going to get from this gang of misfits.

Graham cleared his throat. "Maybe this is a good time to lighten the mood a little. Most of you know it's George's birthday. I brought a cake, and Tony brought his guitar— thank you, Tony, for remembering. Let's all join in and sing a Happy Homefront Support birthday to George."

Tony reluctantly took his guitar out of its case. He hadn't planned on bringing it, but when he mentioned G-dog's birthday to Sharon, she said she thought it was a good idea. It was a nice thing to do for G-dog, and he needed to participate fully in the group if he was going to reap the benefits of belonging. So far, he couldn't list what those benefits were, but he played along. As he picked the basic notes, they all sang, "Happy birthday to you..." If this were *American Idol*, they wouldn't have gotten much further than that. But they croaked and groaned their way through the blessedly short song, and Tony felt a buzzing in his back pocket. He put the guitar down and removed his phone. Sharon.

"Sorry, guys," he said. "I gotta take this."

Tony quick-stepped his way from the room. "Hey, Babe." He tried to sound lighthearted, hoping she would, too.

"Am I interrupting your meeting?"

She sounded normal, Tony thought. Not mad, not ballistic. "It's just about over—don't worry about it. They're just having birthday cake now. What's up?"

"I've been feeling bad about the way I hollered at you

earlier. I'm sorry. That's not how I want to be, especially with you."

"I'm the one who should be sorry," he said. "You're so good to me, and I know I need to get my act together. I know what I need to do, and I promise, I'm going to work on it."

"Tony, I believe you, I do. But you've already sung that song countless times. You need to be more concrete. Hoping to change things won't change them. You need to think of a plan. And I'll help you. I'm good at planning."

"I know, I know," he said. "You're right. Let's work on it... tonight."

"I'll be dead to the world by the time you get home," she said. "What about Saturday? Let's sit down and brainstorm on Saturday, then we'll celebrate by going out to dinner at Ponchos. What do you say?"

"Count me in," he said. But he knew he was just playing a role, putting on a show that said he was okay, that he would try harder. In reality, he had no idea how to get unstuck. Just then, a horrible sound, a violently unmusical cracking of wood and twanging of dissident notes spilled from the meeting room, followed by yelling and a chair falling over.

"I gotta go." Tony didn't even end the call or notice the revolt in his stump as he sprinted back into the meeting.

○ ○ ○

Philip Crenshaw, known to himself as "Sniper," lay like a balled-up sock in his favorite spot in the entire world, his comfort zone, as one of his psychiatrists, he couldn't remember which one, had said. His comfy single bed, his clothes and books and soft blanket hugging his sides, headphones on, the Dead Milkmen ramming it, incredible guitar work, the screechy, or what his parents would call "Satanic," voice wailing. "Now I feel a little better, about throwin' gas on your dad, but you know it's hard to quit, and besides he started it..."

In his mind everything was pale purple, but squirts of liquid flame shot across in the distance, colorfully violent but safe. A virtual reality kaleidoscope. Music was great for that, allowing you to transport somewhere that only existed in your mind. If only...

A sharp banging on his door jarred him back to the gray clapboard house with blue shutters on Oliver Street. The door opened because they wouldn't let him put a lock on it.

"Philip." Aunt Lynn looked at him like a booger on a doorknob. "I've been knocking for five minutes. Listening to music at that volume can't be good for you. You need to get up. Your support group is at four, so you've got about 20 minutes to get ready."

"Sure," he answered, removing the headphones and turning off his iPod. "I just need a minute to clean up."

"Alright. See you downstairs." She turned and left. She would have fit in well in the military. There were rules that only Aunt Lynn knew, and she followed them to the tee. She expected her underlings to do likewise. Although Phil didn't understand, he'd learned one thing in boot camp—never question. Shut up and follow.

Philip was lucky, and he knew it. He made it about six months until his parents couldn't take him anymore. Aunt Lynn and Uncle Harold, super libs who couldn't fathom there was someone 'down on their luck' that they couldn't uplift and remold through their compassion and love and endurance, volunteered to take him in for an undefined period of time. He had a suspicion that period would get defined any time now.

Philip brought his towel and a clean tee shirt with him into the upstairs bathroom. After turning on the shower, he removed the top of the toilet tank and fished out a Maxwell

House coffee can. He dried the can with the towel and sat on the closed toilet lid.

He removed his pipe, lighter, a baggie of weed, and a small glass vial with a pea-sized rock from the can. Although his hands trembled a little as he worked, Phil managed to get some weed in the bowl, and chipped off a fragment of crank with his fingernail and placed it on top of the weed. After returning the baggie and vial to the can, he took two deep breaths, exhaled, then put the pipe to his lips, flipped the Bic, and put fire to his dreams.

The first breath after taking a hit was relatively normal. It was the second breath that hit like a white-cap in Kauai. *Bam!* It took a lot of effort to ground his feet in place and not topple over. Brain full of electric bubbles and damp earth, he replaced his stash, then brushed his teeth. He threw some water in his face and shut off the shower. Before heading downstairs, he opened the medicine chest and took out a Xanax, considered putting it in his pocket, then popped it in his mouth and dry-swallowed it.

Blessedly, as his mother would say, Aunt Lynn wasn't in a chatty mood as she drove him to the VA. Instead, she listened to NPR, where the hosts, with their patented NPR library-certified voices, praised Obama like he was the second Jesus or something. Phil put in his earbuds, skipped past Gorilla Finger, StoneToad, Alice in Chains, and settled on Disturbed. C'mon everybody, get down with the sickness.

"Are you worried?"

"Hunh?" Philip looked over at his aunt, then reluctantly removed his earbuds. "What was that?"

"Are you... comfortable with attending the meeting today?"

"Sure," he said, although it wasn't true.

He'd been to group before. He'd been to dozens of groups before. He'd been to one-on-one with psychiatrists, psychologists, and of course his parents had insisted he talk to Pastor Lewis, and then Bob Carson, one of Dad's buddies who served in Vietnam. None of it made a difference. None of it helped. What he needed was sleep, and sleep couldn't come because the images wouldn't stop. Hell, they couldn't stop. As soon as his mind was unoccupied, and even sometimes when it was, they'd show up quick and random as a firefly on a warm summer night.

A whole block of buildings knocked half-over from the air raid, the other half engulfed in flames, mangled Iraqis strewn everywhere. Osborn climbing a wall, almost over, when a single shot rang out in the blazing heat and took out the left side of his head. Ferguson stepping on an IED and splitting apart like an overripe watermelon dropped on hot concrete, and a staff sergeant screaming at Sniper to pick up the parts. An old Iraqi grandmother pissing herself as he pointed his rifle at her belly.

That's why he smoked, and played the shrinks for all the pills he could get out of them. They could slow the film down, or even blank it out. For a while. Talk therapy was no better than jerking off, although jerking off at least had a happy ending. No thanks, he'd rather skip the support meeting.

But he knew Aunt Lynn and Uncle Harry were starting to realize their left-wing ideals weren't as powerful as they once thought. Maybe they couldn't drive the devil out of their nephew, because Lucifer had found himself a very pliable host. Once they parked, Philip got out, expecting to say thank you to Aunt Lynn for driving him. But she must have read his mind. She got out too.

"I'm going to walk you in. I'd like to make sure you find the meeting and see who else is there. Not sure if I should wait or come back and pick you up."

Question not asked but answered. Philip tucked his

earbuds in his pocket and followed his aunt as she marched in a straight line for the building's front door. The basement of the VA was cool and damp as a crypt, with its government-sanctioned beige carpet and cement walls. Aunt Lynn marched into the presumed meeting room, but Sniper froze. He saw the door and the old black guy on the other side. But he could only pay attention to the VR-like scene happening in his mind, playing like a 3D video. A dead Iraqi family, the kitchen floor covered in blood, some crazy-smelling rice dish starting to burn on the stove. Sarah, the girl in eleventh grade he had an earth-shattering crush on, who never even saw him. Invisible Sniper. Turning the corner of a one-story brick building and seeing the Haji insurgent and his AK mowing down Bravo Company, and he, the Sniper, couldn't pop off a shot because the spineless fucker had kids standing in front of him for protection.

The old black guy introduced himself, then limped over to get coffee. He asked Phil if he wanted any, but he said no—at least he thought he said no.

The old-timer sat next to him, then exchanged pleasantries with the other guys as they arrived. One guy about Phil's age looked kind of full of himself. Another guy, in dumpy jeans and a black hoodie, looked like he had no fight left in him. There was a giant black guy who was either a professional football player or was roided out to the max. A guy who looked a few years younger than him, a scraggly attempt at a beard on his face, came in carrying a guitar, of all things. If these assholes started singing kumbaya, Old Sniper was outta there.

A few minutes passed. While he was puzzling out whether or not to put in his earbuds, a clown who looked right out of "Animal Crossing" showed up. He wore a purple shirt with a lemon-yellow tie, and Phil had to scratch himself to be sure he was there, awake, and not tripping or anything.

But this guy was real, words coming out of his mouth like wriggling wasps spilling onto the ground.

He shook that image from his head, and heard all the guys laughing, so he joined in. Maybe they saw the wasps, too, and thought it was funny. Phil was there for a while, trying to listen. But this group, like the last group, and the group before that, they just blabbered on about their problems. Nothing ever changed. If he was a surgeon, he could cut the faces off these guys and put them on the heads of any other group, and nobody would know the difference. Kind of like *Mission Impossible*, although Phil thought the Tom Cruise character used masks. How much better would it be to use real skin? Real faces?

Sniper was back on patrol in Ramadi. Culley trailed behind him, and they were both hugging the brick wall low, the scorched remains of a car on the street in front of them. Culley touched his shoulder, twitched his head, and then rolled behind the torched vehicle. Keeping low, Sniper poked his rifle around the corner, then one eye. He heard the AK firing steadily, smelled the cordite, saw the fucking Haji with three little kids in front of him. One boy looked like he was a badass, but the littler boy and the girl both looked terrified. He should shoot, he knew, but the kids. Those damn kids, what the fuck.

Culley fired a shot, which went high. Sniper turned to see him in good position, kneeling behind the car, his arms stabilized on the burned hood. He fired again, and a burst of bullet strikes hit the building behind Culley right before...

"Can I ask a question?" Phil asked. It more spilled out of him than formulated, but he needed to break the cycle. He wished he'd pocketed another Xanax or two.

"Sure, Phil." The purple bot said. "That's what we do here. We talk, we listen, we help each other."

"Do y'all believe in ghosts?"

Big Muscles laughed. "Say what?"

"When I was over there," Phil said, "we killed a lot of people."

Dead Iraqis. Dead GIs. Culley's head cut clean off, falling to the pavement with a dull thud that haunted Philip's dreams. The court martial, and all the brass in their shiny uniforms and spit-polished boots yelling at him.

"First Sargent said I 'exsanguinated' something. I don't even know what that means."

Then, although he'd never mentioned it to anyone back home before, he brought up the dogs. After he'd seen PFC Culley, the oldest of three boys born to an Ohio farm family, get exsanguinated, he found what he needed to fire, and the first shot got the Haji right in the neck. The second shot tore that poor little girl's shoulder and arm right from her body. And the blood, God, the blood.

There were a dozen things he knew he should have done, but none of that clicked in. Instead, he ran. He ran, and ran, until he saw a bunch of wild dogs picking at trash spilling out of a dumpster. The Sniper shot them. No, he massacred them—maybe three, maybe five—he emptied his magazine into them, then the only logical thing left to do was to kill himself. But that wasn't the demons' plan. The demons made sure he was out of bullets. The demons entered him, moved some organs around and made themselves comfortable. And now they just haunted him, biding their time.

When Phil checked in again, the bearded guy was playing "Happy Birthday" on his guitar, and everybody was singing like they were all in first grade. Then Animal Crossing guy was passing out cake that looked like it was made of spackling and mud. He offered Phil a piece, but no way was he eating that toxic shit. Instead, he picked up the guitar and started playing. Well, not playing really, since he had no idea how to play. But he thought it would be funny, so he started strumming and singing, "They say I gotta go to rehab, but I said, no, no, no..."

Big Muscles immediately got in his face and told him to put the guitar down. And he meant to, he really did. But the demons had awoken in Sniper, and as he was about to place the guitar back into its velvety case, he raised it high over his head and brought it down on the floor like he was playing that carnival game where you hit a lever with a sledgehammer.

And oh, lord hallelujah, that sound was glorious. That was truly music, and the demons inside him danced with glee. He hammered down again, and the strength—what strength he had. The music of devastation had energized him, and now, now he couldn't be...

Somebody or something slammed into him and drove him to the floor. His head hit the carpet, but that carpet covered government-grade concrete, so his noggin bounced like a mallet on the head of a spike. And that image made him laugh.

o o o

As the others joined the melee, Graham ducked under the table and Isaac stepped back, thinking, *I'm too old for this shit, man.*

Malik managed to rescue the new guy, but not before Tony had done quite a bit of dental work with his fists. Tony fell back to the carpet-covered concrete floor, pressing his palms to his face, tears of rage dampening his beard.

Isaac took a deep breath, asked his maker for guidance, and took Tony by the arm. "Come on." He put his hand out to Tony, pulled him up, and ushered him toward the door. "Let's get outta here."

Once in the hallway, Tony shrugged Isaac off and wiped

his eyes with his sleeve. "What the hell's wrong with that guy? Why would he do that to my guitar? My fucking guitar." By the way Tony's jaw was clenched, Isaac knew Tony was trying to hold back more tears. He looked away from him to protect the guy's pride. He walked to the elevator and hit the up button.

"Sharon gave me that guitar. It's the only nice thing I own. It was, anyway. That motherfucker."

Isaac let Tony get the fury out of his system, until they got to the parking lot. "You got wheels?"

Tony pulled a used napkin out of his pocket and blew his nose. "Yeah, the green Acura over there."

"How 'bout we go get a cup of coffee?"

"I'd rather get a double shot of Jack." Tony unlocked the passenger door and Isaac got in.

Isaac tried to ignore the stale smell of beer and cigarettes as he moved the pile of empty forties from the front floor into the rear.

"I been meaning to clean that up." Tony shrugged. "Just never got around to it."

Isaac said nothing and put on his seat belt.

Tony started the car, then sat, hands on the wheel. "Do you think I should go get it...? Maybe somebody can fix it."

"Ain't nobody gonna fix that," Isaac said. "One of the guys will save the case for you. Let's roll over to Mill Street Diner."

After Tony made another attempt to talk Isaac into hitting a bar, he drove to the diner. It was an old-fashioned, silver train-car-style restaurant. They settled into a weathered booth in the back. Isaac ordered a coffee, while Tony went for a Coke and an order of cheesy fries.

"What was that guy's name again? I'm going to find him and pound the dirt right out of him, then sell his organs so I can buy a new guitar." He shook his head. "I'll never be able to replace that guitar. It was one of a kind. A friend looked at it and said it was handmade. Hand-fucking-made. Some dude named Morris put his heart and soul into it when he made it." His voice cracked. "And that twisted crackhead busted it all to splinters."

Isaac put up a leathery hand in the stop position. "You already done pounded that boy pretty good. I understand you're pissed off. I do. But son, you got to look at the bigger picture."

"Bigger picture? What the hell's that supposed to mean?"

Isaac waited as the waitress set their orders down. "Thanks." He sipped his coffee, lukewarm and probably leftover from the morning, and collected his thoughts. "What was that you played at the meeting today?"

Tony hesitated. "You talking about 'Happy Birthday'?"

"Yeah." Isaac tried to arrange his thoughts so the kid would understand. "Look, I ain't no college professor. But what I'm saying is, a song is made of notes, right? Hundreds of notes, thousands of notes. Each one's important, but, when you put them all together, the song, the end product, is bigger, beautiful even. You feel me?"

Tony shrugged.

"Today was a note. A bad note. Seems like you been havin' a lot of bad notes lately. But son, your song is long. You need to focus on the whole song, then work on the notes, one by one, day by day."

Tony shoved several fries, slathered in gooey cheese, into his mouth. After he gobbled them down, he reached for a napkin and wiped the grease from his face. "I got no idea what you're talking about." He tossed the napkin to the table, leaned back, and crossed his arms.

Isaac closed his eyes. In the Bible, God would just put the words into the mouths of the prophets. He needed the right words. Now.

He opened his eyes and spoke the words that came to him. "When I come home from Nam, I was a mess. Like all combat vets, I saw a lot of action, and done a lot of stuff I'm not exactly proud of. But, at the time, I did what I thought was best for our country." He reached over and took one of Tony's fries, popped it into his mouth, and immediately regretted taking in that greasy glop. Like he'd done a thousand times with military chow. He didn't think, just swallowed. Then he went on.

"Like you, like the other guys, I changed when I was over there. And when I came back, I just didn't fit in. Nowhere. But I bluffed—or at least, kidded myself I was bluffing. I got a job driving a fork truck in a warehouse. I went out with the guys and got plastered most nights. I met a beautiful lady, sweet-talked her into marrying me, and two years later we had a baby. Little Daisy. Best thing I ever did, that baby. But you see, I wasn't focused on the big picture. I was living day by day and letting the little shit in life get to me. Then I did the only thing I knew to do—I went at it full bore, kicking and scratching and punching with both fists."

Isaac could tell by the way Tony leaned forward and uncrossed his arms that he had his attention. Everyone in the group told stories like this, and once a guy heard them a dozen, two dozen, five dozen times, all the stories just sort of blended together and meant nothing.

"One day I come home after grabbing a few beers and a couple of shots with the guys after work. Paulette and Daisy were gone." Isaac looked away, his jaw muscles working, his eyes closed. Telling this story, even after all those years, still felt like he was picking at a scab with an infection underneath, a wound that wouldn't heal. "They never come back." He took another sip of coffee, nodded, and went on. "Paulette read me the riot act a dozen times. She told me to go to counseling. But, no, that crap wasn't for me. I was a man, I'd fix me, myself. So, instead of hanging on to my wife and daughter, I hung on to the anger."

"Did you hit her?" When Tony spoke, Isaac saw something in his eyes. Sadness, maybe? Or understanding?

Isaac paused. He'd always been loaded at the time, and he'd certainly tried to wash away the memories with Miller and Jim Beam. But they were still there, always ready to bob up to the surface and spill. He also remembered doing the steps, so he swallowed and said, "Yeah, I hit her."

"Shit," Tony said. "That sucks."

"Yeah, it does." Isaac swirled the dregs of coffee in his cup. "That's what I'm trying to tell you. I know you're dealin' with stuff. But you got someone special who is dumb enough to love you. Don't go throwin' that away."

"I understand what you're saying, Isaac. I'm just having trouble getting my ass going. I mean, today, well, I told you about today. Then that tweaker went and busted up my guitar. I mean, what the hell?"

"That guy's a mess, Tony. There's no explaining it. It's probably the drugs, but Lord only knows what happened to turn him that way. He experienced some terrible stuff over there. Probably not too different from things you saw and did. Some guys can handle it better than others. We're all broken, Tony. It's what makes us human." Isaac sipped his coffee, picked up his napkin, and wiped his mouth. "You said your girl gave you that guitar, while you was still rehabbing, right?"

Tony nodded.

"And you didn't know how to play at all. But you read books or watched videos or whatever you did, and taught yourself some notes. Then some chords. Then you learned to string them together into a song. That, whatever you want to call it, drive, is what got you from knowing nothing to playing like Chuck Berry. That part of you wasn't in the guitar, it's in you, and nobody can take that away from you, 'cause it's you, man. In your core. It's indestructible."

He looked at Tony, who was staring at his plate and the few fries still swimming in fat. By the way the kid's shoulder sagged, the way his face softened, Isaac could tell some of the anger was out of him.

"You got to find a way to tap into that inner strength, son. That's the real you. That's the you that God wants you to be."

"Jesus—you're not going all holy-roller on me, are you?"

Isaac laughed and shook his head. "I'm just telling you what you already know. There's a part of each and every one of us that wants to feel good, to be happy. In order for that to happen, you got to let the negative shit go. And a good way to start is to quit drinkin' forties before group."

Tony nodded, and Isaac figured the kid couldn't take much more lecturing.

Isaac put his cup down and fished in his pocket. He pulled out several wadded bills.

Tony looked up from his plate and said, "I met this sailor when I was still in the hospital. His name was Brian. Some of the guys called him Torch behind his back, 'cause, you know, he was all burnt up. Anyway, he told me he thought God was music. Not that, exactly, but that God is in the music. He called it the universal language."

Isaac thought of Christmas Eve, sitting at church, and how he couldn't keep himself from crying like a baby as the folks all sang "Silent Night" or "O Come, All Ye Faithful." Then, he heard Dusty Springfield in his head, singing about the son of a preacher man with a voice sweet as honey. Wilson Pickett. Aretha Franklin. Little Richard. Ray Charles and so many more. The anger in today's rap music. The pain at the root of the blues. How Etta James's voice could make your skin burn and a chill boogie down your spine at the same time.

"I never heard that," Isaac said. "But it makes sense to me. People pour their feelings into their music. They expose themselves, asking us to understand. They help us find beauty in all the pain. I believe that's what God, or whatever you want to call it, wants from us. Compassion."

"Everybody likes music," Tony said. "I'm not big on God, but I'd agree that there's something relatable in music. I always wondered why, when bands tour in Europe or Russia and Japan, fans there all go nuts, even though they don't understand the language. But music's got it all—heartbreak and dancing and falling in love. And that comes through."

"Ain't heartbreak and falling in love the same damn thing?" Isaac laughed and left a twenty on the table. "First rule—stop drinking. Second rule—always be good to workin' folks. Now, let's get outta here."

Approaching the car, Isaac asked, "Can you give me a lift home? I could walk, but it's pretty far."

"'Course," Tony said. "Just tell me where to go."

As the Acura rattled to life, Tony turned on the radio. "What kind of music you like?"

"Motown's my favorite," Isaac said. "But I'm not picky. Try 94.5, WBLW. It's a tiny little station out of Baltimore. They play hip-hop during the day, but R and B at night."

Static crackled as Tony tuned it in and they listened as a tinny voice recorded back in the day sang,

"But people just don't understand, now, what makes a man feel so blue..."

"Mr. Pitiful," Isaac said.

"You know this old stuff?"

"My man Otis was big when I was in high school. Guys like him and James Brown. They were the first to sing about things a brother could relate to. Right up here on Whitmore," Isaac said.

Tony turned, and they rode in silence, listening to Otis, watching as evening spilled over the strip malls and rowhouses.

"You ever see a shrink?" Tony asked when the song finished. "I mean, after your lady took off?"

Isaac hesitated, suddenly feeling tired and old, deep in his bones. "Naw. Back in the day, only pussies needed therapy. Real men drank their pain away. But these days, I think it's more acceptable. I think if you find the right one, it maybe could help." Isaac used a finger, indicating to Tony to turn left at the light. Halfway down the block, he said, "Here, pull over and park here."

"Here?" Tony asked. "You can't live here—it's all stores."

"I know." Isaac unbuckled his seat belt. "I want to stop by The Music Guild across the street. I happened into some extra money today. I want to see if they got a used guitar that suits you. Maybe even pick up your lady friend some flowers."

Tony shook his head. "Why you doing this? You don't even know me."

"Back in Khe Sanh, a guy I barely knew kicked a grenade and saved my sorry ass. He wound up in a wheelchair, and years later I asked him why he done it. You know what he told me?"

Isaac got out of the car. Tony joined him at the curb and said, "What?"

"Semper Fi, motherfucker. Semper Fi."

The two men, one old and limping from the scars of a lifetime of struggle, the other young and confused and uncertain, crossed through the sounds of traffic. The air was heavy with humidity, exhaust and the smells of burgers and fries and pizza from nearby shops where working men and women were earning enough pay to make their way through another day, another week. The music store door was open.

Someone inside was picking out a melody on a well-worn guitar. Together, Isaac and Tony walked toward the notes, the chords, and the song that seemed to call them home.

> *"But I won't cry for yesterday,*
> *there's an ordinary world,*
> *Somehow I have to find*
> *And as I try to make my way,*
> *to the ordinary world,*
> *I will learn to survive."*

– "Ordinary World" by Duran Duran

ANOTHER'S NOTE

You finished! Thanks for reading *Morris*, and I hope you enjoyed it.

It's come to my attention from a few of my early readers that these stories might be perceived as less than uplifting. One reader actually used the phrase "stick my head in the oven," but I'm sure they were just being dramatic. Hope so.

Anyway, if this collection of regular people experiencing the pleasures and pains of reality has left you feeling blue— please turn the page and give me five more minutes of your time. I promise you'll feel better.

CHEESECAKE

"A long, long time ago
I can still remember how that music used to make me smile
and I knew if I had my chance that I could make those people dance
and maybe they'd be happy for a while"
– "American Pie" by Don McLean

From: Daisy Stone
Sent: Sunday, January 9, 2014 9:08 PM
To: Isaac@StoneBread.com
Subject: cheesecake

Hey Dad,

It was so great seeing you this past weekend! I'm so glad you got the chance to meet Malcolm. We are both thrilled that you and Mom are talking again and agreed to walk me down the aisle. I can't tell you what that means to me. For so many years I felt a void in my life, like a piece of my heart was missing. It felt better once Malcolm and me got together, but I didn't feel whole, didn't feel complete, until you came back into my life. I know we are still getting to know each other better, and we are bound to have some differences, but it feels so right being a family again.

Speaking of family and walking me down the aisle, I also wanted to thank you for putting me in touch with your friend Tony. You were right—he's a fantastic guitarist—so I've asked him to play during the cocktail hour between the wedding and the reception. He's agreed, but refuses to let us pay him.

He says you're family, so I'm family. He's a sweetheart, as is his wife, so I won't argue!

Finally, Malcolm and I were so impressed with the chocolate raspberry and the lemon coconut cheesecakes you brought, I decided to run something by you. Since the wedding will only be about 40 people, we were hoping you might be willing to make several different cheesecakes for us instead of a wedding cake. We're not really very formal/traditional people, and those cheesecakes were absolutely delicious! Please let me know what you think.

Okay, I'm exhausted and need to get ready for bed. Thanks again for coming over this weekend, and let's do it again real soon.

Love,
Daisy

ACKNOWLEDGMENTS

I've had a lot of help in putting this book together. Firstly, I have to thank my wife, Christine. Without her love and support and never-ending patience with my, shall we call it quirky, sense of humor, none of this would be possible. Together we make a great team.

Next, I got a great deal of helpful input from my friends Abby Astor, Marleen Pasch, and Bridgit Keunnig Pollpeter.

I'd also like to thank my first readers, the Links critique group: Scott McFadden, Dana Evans, Kathy Coleman, and Kati MacArthur. You guys always keep me on track.

My kids, Nick and Grace, were a big help in editing and brainstorming marketing ideas. My niece Anna built my website, www.chriskuell.com, and I'm so grateful for all they have given me.

Lastly, I'd like to thank the folks at Atmosphere Press.

THE PLAYLIST
Recognition of lyrics, songs, and artists

The power of music is an obvious theme in these stories, so I wanted to be sure to credit all the songs referenced or quoted in this collection.

"The Ballad of the Green Berets" by Barry Sadler, January 1966

"Windy" by The Association, 1967

"Light My Fire" and "The Crystal Ship" by The Doors, from the album *The Doors*, April 1967

"White Rabbit" by Jefferson Airplane, from the album *Surrealistic Pillow*, June 1967

Sgt. Pepper's Lonely Hearts Club Band, an album by The Beatles, May 1967

Cosmo's Factory, an album by Creedence Clearwater Revival, July 1970

"Blowin' in the Wind" by Bob Dylan, from the album *The Freewheelin' Bob Dylan*, August 1963

"Born to be Wild" by Steppenwolf, from the album *Steppenwolf*, June 1968

"Strange Days" by The Doors, album released September 1967

"Just My Imagination (Running Away With Me)" originally by The Temptations, January 1971. I have to admit a glitch in time with this musical reference, as I heard The Stones perform the song live in 1983, and "Idle Talk" is set in the late 1970s. Let's call it artistic freedom.

Stone Toad is a fictional band I dreamed up for the story "Q and A." A quick Google search does show that a Boston hard-rock band called Stone Toad formed in 2017. In addition, the Stone Toad was a popular music club in downtown Milwaukee for much of the 1970s and 1980s.

"Dust in the Wind" by Kansas, from the album *Point of No Return*, January 1978

"Tennessee Waltz" by Pee Wee King, recorded December 1943

"Old Man" by Neil Young, from the album *Harvest*, 1972

"Ring of Fire" by Johnny Cash, from the album *Ring of Fire*, April 1963

"Rocky Racoon" by The Beatles, from the album *The Beatles (White Album)*, November 1968

"Take It Easy" by The Eagles, from the album *Eagles*, May 1972

"Puff, The Magic Dragon" by Peter, Paul and Mary, from the album *Moving*, January 1963

"Buckets of Rain" by Bob Dylan, from the album *Blood on the Tracks*, January 1975

The lines "Crying won't help you, praying won't do you no good" come from the Led Zeppelin version of the song "When the Levee Breaks," originally by Memphis Minnie and Kansas Joe McCoy, recorded in 1929.

The Best of Bread album released March 1973

Purple Rain by Prince, album release June 1984

"Dear Prudence" by The Beatles, from the album *The Beatles (White Album)*, November 1968

"Seagull" by Bad Company, from the album *Bad Company*, June 1974

"Two of Us" by The Beatles, from the album *Let It Be*, May 1970

"Katmandu" by Bob Seger, from the album *Beautiful Loser*, 1975

"Don't Disturb this Groove" by The System, from the album *Don't Disturb This Groove*, January 1987

"Bohemian Rhapsody" by Queen, from the album *A Night at The Opera*, October 1975

"We Are the Champions" by Queen, from the album *News of the World*, October 1977

"Bicycle Race" by Queen, from the album *Jazz*, October 1978

"Love of My Life" by Queen, from the album *A Night at The Opera*, November 1975

"9 to 5" by Dolly Parton, from the album *9 to 5 and Odd Jobs*, November 1980

The black ties are a fictional band that the author dreamed up for the story "The Letter." However, a Google search now shows a Facebook page for a four-piece rock band called the Black Ties in Central Jersey.

"Talkin' 'bout a Revolution" by Tracy Chapman, from the album *Tracy Chapman*, July 1988

"Suspicious Minds" by Mark James, recorded by Elvis Presley, August 1969

"Torn" was written by Scott Cutler, Anne Preven, and Phil Thornalley, performed by Natalie Imbruglia, from the album *Left of the Middle*, October 1997

"Folsom Prison Blues" by Johnny Cash, from the album *Johnny Cash with his Hot and Blue Guitar*, December 1955

"Wanted Dead or Alive" by Bon Jovi, from the album *Slippery When Wet*, March 1987

"If You Love Somebody, Set Them on Fire" by The Dead Milkmen, from the album *Metaphysical Graffiti*, June 1990

Gorilla Finger Dub is Maine's premier Reggae band. Check them out at gorillafingerdub.com.

"Down With the Sickness" by Disturbed, from the album *The Sickness*, October 2000

"Rehab" by Amy Winehouse, from the album *Back to Black*, 2006

"Mr. Pitiful" by Otis Redding, from the album *Sings Soul Ballads*, December 1964

ABOUT ATMOSPHERE PRESS

Atmosphere Press is an independent, full-service publisher for excellent books in all genres and for all audiences. Learn more about what we do at atmospherepress.com.

We encourage you to check out some of Atmosphere's latest releases, which are available at Amazon.com and via order from your local bookstore:

Icarus Never Flew 'Round Here, by Matt Edwards

COMFREY, WYOMING: Maiden Voyage, by Daphne Birkmeyer

The Chimera Wolf, by P.A. Power

Umbilical, by Jane Kay

The Two-Blood Lion, by Nick Westfield

Shogun of the Heavens: The Fall of Immortals, by I.D.G. Curry

Hot Air Rising, by Matthew Taylor

30 Summers, by A.S. Randall

Delilah Recovered, by Amelia Estelle Dellos

A Prophecy in Ash, by Julie Zantopoulos

The Killer Half, by JB Blake

Ocean Lessons, by Karen Lethlean

Unrealized Fantasies, by Marilyn Whitehorse

The Mayari Chronicles: Initium, by Karen McClain

Squeeze Plays, by Jeffrey Marshall

JADA: Just Another Dead Animal, by James Morris

Hart Street and Main: Metamorphosis, by Tabitha Sprunger

Karma One, by Colleen Hollis

Ndalla's World, by Beth Franz

Adonai, by Arman Isayan

The Journey, by Khozem Poonawala

ABOUT THE AUTHOR

CHRIS KUELL is a writer, editor and advocate living in Connecticut. A former research chemist, he lost his sight as a result of diabetic retinopathy. He learned how to use a computer with speech output and turned his efforts to writing. His essays and stories have appeared in a number of literary— and a few not-so-literary—magazines, journals and newsletters. He has edited several books and anthologies, and is the editor of *Breath and Shadow*, an online literary journal of disability culture and ideas.

Please visit **www.chriskuell.com** to learn more.